Desire

and

Duty

A Sequel to Jane Austen's
Pride and Prejudice

Ted and Marilyn Bader

© Copyright 1997 by Revive Publishing
1790 Dudley Street
Denver, Colorado, USA
Voice/Fax 800-541-0558

Authors: Ted and Marilyn Bader

Library of Congress Catalog Card Number: 96-92575

ISBN: 0-9654299-0-3

10 9 8 7 6 5 4 3 2

This book is dedicated to our parents:

Dean and Geraldine Bader
and
Edgar and Muriel Taylor

who first taught us about love and loyalty.

PREFACE

In 1850, Catherine Hubback, a niece of Jane Austen, published a continuation of her aunt's unfinished novel, *The Watsons*, thus launching the enterprise to which another niece, Anna Lefroy, a great grandniece, Edith Brown, and a great-great-great niece, Joan Austen-Leigh, at varying intervals gave further impetus with pastiches of *Sanditon, Mansfield Park, Emma*, and yet again, *The Watsons*. As early as 1890, however, without benefit of kinship, Andrew Lang made a brief foray into this family demesne. Predictably his audacity emboldened others to venture incursions of their own. Most audacious, at the outset, was Sybil Brinton who, in 1913, thrust into print a novel of near epic scale (as such productions went), in which she found roles for every character of major consequence met with in the six major Austen novels.

In 1975 the bicentennial of Jane Austen's birth was celebrated throughout the civilized world. Even the hidebound British postal service, accustomed to reserving its homage for monarchs, put tradition aside to issue a set of Austen stamps, a gesture which gratified philatelists recognized as long-overdue, appropriate response to a query first propounded in 1909, by William H. Helm: "We call one unwedded queen 'Elizabeth'! Why should we not call another 'Jane'?"

The Austen bicentennial ushered in, as well, an upsurge of Austen scholarship that has seen, newly published, in the ensuing score of years, more than 2,500 books and articles on Jane Austen and her works. Prominent among these publications are more than two dozen continuations of the novels. In themselves these attest to the soundness of E. M. Forster's shrewd assessment of Jane Austen's work: "Her novels are microcosms of humanity because they are ready for an 'extended life.'" In 1975 itself Marie Dobbs (modestly identifying herself merely as "Another Lady"), set the standard with her best-selling continuation of *Sanditon*, the novel that Jane Austen was writing when, at forty-one, illness told her that the time had come for her to cease her earthly labors.

It is in the context of this legion of continuations of the novels of "the divine Jane" (to use William Dean Howells inspired phrase), especially of those that have undertaken to carry on *Pride and Prejudice*, E. Barrington, Bonnavia-Hunt, T. E. White, Emma Tennant, and Julia Barrett, that we come to consider *Desire and Duty*. To extend *Pride and Prejudice* is, of itself, an audacious undertaking. The labor of many years, Austen spared no effort to bring it to a state of perfection. She left *The Watsons*, and *Sanditon* unfinished. At the end she held back *Persuasion* and *Northanger Abbey*. They, too, she thought, fell short of completion. Here then, there was ample reason for continuators to come forward. Fortunately, Jane Austen opened the way for others to extend her other novels, too, if they chose to do so. Her closures never were hermetically sealed. Even after a manuscript passed into print her characters continued to live in her mind. Sometimes, to those around her, she spoke of the subsequent history of Kitty and Mary Bennet, Mr. Woodhouse, Jane Fairfax. Here the aspiring continuator finds authorization to pick up the thread of the narrative. To do that, of course calls not only for audacity but for a sure grasp of Jane Austen's mind and art.

"A full appreciation of the genius of Jane Austen," Montagu Summer tells us, "is the nicest touchstone of literary taste." Many think they have arrived at such a state, some, perhaps, because, as Katherine Mansfield observed, Jane Austen has a way of making every reader feel she is a personal friend. But consider another point Summer makes: "Jane Austen, Jane Austen and life, which of you two copies the other?" Here, indeed, are keenness of intellect, wit, and judgement needed copiously to hold one's place in Jane Austen's company.

To take intimacy with the mind of Jane Austen for granted approaches hubris. To presume intimacy with the full workings of the minds of Elizabeth and Darcy is scarcely less formidable. No reasonable continuator would consider doing it save for brief exchanges. But it is not intrusive to dwell on the welfare of those who hitherto have been an essential part of Darcy's entourage and, in the natural order of things, would continue to be so. Most especially is it desirable that the fabric of that world be consistent with the moral tone of what has gone before, manners not excepted.

The Baders, Ted and Marilyn, bring to *Desire and Duty* an intimate knowledge of the society that made Elizabeth Bennet and Fitzwilliam Darcy, Wickham and his Lydia, and even Lady Catherine and her Mr. Collins, possible. No rent sunders that fabric as the Baders' extended narrative brings us again into the presence of Jane Austen's glorious troupe of Georgian performers. Unlike Dickens they do not make their villain too steep, their heroine irresponsible, their hero moonstruck. Social awareness gives fiber to their narrative as it did Jane Austen's, but, like Austen, as Archbishop Whately wrote, with commendation, they do not preach but let reason and conscience prevail.

Here is Georgiana Darcy's subsequent history laid before us with such skill that we move into the narrative, out of Longbourn into Pemberley, without a ripple of adjustment. The Baders' sequel to *Pride and Prejudice* not only extends Jane Austen's narrative with a grace that promises to endure, for fastidious readers of today, and tomorrow, it will be welcomed as a worthy companion volume to its predecessor--in effect extending the Austen canon itself! by ordinary mortal reckoning, a fair bid to immortality!

Professor John McAleer, Ph.D.
Professor of English
Boston College
Permanent Fellow, Durham University (England)
25 December 1996

(Publishers' Note: Professor McAleer is probably the world's foremost authority on Jane Austen. He has been commissioned to prepare a definitive biography of Jane Austen which will be titled *Chawton Benefaction*. A product of 900 typewritten pages and twelve years of work, this monumental effort should be available in the near future. His last biography on Ralph Waldo Emerson was nominated for a Pulitzer Prize.)

Authors' Foreword

The ending of Jane Austen's *Pride and Prejudice* begs for another episode. We hope you will enjoy this story as much as we did while writing it. The book is made to stand alone; however, readers will derive more benefit by understanding its predecessor.

While Pemberley and Westbrook Halls are mythical places, Staley Hall actually exists on the border of Derbyshire. One of the authors, TFB, is a great-grandson of Leah Belle Staley, a descendent of Staley Hall.

Jane Austen writes from a third person, single viewpoint with occasional omniscient glimpses for the reader. What this means is that the story is written from the heroine's perspective, but in the tone of a third person. Occasionally, the reader is told things that the heroine may not know. The basic story line in each of her six novels is that of a young heroine who experiences difficulties and growth in maturity while searching for a husband.

Many customs of the early nineteenth century are explained in the context of the story. If not, an extensive section of historical notes, subdivided by chapter, exist at the end of the book.

Ted and Marilyn Bader

Section One

December, 1805
Derbyshire England

Chapter One

"Be off with you and finish polishing the brass," Mrs. Reynolds said firmly to one of the maids. "Master Darcy is finally returning to Pemberley with his bride and I want everything in the household to be perfect for them!" Mrs. Reynolds, the respectable-looking, elderly housekeeper, had known Mr. Darcy from the age of four to his current age of eight and twenty. She and Mr. Reynolds, an equally respectable-looking husband, were in charge of the Pemberley household.

"Mrs. Reynolds, do you think my brother will be happy with Elizabeth?" asked Miss Darcy.

"Undoubtably, Ma'am. From the first time I saw Elizabeth here last summer, I thought she was most unusual. Then, with her return a few days later, I saw how much Mr. Darcy regarded her. Since his visits to Longbourn during the courtship, I have seen him smile and heard him humming-- actions which are new to him and do him good. I have no doubt she is the perfect woman to make Mr. Darcy happy and to fill Pemberley Hall with laughter."

Miss Darcy, age sixteen, waited for her brother and new sister-in-law to arrive by pacing back and forth in front of the large window in the parlor room next to the entrance hall. She was perceived as a tall young woman since she stood five feet and nine inches. Her black hair, put up in ringlets to frame the face, contrasted with the white muslin dress covering her well formed figure.

"Should they not be here by now?" Miss Darcy queried as she stopped to peer into the early winter twilight for the coach.

Mrs. Reynolds reassured her, "The carriage must come soon. Mr. Darcy would have sent a messenger if their plans changed."

Even though it was only a few weeks to Christmas, and frost was on the ground, a large group of tenants and staff were gathering in the front of the hall in anticipation of the wedded couple's return. The fragrance of the evergreen boughs festooning the mantels and the warmth of the blazing fires in the entrance hall spilled into the large parlor room creating a cheery atmosphere.

Shouts and muffled sounds of an approaching carriage were heard. Miss Darcy walked to the front hall, beyond the point where the two large doors were to be opened, so she could be at the head of the welcoming line. Mrs. Reynolds was standing next to Georgiana (Miss Darcy's given name) and the more important household help lined up in order next to Mrs. Reynolds.

Mrs. Darcy was first to enter the hall. Miss Darcy saw the red glow on Elizabeth's face and admired her healthy, beautiful appearance. Slightly shorter than Georgiana, she came to Miss Darcy and hugged her. "I am finally here, Georgiana. How is my dear sister?"

"I am filled with happiness to see you come to be mistress of Pemberley," replied Georgiana.

"I hope you will not be jealous at my assumption of that title," Elizabeth cautiously ventured.

"Not at all. I am too young to be mistress of anything. I am quite relieved with your coming," Georgiana earnestly replied. "Since my mother died, Pemberley has wanted a lively feminine touch. I hope you will bring a special presence to our house."

"Thank you. I shall do my best."

"The double wedding with your sister Jane and Mr. Bingley was simply lovely. I am sorry to have had so little time with you beforehand."

"Yes, and I wanted more time with you, also," Elizabeth replied. "I have enjoyed your numerous letters, filled with sisterly love."

"Your letters have given me much laughter." Georgiana smiled as she turned part way towards Mrs. Reynolds and said, "Mrs. Darcy, you will remember Mrs. Reynolds."

"Indeed I do. I will be forever grateful to you, Mrs. Reynolds, for enlightening me on the true nature of my husband's character. Your statements of 'never hearing a cross word from him', 'sweetest-tempered, good natured' and the 'best landlord and best master' were instrumental in correcting my prejudicial ideas about him. Certainly, I have found your descriptions of his amiability perfectly correct."

"I am glad to be of help to you Ma'am. I will be at your service to begin running the household the way you should want."

"Mrs. Reynolds, I shall need your help. I never dreamed of being the mistress of such a large estate and I shall rely heavily on your advice. Pardon me, if I do not respond to the title 'Mrs. Darcy' as it is still not familiar to my ears."

The line looked towards the door as Mr. Darcy entered. Tall, strongly built, he came through the doorway with a smile on his face. He walked up to Georgiana and embraced her. Somehow Georgiana felt her brother was more complete being married. He certainly was happier. A tear escaped from her eye and landed on his cheek.

"Sister, what is the tear I feel? Surely you are not unhappy?"

"Quite the contrary. I am so happy for you and Elizabeth."

"I am glad you feel so. I shall not only be a better brother to you, but I have brought home the sister for whom you have always longed."

Mr. and Mrs. Darcy proceeded down the line of household help with introductions and acknowledgments.

Chapter Two

The next morning the sunshine poured into the dining parlor of Pemberley where Elizabeth and Georgiana were standing and waiting for Mr. Darcy. He entered the room with riding coat on and hat in hand, only to have Elizabeth exclaim, "Mr. Darcy, you must have breakfast with us."

"The steward has something down at the trout ponds he would have me look at," he replied.

"No. No. No, my dear Fitzwilliam," Elizabeth importuned as she came up to him and adjusted his lapel. "Your business must wait. You shall come and have breakfast with us."

"I have been gone too long, though I must say for the loveliest reason standing in front of me, and many things must be attended to. I seldom took breakfast before we were married."

"Then you must change your old stodgy bachelor ways and begin to pay attention to your family." Elizabeth said continuing with a smile, "It will help you to start your day with less seriousness."

He paused, to look at her attractive eyes and her fresh look of one and twenty years, and replied, "I yield to my lady. I forgot that you need to teach me liveliness and a less serious approach to life."

"Yes, and do not forget I need you to teach me about the business of the world and of this large estate," Elizabeth replied playfully, "and I shall never learn if you cannot stop to teach me."

Mr. Darcy motioned to the servant to take his hat and remove his coat. He then moved to seat Mrs. Darcy across from Georgiana with himself in between. Georgiana observed the glow on their faces and was quite satisfied with the atmosphere at the breakfast table.

"Elizabeth," Mr. Darcy addressed his wife, "the breakfast china is a Wedgewood pattern my grandmother brought to the estate. Feel free to order a different pattern for this or any other service. Remember, you are the lady of Pemberley, not our ancestors."

"I do not wish to make any immediate change. I want to feel the presence of the great house for many months before adding my touch." Her finger glided over the coffee cup and she continued, "the green and gold pattern on this service is quite beautiful and seems most appropriate for this morning."

Georgiana ventured to converse by inquiring why her aunt, Lady Catherine de Bourgh, did not attend the wedding. The atmosphere at the table suddenly became frosted, like the December ground outside; then, her brother and Elizabeth laughed simultaneously.

Mr. Darcy replied, "I see we have been too circumspect with you by avoiding the real story in relation to our aunt. Before we start the tale, please bear in mind that she, in her own perverse sort of way, helped us get together much sooner than we might otherwise have had courage to do."

Elizabeth began the story of the fateful day of Lady Catherine de Bourgh's visit to Longbourn, by reciting her demands, "Tell me once and for all, are you engaged to him? . . .And will you promise me, never to enter into such an engagement?"

Georgiana's face turned crimson when Elizabeth told

the part of Lady Catherine de Bourgh's second shocking demand that Elizabeth should promise never to become engaged to Mr. Darcy. "I am so ashamed of my aunt," Miss Darcy replied.

"Do not let it vex you, sister," assured Mr. Darcy, "for it was Lady Catherine de Bourgh's report of Elizabeth's refusal to comply with such a promise that gave me great hope for the future. It was not long after the argument with my aunt that I asked Elizabeth to be my wife and had the joy of her acceptance. What our aunt intended as evil turned out for good."

Georgiana looked at both Elizabeth and Mr. Darcy incredulously, but found only warm reassurance in their eyes and began to believe their statements about her aunt. Miss Darcy had always been terrified of her aunt and found it hard to believe that her brother and sister-in-law could stand up so well to the presence of Lady Catherine. Obviously, some of that strong personality of her mother's family had been transmitted to her brother. She wondered if she herself would ever have that kind of courage.

Finishing his plate, Mr. Darcy rose and asked for his coat.

Elizabeth said, "Now, dear, your sister and I shall want you to come to breakfast each morning to acquaint us with the daily news of the estate."

"I shall be glad to do so," he replied with a smile. He then strode with strength and dignity from the room.

Georgiana turned to Elizabeth and said, "Shall I begin to show you my favorite parts of the garden? The weather seems a little cold for December, but the sunshine will help."

"I should be delighted," replied Elizabeth.

They stood and, after having their coats placed, went out the large front doors into the southern gardens.

"Elizabeth, this is my favorite path," Georgiana continued. "The walk is smoother and continues around about one quarter of a mile. The underbrush is kept clear and the bushes well trimmed."

"Georgiana, I must have you call me 'Lizzy' in the manner of my favorite sister, Jane. Elizabeth or Mrs. Darcy should be reserved for more formal situations."

"I was hoping you would allow me to do so," replied Georgiana. After walking a short distance, she continued, "My special dog, Phillip, usually accompanies me on this walk. I have not introduced you, Lizzy, to my dear Phillip. He stays with me in my bedroom at night and often accompanies me during the day. During meals, I let him loose outside since he can get underfoot of the servants. I wonder where he is now?"

Her question was soon answered by a short series of excited barks ahead of them. As they approached, the small black and white spaniel appeared to be anxiously looking and scratching at something in the ground. At the sound of their approach, he turned and approached with tail wagging. Georgiana bent over and took him in her arms. Patting him, she told Phillip of the new mistress of Pemberley Hall and how he must now recognize and be kind to her. His eager look and allowance of Elizabeth to pet him told Georgiana that Phillip had already followed her command.

"My brother bought him for me one year ago. Phillip has been such a companion particularly when my brother is gone on business into London. I thought a name for him meaning 'brotherly love' most appropriate."

"I can see you love him," Elizabeth replied, "It has been my observation that people who love animals are more likely to love people. This speaks well of you." After walking further, Elizabeth asked "When is the next gathering or dinner party for Pemberley Hall? Do you invite gentry from around Derbyshire?"

"We usually have a dinner party and gathering on the penultimate eve of Christmas. Our long-time family friends, the Staley and Westbrook families, are always invited. You have probably heard of the Earl of Westbrook. The Westbrook estate borders the western aspect of Pemberley Manor. The family is tolerable. The younger brother is Henry, who is two and twenty years old. They have an elder son, Lord Alfred, who is four and twenty."

"And the Staleys?"

"Staley Hall is not nearly as grand as Pemberley or Westbrook. Sir William Staley is a baronet with a good size estate, which borders Pemberley on its northern aspect. However, they have had financial difficulties in the past few years and have had to sell some of their land."

"And the family?"

"They have two sons: the older is named George who is three and twenty; the younger is eighteen and named Thomas."

"Are you partial to any of these young men?" asked Elizabeth.

"Oh, Lizzy, do not tease me. If you mean, do I love any of them? No. Lord Westbrook is not very interesting. His younger brother, Mr. Henry Westbrook, is sensitive but amiable. Mr. Thomas Staley is the friendliest of them all. He enjoys reading and music, like myself. His older brother, Mr. Staley, is wild and often disagreeable."

Coming to the first short turn, Elizabeth said, "It is becoming cold. Shall we return inside?"

"Yes. We can finish this walk tomorrow."

"I am anxious to explore the halls of Pemberley. Which room is your favorite?"

"I believe I like the library most," replied Georgiana.

"Oh! Oh, yes, the great library of Pemberley," laughed Elizabeth, "it was one of the first things I heard about this estate during the time my sister, Jane, was convalescing at Netherfield. I love to read. Let us go and see it at once."

Returning inside the entrance hall, they ascended the

grand semi-circular staircase, which wound to the left.
Coming to the landing, they were soon met with a larger than
average hand-carved door. Opening it, Georgiana saw
Elizabeth hold her breath momentarily as she entered the
long and rectangular room. The walls of the room were
covered with bookshelves filled with books.

"I love the paper and leather smell when I enter here.
The room is forty by twenty feet in dimension. As you can
see, there are three large windows facing the east,"
described Georgiana. Walking towards the middle window,
she continued, "This bay window is my favorite area since it
projects out at the second story height. Here, I can often see
my brother as he is about on the estate."

"With this large fireplace across from it, I imagine you
spend much time here," replied Elizabeth.

"Oh, I do. There are days when I only leave to
practice on the pianoforte and to eat meals."

"I should like to come here often and spend time
reading. Would it bother you for me to do so?"

"Not at all. Your presence shall be most agreeable."

Stepping up to the shelf adjacent to the middle
windows, Elizabeth reached up and pulled down a beautifully
bound copy of *The Rise and Fall of the Roman Empire* by
Edward Gibbons. "This is the type of reading which I need to
do," sighed Elizabeth and continued, "I am afraid my favorite
reading has consisted of novels such as those by Fanny
Burney."

"Don't tell me!" exclaimed Georgiana.

Elizabeth replied with raised eyebrows, "What?"

"That you like *Camilla?*"

"Yes, very much so."

"I thought I was the only one who loved *Camilla*! You
shall be my dear sister after all. Here are the five volumes of
Camilla across from the window. Miss Burney made it seem
to last   forever before Edgar and Camilla got together,"

exclaimed Georgiana.

"Yes! And remember Edgar's interfering friend, Dr. Marchmont? He advised the reflective Edgar to say to himself about Camilla, 'How should I like this, were she mine?'" mimicked Elizabeth in a low voice, which resulted in both of them trying to repress giggles.

After a few moments, Georgiana continued, "We also have *Evelina* and *Cecilia*, her two other books, next to *Camilla*."

"Have you heard that Miss Burney had to write her first book, *Evelina*, in secret?" asked Elizabeth.

"No, I had not."

"Apparently, Miss Burney had been told by her stepmother that she should not 'scribble' (and she agreed she ought not), but nevertheless, she could not resist going upstairs, under pretense of doing something else, to write in brief bursts of activity."

Georgiana loved to hear information about her favorite author. "I can see we will have much to discuss this winter. Next to Miss Burney's books are those of my favorite poet, Cowper. Now, let me show you other aspects of the library." She led the way to a distant corner of the large room, "These are the oldest books in our collection. Some of them are more than two hundred years old. As you can see, the bindings are falling off and dissolving. We hope to find an expert in bookbinding to repair them."

Turning to another bookcase, Georgiana continued, "Here are books on aspects of family and home." Pulling down one book she added, "And here is one on embroidery. I have attempted this art, but have had no woman to show me how to advance beyond the basic stitches."

Elizabeth exclaimed, "I will be happy to help you. It is a marvelous way to occupy an afternoon and to decorate clothes." Flipping through the pages she continued, "Some of the designs are quite interesting."

After awhile, Georgiana started moving towards the library door and said, "The next portion of the house I want to show you is the chapel." She and Elizabeth proceeded to descend the circular staircase and turn to the north hallway. The north hallway had paintings of the Darcy's ancestors. Mid-way, Georgiana stopped and pointed to a life-size picture of a beautiful dark-haired lady in a white gown and said, "This is Lady Anne, my mother. She died when I was age six; so, unfortunately, I do not remember much about her. Next to her is my father, Mr. Darcy. It was much more difficult for me to lose him five years ago, as the loss of the second parent is always much more severe. My brother, in whose care I now am, is as loving a brother as a sister could have."

Elizabeth exclaimed, "Your mother was very beautiful. Her eyes are so expressive. It almost appears as if she wants to tell us something."

"I often sit in front of her picture and try to imagine what it would be like if she were here now."

Restarting down the hall they soon stopped. Georgiana opened a door, similar to the library door, revealing a small, but richly colored chapel. Red, blue and yellow colors were splashed over all the walls due to the sun shining through the stained glass windows.

"The chapel is only thirty feet long by twenty feet wide," Georgiana said as she walked up the main aisle between the pews.

"Are these real mahogany benches?" inquired Elizabeth.

"Yes, they are. I come here every day for prayers," Georgiana said softly and continued, "The family and servants used to have daily morning and evening prayers, but these were left off in my grandfather's day."

"I wish my religious life were as dutiful as yours. Does Mr. Darcy ever come?" asked Elizabeth.

"Yes, he joins me on Sunday morning before we attend the parish church."

"Then, I shall do the same as Mr. Darcy," replied Elizabeth with a smile.

"There is one other room, important to me, which I desire you to see."

Leaving the chapel, they retraced their steps down the north hallway, crossed the entrance parlor, and opened a door to the dining room. They went through it and opened another door. "This is the state music room. You can see the pianoforte in front of you and the harp on the other side of the room. You are familiar with this room, since you have played this instrument once before for our pleasure."

"Not with any measure of skill that you have, Georgiana. Tell me about your training in music."

"After my mother died, my father and brother encouraged me to pursue the musical talent my mother had. My teacher on the pianoforte, for the first three years, was Lady Marilyn Staley, of the Staley Hall previously mentioned this morning. She would either come here or I would visit Staley Hall. Unfortunately, she died when I was nine and from thence until age fourteen I attended music school in London. Except for the musical training, I hated the school and the dismal air of London. I have stayed here at Pemberley since I saw you last summer."

The afternoon continued in similar discussion of the estate by Georgiana and Elizabeth. The hoped for felicity in their relationship was becoming reality.

Chapter Three

"I am so glad Mr. Darcy invited my family to Pemberley for Christmas. They are to arrive this afternoon, and we expect the Staley and Westbrook families tomorrow on the 23rd," Elizabeth said to Georgiana at the breakfast table.

Mr. Darcy interjected, "Did I not tell you, Lizzy, that the Staleys are coming late this morning? Sir William needs to speak to me of some matters and he thought it would be better to come today and return to Pemberley again tomorrow."

"Well, my love, I am glad you informed us now so we can plan this evening. There should be no problem with the supplies we have stocked for the dinner tomorrow night. The large dining hall here makes it easy to accommodate any number of visitors," replied Elizabeth.

The carriage arrived a few hours later and Sir William Staley stepped out. He was a distinguished looking man, sixty years of age, with white hair. One could tell he had been a very strong man in his youth because of his large frame.

He was introduced by Mr. Darcy to Mrs. Darcy as his son, Thomas, stepped down behind his father. Thomas, though only eighteen, had similar broad shoulders and the same six foot height of his father. Georgiana thought his face only mildly handsome, but his curly brown hair made him more attractive than he otherwise might be. That he was three inches taller than she, also made a favorable impression. Her height, taller than many men, was a feature that exacerbated her shyness.

Sir William Staley bowed and said in a sure to please voice, "Now I have the privilege of meeting you, Mrs. Darcy. The reports of you by Mr. Darcy make you the most accomplished and pleasing woman in the world."

Even Elizabeth could not help blushing a little as Mr. Darcy beamed, "And she has made me more happy than I thought any woman could."

Turning to Georgiana, Sir William continued, "You are no longer a child, my dear. Your beauty grows with each visit."

Georgiana curtsied in reply to his statement. As Mr. Darcy and Sir William started to walk away, Georgiana introduced Thomas to Elizabeth with, "and this is Mr. Thomas Staley, my long-time friend. Please meet my new sister, Elizabeth," Georgiana said with the pride of a new possession.

After bowing, Thomas commented to Elizabeth, "From what I have heard, you are just the person that Georgiana needs. For too long she has been the only feminine presence at Pemberley. Now I shall have two pleasant women to visit here instead of one," as he looked at Georgiana.

To turn the subject away from herself, she walked up to Thomas and asked "Do you want to walk with Mrs. Darcy and myself? We were just getting ready for our morning excursion when you arrived."

"As I am not needed by my father, and the day is pleasant for December, I should like very much to walk with you," he replied.

As the three of them approached the walk to the south gardens, Georgiana asked, "Where is your brother, Mr. Staley?"

"He had to finish some business at Cambridge and

stayed over the term." Turning to Mrs. Darcy, he asked, "How do you like the Pemberley estate, now that you are mistress of it?"

"To be honest, I little understood the inner greatness of the hall before my marriage. I still do not completely believe that I am actually here. I fear that I will wake up from this wonderful dream and be told to start living again. And will you, Mr. Thomas Staley, tell me of your acquaintance with Pemberley and my sister, Georgiana?"

"Pray, call me Thomas. The formal name seems so stiff. . . .. As Georgiana can tell you, the Staleys and Darcys go back as neighbors for many generations. From the frequent intercourse of our families, Georgiana and I were great friends as children--amusing ourselves together many a time. However, we were separated for a long time until her return to Pemberley last summer." Turning to Georgiana, he continued, "Is there anything left of the three-quarters size play house your father built for you years ago?"

"I am afraid not. Since my musical education began ten years ago, I have shamefully neglected it. We can head towards the remains of it," replied Georgiana.

"Do you remember when we used to play 'wiggles' in it?" asked Thomas.

Georgiana laughed and Elizabeth looked quizzical. Glancing at Elizabeth, Georgiana continued, "Do not feel remiss that you do not know the meaning of 'wiggles'. It was a game that Thomas and I made up to entertain ourselves."

At that moment, the three heard an agonizing bark of a dog in pain.

Georgiana screamed, "Phillip! Are you hurt Phillip?" She began running down the walk toward the plaintive, repetitive hoarse sounding barks. Elizabeth and Thomas hastened to follow her.

After a few moments, Georgiana found Phillip entangled in the exposed roots of a lilac bush. Fearful of hurting her pet any further, she hastened to reassure him by sitting down next to him. She talked in a broken manner, "What is the matter. . . Phillip, where does it hurt?"

Thomas knelt down and began to examine how he could extricate the dog. After pulling several roots, the trapped paw was loosened and Thomas slid the dog away from the bush. Thomas began to pet Phillip on the head while he gently examined him; his barking ceased and his breathing became more regular. Thomas looked at Georgiana's frightened face and said, "It appears his left rear leg is broken at the tibia. I am afraid he is in great pain."

"What can we do?" Georgiana asked anxiously.

"Because you are his mistress, he will probably only let you pick him up. Let us take him over to the stables so we can find a splint for his leg and perhaps a horse sedative before we apply it," Thomas said in a commanding tone which suggested he knew exactly what to do.

"Elizabeth, will you go tell my brother what has happened and tell him to send someone to help us?" Georgiana implored.

Elizabeth turned and started walking quickly back to the hall. With Thomas patting Phillip's head, Georgiana slowly placed her arms under her beloved dog and picked him up. Phillip groaned and started to pant quickly for a while.

Later, in the stable, Mr. Reynolds found them standing in front of a table where Phillip was resting quietly from sedation. "Phillip is all right now, Mr. Reynolds. Thomas has fashioned a very good splint for him and he appears comfortable. Do let Mr. Darcy know everything is all right. I shall carry Phillip up to my room where he can stay tonight." She began to put her hands underneath him and he became restless. Her hands started to shake. Thomas noticed her unsteadiness and asked if he could carry Phillip up to her room. He gently took the sedated dog and began walking carefully towards Pemberley Hall. The December twilight slowed the march. Entering the large doors in front, a procession of the household formed going up the wide semicircular stairs to the second floor. Mrs. Reynolds and Elizabeth were allowed by the others to follow closest behind Thomas and Georgiana.

Laying Phillip down on a large pillow on the floor, Thomas straightened his back and sat down. Georgiana walked up to the side of his chair and spoke softly, "Thank you, Thomas, for the way you have helped Phillip. I am sure he and I will never forget it."

He took her hand in his and squeezed it in a friendly manner.

Mrs. Reynolds said, "Miss Darcy, I will watch Phillip for now. You do not look entirely well. Please go downstairs and tell your brother what has happened. He is anxious to hear how Phillip is doing. He said to interrupt him, if necessary."

"No, I want to stay with Phillip for the evening," she replied.

Mrs. Reynolds and Elizabeth implored her to go downstairs and she finally yielded when they said she would be needed later to help watch Phillip during the night.

Elizabeth, Thomas and Georgiana moved downstairs to the drawing room and Georgiana gladly received a cup of tea from a servant. After drinking several sips, she said, "There, I feel better now. I think the shakiness is gone."

"Good, I think Phillip is going to be fine. The splint looks wonderful," Elizabeth soothingly replied.

Mr. Darcy and Sir William entered the room and walked over to where Georgiana and Thomas were seated in separate chairs. Thomas explained the events and the condition of Phillip, while Georgiana nodded in agreement with the story.

A servant came announcing the arrival of Elizabeth's

family, the Bennets. All of those present in the drawing room moved to the welcoming hall. Elizabeth led the way in introductions. Mr. and Mrs. Bennet, along with her sister Kitty, were introduced to the Staleys.

"Mamma, where is Mary?" Elizabeth asked Mrs. Bennet.

"She has decided to stay this time with her Aunt Phillips." Lowering her voice to Elizabeth, although Georgiana could hear, she continued, "I think she has become interested in one of your uncle's law clerks. I thought she would never get interested in a man, so I prevailed on Mr. Bennet for her to stay in Meryton." Then, with a whisper she added, "Pemberley is even grander than you described in your letters."

Kitty seemed insensible to the grandeur; as the men moved back to the study, she began asking Elizabeth about Thomas. Her questions about him quickly exhausted her elder sister's knowledge. Elizabeth began to refer Kitty to Georgiana for answers. When Kitty looked at Georgiana, she abruptly stopped and said politely, "Miss Darcy need not answer me. I am being too inquisitive to be courteous."

During the dinner hour, Kitty engaged the attention of Mr. Thomas Staley more than Georgiana could. As the Darcys and Bennets bid goodbye to the Staleys for the night, Georgiana sensed a new emotion, unwarranted irritation, towards Miss Bennet and could not understand why. The thought flitted through her mind that she was jealous--but she quickly dismissed it. Due to her education being entirely private at Pemberley and in London, she had few close female companions until the arrival of Elizabeth. As a result, Georgiana never had to compete for the attention of a young man. She had always considered Thomas an amiable friend, even a brother. When Mr. Thomas Staley visited, she did not have to share his attention with any other woman her age. The inquiries of Kitty elevated Thomas in her esteem, but Georgiana understood neither the jealousy nor the esteem.

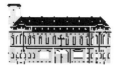

Chapter Four

The next morning, Mr. and Mrs. Bingley were to arrive at Pemberley House. Mr. Charles Bingley, a jolly young man, had a good opinion of everyone. Mrs. Bingley, known as Jane to her family, was the eldest among the five girls born to Mr. and Mrs. Bennet. Elizabeth considered Jane her dearest sister.

Upon arrival, Jane and Elizabeth hugged each other while Georgiana greeted Mr. Bingley. As the sisters embraced, Elizabeth said, "I am delighted you are so early; however, mother and Kitty are still getting ready and will be down soon." Pulling back and looking at her sister, she asked, with a twinkle in her eye, "Now, then, how does it feel to be an old married woman, Jane?"

"Lizzy, I have been married only two months, and not one second longer than you!"

"Yes, you have; you said 'I do' ten seconds before I did at our double wedding."

"Oh, Lizzy, I can see you have not become overly serious yet!"

"Nor shall I ever," said Elizabeth with a smile. "Jane, I know you have met Georgiana. She is becoming my dearest feminine friend besides yourself."

Georgiana curtsied.

"Georgiana, this is a very high compliment to you. Lizzy chooses her friends quite carefully."

"And I mine. Lizzy has also become my dearest

friend."

"I hear you are very accomplished at playing the harp and pianoforte," said Jane.

"I will admit to playing them," replied Georgiana.

"Please, let us hear you this evening. It has been much too long since I have heard a harp played," Jane said earnestly.

Elizabeth turned to Mr. Bingley and said, "Mr. Darcy and my father have been walking the gardens since early this morning. You should find them in the hothouse by now."

Mr. Bingley walked away towards the garden as Elizabeth led the ladies to the entrance parlor. Jane said, "I bring a letter from our Uncle and Aunt Gardiner. I have not opened it but it is my understanding they will not be able to come to Pemberley for Christmas."

Elizabeth sat down and read the letter. She handed it to Jane who, after perusing it, forwarded it to Georgiana who read:

My Dear Elizabeth,

I am greatly disappointed to write that your uncle and I will be unable to come to you this Christmas. Your uncle has pressing legal business which could not wait until after the holidays. He hopes to complete much of it by spring and break away to see Derbyshire in April.

At that time, I shall want to ride the perimeter of the Pemberley grounds in our phaeton with little ponies as we have talked about so often.

Give our love to Mr. Darcy. We are most proud of your marriage to him. We are humbly glad to have been of service in helping to unite you.

Sincerely,

Your Aunt Gardiner

"Lizzy, what does your aunt mean by helping to unite you and my brother?" Georgiana inquired in a soft voice.

Elizabeth and Jane glanced at each other and laughed.

"Only Jane and Mr. Darcy know the entire story, but I can see that you should be told so we have no secrets," replied Elizabeth.

With a sigh, Elizabeth told the story of her visit to Rosing Park in the spring and how she turned down Mr. Darcy's first proposal.

Georgiana gasped, "You turned my brother down once?"

"Yes, I am ashamed to admit my own stupid reasons of pride and prejudice; though, I still think properly, that a woman should marry only with affection. At the time, I had no affection and thus I did not wish to marry," replied Elizabeth.

"I agree, Lizzy. It is so important for a woman to marry with affection. Too many of our sex marry only for duty, particularly when they can improve their lot," said Jane.

"My brother was probably quite upset at your refusal," said Georgiana.

"You will have to ask him about his reaction. Only, I prefer you not dwell on my past foolishness." Continuing the story, Elizabeth related how Mr. and Mrs. Gardiner took her on a tour of Derbyshire. Elizabeth was curious about Pemberley and thought she was touring it when none of the Darcys were home; however, a chance meeting occurred when Mr. Darcy returned unexpectedly, and the rest was common knowledge to Georgiana.

"Despite our difficulties in getting together, Mr. Darcy is the kindest, most affectionate husband any woman could have," said Elizabeth. As she looked at Jane she continued, "Though, I suppose, Jane would disagree with me and say Mr. Bingley was the best."

Jane smiled, but Elizabeth cried to Georgiana, "However, Mr. Bingley and Jane only smile, while your brother and I laugh!" After their laughter subsided, Elizabeth continued, "Jane, let Georgiana and I show you some of

Pemberley." Turning to Georgiana, she asked, "Will you help with a tour of the house for Jane and the rest of my family?"

"Certainly. First, I must go check on my dog, Phillip."

Elizabeth rejoined, "I would also like to see how he is doing." Looking at Jane she explained, "Phillip broke his leg yesterday. Shall we check in on him and then find Mother and Kitty?"

Entering the bedroom, the women could see that Phillip was now awake. His eyes were bright. He barked softly when he saw Georgiana. He tried to come to her, but with his left rear leg dragging in a splint, he managed to elicit pathetic looks from the women. Statements of pity and love poured forth from them, particularly when Georgiana picked him up in her arms.

"Now, Phillip, it is important that you rest and eat well." Phillip's eyes looked as if he wanted adventure rather than convalescence. He eagerly accepted the patting of the women before being placed back in his basket. He was reassured that Georgiana would return after the tour with Elizabeth's family.

The ladies enjoyed viewing the house and had a brief time of rest and preparation before gathering in the parlor for the 5 o'clock dinner hour. When they were all present downstairs, a servant announced, "The Earl of Westbrook and his family have arrived."

The Darcys, Bingleys and Bennets went outside to greet the visitors. The Earl, a fat man of medium height, stepped out first. His wife, Countess of Westbrook, who had a proud and serious face, was close behind. His older son, with the courtesy title of Viscount of Derby, and who was known as Lord Westbrook, stepped down. The younger brother was introduced as the Honorable Henry Westbrook.

Lord Westbrook (the son) approached Georgiana

and said with a sigh, "How is my Miss Darcy?"

"Good. Thank you, and yourself?"

"For myself, the journey here was quite tiring. Coach rides in December should be avoided. One never has enough energy for them."

"Step aside, Alfred, so I also can greet Georgiana," said Henry Westbrook. Moving in front of his brother, "It has been too long since I have seen you."

At that moment, two other carriages arrived. One carried Mr. Bingley's sister, Miss Caroline Bingley, and the other, the Staleys. Miss Bingley stepped out of the carriage in her usual fine dress. The younger Lord Westbrook spied her and quickly went over to introduce himself. Then he escorted her back to the group.

Caroline Bingley was the proud woman who had set her cap for Mr. Darcy and disdained Elizabeth's chances for engaging him. However, when she lost, Miss Bingley was quick to make amends with Mrs. Elizabeth Darcy in order to continue her social contacts at Pemberley.

Mr. Darcy introduced Elizabeth to all of the Westbrooks. The Staleys and Westbrooks knew each other. The Bennets and Bingleys were introduced all around. The families then entered the large, welcoming doors of Pemberley.

As the group settled in the parlor, Elizabeth whispered in Georgiana's ear, "Come with me to the dining room." When they were alone, Elizabeth said, "I have never had the responsibility of seating guests at a large dinner party before. I shall need your help."

Georgiana said, "I am sure you will do fine."

Elizabeth replied, "But, I am not entirely certain of everyone's social rank. Further, I am not sure who will converse well with each other. I could consult *Burke's* at this point to get things straight, but you have had your friends over before and know their social status."

"Indeed, what is familiar to me might be confusing to you. Clearly, my brother should escort in the Countess. You will need to escort the Earl. Lord Westbrook and Mr. Henry Westbrook should be seated next. I will then sit next to Mr. Thomas Staley, although we can interrupt the usual sequence for relations sake and Kitty may be advanced to sit beside one of the Westbrook sons. Then, I shall not have to be flanked by three men, although I do not mind sitting next to Thomas. Then, you should seat Mr. and Mrs. Bingley, Sir William Staley and, finally, you can place your parents, the Bennets."

Elizabeth replied, "I can not help but notice you omitted Miss Bingley. How far away from Mr. Darcy can we seat her?" she asked mischievously.

"What did you have in mind?"

"I should prefer seating her in the library, if that were possible."

Georgiana laughed and Elizabeth was smiling as Mr. Darcy entered the room. His face inquired the reason for the gaiety and Elizabeth explained, "Georgiana and I were discussing the seating arrangement for tonight. Since Miss Bingley is an old flame of yours, we were wondering about the propriety of exiling her to the library during the meal."

Darcy replied, "My dear Lizzy, I can assure you that the heat was all on Miss Bingley's side, not mine; I believe she desired Pemberley more than its master."

Mrs. Darcy approached her husband and kissed him on the cheek. "I know Caroline Bingley has made amends to me, but I am still uncomfortable with her being near you, my love. I expect my discomfort will disappear eventually."

Darcy pulled her closer and returned her kiss. "You have no need for concern about the matter. You are the only one to command my attention." He sighed, "Duty calls and I must return to our guests; but you, my loveliest Elizabeth, will remain in my thoughts." He reluctantly released her, winked at his blushing sister, and left the room.

Elizabeth resumed the conversation with Georgiana, "Thank you for helping me with the seating order. I believe we will seat Caroline Bingley next to Lord Westbrook. I spent this morning going over the other details for the seven course meal. I assume the service will be á la francaise."

Georgiana replied, "Yes, that is our practice here. My brother is quite adept at carving the venison that you are planning for this evening."

The meal went as smoothly as could be expected. Georgiana observed that Mr. Henry Westbrook and Kitty Bennet were talking pleasantly. She even heard them laugh together several times. Georgiana had a discussion with Thomas of several books she had been reading lately. When the meal was done, Mr. Bennet said, "Where are the glasses for wine?"

Mr. Darcy rose and said, "Mr. Bennet has asked a reasonable question about the cups for wine. Some of you around the table know that seven years ago tonight my own dear father was finally able to give up his habit of alcohol. For too long, it had ensnared him and caused a decline in his health. He lived for two more years before dying of cirrhosis of the liver. Tonight, not for any moral reasons, but in memory of my father, I thought we should have only coffee and tea."

Finishing this, Mr. Darcy looked at Sir William Staley who stood, "Thank you, Fitzwilliam. Your father was a good man with a bad habit. As you know, I, too, was caught up in this struggle. Your father and I worked through the difficulty together. I appreciate your decision this evening to avoid it. To our new visitors here tonight, we hasten to add that if you drink alcohol, you will not offend those of us who choose not to imbibe it. We only beg your indulgence in our forbearance of it this evening."

Mr. Darcy added, "Mr. Bennet, we are happy to bring

you some wine, if you desire."

Mr. Bennet stood and replied, "In memory of your great father, I am quite happy to join you in honoring him in this way. It is good for a man to practice forbearance." He paused for a moment and then said, tongue-in-cheek,

> Anything that might prolong my life
> has the approbation of my wife;
> who, as most of you know, holds her breath
> over losing our estate upon my death.

Everyone laughed. With the after dinner speeches done, the ladies stood and proceeded to the parlor for coffee.

When they reached the parlor, Mrs. Bennet said directly to Kitty, "Now Kitty, Mr. Henry Westbrook is quite a man, being the second son of an earl. He also seems interested in you; he is the one you want to set your hat for, not this other fellow, Mr. Staley--he is only the second son of a baronet!"

Though the latter statement was not made to the entire group, Georgiana heard it and disliked her friend being described in such a disparaging manner. After all, a baronet was a respectable title for a gentleman! A baronet was not as high in status as an earl, but it mattered little since second sons were unlikely to inherit the family title anyway.

After thirty minutes discussing the politics of Derbyshire, the gentlemen rejoined the women in the parlor.

The conversation was initially started as to who was going to go to London for the "season." "We are escaping the countryside to return to London in less than a month," the Countess stated. "Miss Darcy, are you returning soon?"

Georgiana said, "No, since my brother and Elizabeth are staying at Pemberley, I shall remain with them. I should prefer to never return to London, since I do not enjoy either the air or the society there."

Caroline Bingley remonstrated, "Now, Georgiana, surely you do not desire to avoid London for the season. St. James' court and the society there make life meaningful. Further, how will you progress in your musical talent?"

"I am far enough along to where only continued practice is needed for improvement."

Georgiana looked at Elizabeth for help, who added, "My sister is a shy girl with little desire for any society beyond that of a rural country life. As to her musical talents, she far exceeds my own and has become the official musician of Pemberley Hall. Georgiana, would you favor us with a song on your harp?"

She moved to play it and, during the first number, she was particularly pleased to note the approbation of her playing shown on Thomas' face. The group clapped at the end of her second number. How different was her musical personality from her public persona! Once playing, she could do so without fear or shyness; but when speaking, other than to her family or friends, she would revert to silent shyness.

Henry Westbrook approached Kitty and said, "Your bonnet and scarf are quite handsome. Did you buy them or make them?"

Kitty bashfully replied, "I bought them, sir." She began coughing, rose, and excused herself from the room.

As Georgiana approached, Thomas inquired of Henry, "Tell me how your studies are going at Cambridge."

"I have one more semester to finish and then I hope to take holy orders and find a living. As you know, second sons of gentlemen have few options. Since we do not inherit the estate, we can be soldiers, sailors, teachers or clergymen. I am too slow physically to be a good officer; and as to teaching, I would rather teach morals than history or mathematics, since morals have such an important impact on all other aspects of our lives."

Georgiana replied, "I agree entirely."

Thomas nodded in assent. Kitty returned to the group and asked Henry, "Pray, Mr. Westbrook, tell me about your estate."

He replied, "Please call me Henry." She nodded her assent and he continued, "It is not as grand as Pemberley, but larger than your average gentleman's estate in Derbyshire. The house is as large as Pemberley House, but we have only half the land. . . . How long will you be here Miss Bennet?"

"I am uncertain." Kitty went over to her father, Mr. Bennet, and asked, "May we stay at Pemberley for several months?"

"Something's caught your eye, eh?" her father replied with a half serious grin and continued, "Shall I need to remain to chaperone you?"

"Oh, how awful Father," Kitty replied and coughed again.

Seeing her hurt expression he said reassuringly, "I am only engaging in a diversion. I see no militia men here that will whisk you off for an elopement."

"Be serious Father," replied Kitty.

"Your mother and I must return within a week, but if your sister and Mr. Darcy do not object, I see no reason why you could not stay here a month or two."

"Oh! Thank you, Father," was Kitty's delighted reply.

Mr. Henry Westbrook approached his mother the Countess and asked, "May we invite the Bennets and Staleys to our estate for a ball?"

The Countess replied, "Of course, my son. It will help relieve some of the boredom we endure here before returning to London." Turning to her elder son, she asked, "What is this I hear about Mr. Thomas Staley working in the fields last summer at Staley Manor?"

"I cannot believe the rumor is true, Mamma," said her older son, who as he spoke, pulled out a handkerchief to pat his face. Continuing, "A gentleman should never work, and

I, for one, desire never to do so."

"Have Mr. Thomas Staley brought over here to explain himself," the Countess said in a commanding tone. Hearing this, Thomas approached her and sat down.

"Thomas, is this true you worked in the fields of Staley Manor last summer?"

"What do you mean by work? Surely a gentleman needs to be out during the harvest of his estate?"

"I do not mean supervision of the tenants. I mean actual field work and cutting of the wheat. Using the scythe and sickle and all that," she replied.

"I cannot deny that I have done so. Hard work makes me feel so much more alive."

"You should get your exercise by fencing or some such sporting thing. The tenants need to understand their class; only by the gentry staying aloof will the lower classes remain respectful."

"What? And have the harvest go bad, my lady? We have a labor shortage, with many of the tenants moving to Ashton to work in the cotton mills."

Georgiana became anxious about Thomas having to defend himself before the Countess.

Jane sensed this and tried to soften the conversation by saying, "Let me apply to Mr. Darcy. Surely, Ma'am, he can arbitrate this. His family has descended from the D'arcys of Norman times, the original gentility."

"What do you say, Mr. Darcy?"

"I must warn you, I have a strong opinion on the subject," Mr. Darcy replied and paused. "Pray continue," the Countess said.

"While it is true that the principal definition of a gentleman is that he does not have to work, this definition does not prohibit such action. I, myself, like to supervise the estate."

"Well, certainly no one objects to 'working' in that

sense. Our large manors need supervision just as we need the House of Lords to help govern the nation."

"I would not limit it only to that, my lady. I worked in the fields, sometimes, when I was Thomas' age for the sheer joy of doing so. It helped me to understand the tenants."

"The tenants do not need to be understood," the Countess barked. "They need to do their work and pay their respect."

Mr. Darcy, tiring of the duel, walked away during the last statement.

Georgiana continued to be quiet. She was reticent in such company. However, the provision of such information helped her understand why her brother was so well liked and respected by the tenants of Pemberley. He had condescended to work among them and by doing so had earned their respect. Georgiana could see that Thomas enjoyed the jousting between Mr. Darcy and the Countess; both Mr. Darcy and his opponent were strong personalities that most people found difficult to contradict.

Not letting up, the Countess turned once again to Thomas and said, "Are you involved with those religious dissenters?"

"Do you mean the Methodists?'

"Are they not all the same? They all disagree with the true church of England," she replied.

"I should think not. The Methodists are not outlandish like the Clapham Sect, for example."

"Do not try to divide and conquer me young man," she ordered. "Tell me your position."

"My family has been involved in Methodism for a long time. John Wesley, himself, visited Staley Hall in 1745. But as you know, since he lived during your lifetime, he did not desire to start a new church, but merely to reform the church of England. He died a church priest."

With a frown she said, "I never liked John Wesley. He was always preaching to the masses and riff-raff. He has guilt by association with the lower classes."

"Do you not consider it likely, ma'am, that his revivals with the masses of England probably prevented a replication of the French Revolution from occurring here? Indeed, you may owe your **head** to him."

The Countess flushed with anger at the reference to the guillotine and continued the offensive, "Enough of John Wesley. Are you or are you not a melancholy Methodist?"

"I am not certain. I attend the Sunday morning services at the parish church and the Methodist society during the week. I do not know if I believe either."

Several gasps went up from the group. Caroline Bingley sneered, "Do you mean to say you are a faithless, nonbeliever? Is this what dabbling in non-conformity has done to you? Someone who may even become a heretic?"

Georgiana's heart sank. She was developing such respect for Thomas; but, now, his questioning of Christianity had the potential to grievously injure her opinion of him.

"I did not say the doctrines are untrue. I merely said I am uncertain whether I should believe them. For example, Christmas will be here in two days. The Christian doctrine says that the incarnation occurred; or, in other words, that God became a man and dwelt among us. If that is so, then it is an awesome doctrine and the most important historical event ever to occur. If I should submit to these ideas, I think they would make me more radical than the average yawn the doctrines seem to elicit from many in the Church of England."

"My son, do not mistake quiet thinking with weak faith," she said.

Mr. Darcy had heard the entire inquisition by the Countess and returned to the conversation circle. Elizabeth turned to him and asked, "And what do you think, Mr.

Darcy?"

"I do not blame Mr. Thomas Staley for his position. I think it is good if a young man is skeptical of his faith. Eventually, it will either make him a much better Christian or an honest sinner," he finished.

Mr. Darcy, as always, was a hard man to contradict. This statement seemed to end the discussion about religion and Thomas' role in it.

While Georgiana admired Thomas' pluck, she was uneasy about some of his statements. She did not worry about his leanings towards Methodism. What worried her was his doubt of the doctrines. How could someone who had grown up with her be skeptical of such verities?

Mrs. Jane Bingley, sensing the discomfort of the Darcys, stood up and proposed, "Come, let us play whist. Who is going to play cards?"

Mr. and Mrs. Bingley formed a table with Mr. Henry Westbrook and Miss Bennet while Miss Bingley joined Lord Westbrook, Mrs. Bennet, and the Countess. The four older men chose to sit by the fire leaving Mrs. and Miss Darcy sitting by Thomas Staley.

In a lowered voice, Mrs. Darcy said, "Do not let the Countess bother you Thomas; she is insufferable to everyone, including me. If I had an opening, I should have liked to defend you."

Thomas replied, "Do not let it vex you, Mrs. Darcy. I find I must be truthful about these things and, if I am attacked for such a position, so be it. I must say, however, I enjoyed your husband's responses."

Georgiana was relieved at Elizabeth's opinion of the conversation between the Countess and Thomas. She also admired Thomas' courage for not fretting about the opinions of others.

The evening wore on. Finally, after two games of whist, Mr. Bingley jumped up and went to Mr. Darcy and said loudly, "Let us liven up the party with a dance!" He looked at his wife, Jane, who smiled in agreement. Bingley nudged Mr. Darcy again, "Come on, old man, let us dance with our brides!"

Mr. Darcy smiled and asked leave of his fellows. He approached Elizabeth and took her hand as she stood. They turned to ask Georgiana if she wanted to play the pianoforte or dance. Before she could answer, Mr. Bingley, who had followed Mr. Darcy over to where Elizabeth and Georgiana were sitting, said, "She must dance. My own sister, Caroline, will play for us tonight." Georgiana turned and looked to Thomas for help; he immediately strode over to ask her to dance.

Henry Westbrook asked Catherine Bennet to round out the foursome and the party was gay for some time. Later, even the young Lord Westbrook danced with Miss Bingley and once with Kitty Bennet, but then he sat down and declared it too much exertion. Georgiana observed more than passing interest between Kitty and Mr. Henry Westbrook during their dancing.

She heard Henry say to Kitty, "How long will you be visiting Pemberley?" and her reply of "At least one month."

"This is a very fine estate for you to visit."

"Yes," she replied, "and I find the company interesting."

"We shall want you to visit Westbrook manor sometime this month. We are only five miles away."

Georgiana was pleased that Henry showed interest in Kitty and that Miss Bennet seemed to return his attention.

Chapter Five

Christmas morning came to Pemberley. Georgiana was glad to have the house fuller than it had been in a long time. Mr. and Mrs. Bingley brought a happy atmosphere with them. Mr. Bennet's sly comments about life balanced out Mrs. Bennet's silly comments. Mrs. Bennet continued in awe of Mr. Darcy and seldom said anything in front of him.

With Kitty no longer asking questions about Thomas, Georgiana ceased feeling there was any distance between Kitty and herself. Georgiana was glad to see her loving sister, Elizabeth, as the bridge with all of the visitors. It was both a pleasure and a learning experience for her to observe Elizabeth's encouragement and lively repartee with her family and friends. Even Miss Bingley talked nicely to Elizabeth and remained friendly.

Two days after Christmas, the servant brought a letter to her. She took the letter and went to her room and read:

> Dear Georgiana,
>
> Do not be alarmed at the conversation after the dinner party about my beliefs or lack of them at the present time.
>
> I want to believe in the Christian doctrines, but feel unable to do so at present. I hope my asking, seeking and knocking will be rewarded someday.

We did not have time to talk extensively.
As you know, I wish to attend college. I am
hoping for an assistanceship from the
library at Cambridge that will allow me to
attend the next session. Otherwise, I may need
to leave Derbyshire to seek work.

I dare not promise to write. Men are such
poor letter writers. What women will write
a page about, a man will write only one sentence. My warmest regards to your family.

Sincerely,
Thomas

Something about the letter touched Georgiana. She
was pleased that Thomas would write and show concern for
her opinion of him. She read the letter many times and then
placed it in a drawer where she kept her valuables. She was
uncertain about her feelings for Thomas. Was this love?
Even after thinking about it at length, she remained
undecided. She esteemed his intelligence and amiability. She
concluded he was, at the least, a good friend. Her thinking
was diverted by thankfulness that the loneliness of
Pemberley was being filled with friends and family.

She wrote the following reply to Thomas:

Dear Thomas,

Your letter arrived today. I am trying to understand your heart seeking for the
truth. I will pray for you--that you will be
guided into understanding which will help you
accept our religion. Perhaps, we can discuss
this further in the future.

I trust you will be able to attend
Cambridge and not have to delay your education. I know how important this is to you.

As you know, a ball is being planned next
week at the Westbrook Manor. I hope you
will be able to attend; your presence always
makes me feel more comfortable at social affairs.
Regardless, I remain,
Your friend,
Georgiana

The day for the planned ball dawned and it began to
snow lightly. By breakfast time, only an inch or two had fallen;
however, the skies appeared uncertain. At the breakfast
table, Kitty worried, "I suppose this will mean our ball is
canceled tonight?"

Mr. Darcy replied, "In view of the storms effect on
the older among us, I believe the Westbrooks are likely to
postpone their ball."

Elizabeth said, "I am certain the young people will be
quite disappointed. Perhaps, some other activity could be
substituted for them."

"Dear Brother, would a sleigh ride be possible?"
Georgiana asked.

"Excellent idea," cried Caroline Bingley.

All eyes focused on Mr. Darcy.

"Will you allow it?" Elizabeth asked.

Mr. Darcy finally smiled and said, "This can probably
be arranged; however, should the storm, which appears mild
now, turn to bitter cold or blowing snow, we shall have to
cancel it."

Servants were sent to the adjoining manors and
returned with favorable replies for the sleigh ride. It was
agreed that if the weather turned more severe it would not
take place. The plans called for the young people to gather
at Pemberley and the Westbrook brothers should bring
their three seat sleigh.

At the appointed time of four o'clock, the

Westbrooks arrived with their sleigh, and Thomas came soon after. Only three inches of snow had fallen, but a light snow continued, without any wind.

As they all gathered in the entrance hall, Caroline Bingley said, "How delightful this shall be, a sleigh ride in the country. I anticipate how jealous my friends in London will be."

Georgiana said, "Now, are we all bundled up enough?"

Elizabeth, who was standing nearby, spoke up, "In addition to your coats, we have some very warm lap robes that you may use."

As the young people assembled in the area outside the entrance doors, a silent drama took place. The young women had thought much about their respective positions in the sleigh; and the men, evidently, less so. Kitty looked imploringly at Henry Westbrook who decided to ask her to sit with him in the middle seat. That being settled, Thomas had little desire to sit with Miss Bingley or Lord Westbrook and was inclined by friendship to ask Georgiana to sit with him in the back seat. This left Caroline Bingley with her desired choice, Lord Westbrook; she went up to him and took his arm saying, "Well, my lord, that leaves us to take the front seat."

Lord Westbrook, whose face appeared to never have thought about the relative positions in the sleigh, readily consented with, "It will be a pleasure, Miss Bingley. I hope the front seat is not too cold for you."

"Come, come, Lord Westbrook. I shall be fine," she replied.

In a minute they were off. Georgiana enjoyed the gentle gliding of the sleigh over the new snow. She liked having Thomas at her side. Despite her misgivings about his religious devotion, he was a childhood friend whom she trusted and with whom she could easily converse.

"Do you like the ride so far?" Thomas inquired of her.

"Oh, yes, very much so. I like having an occasional snowflake land on my face; and do you, Thomas?"

"I agree. Being out like this makes me feel very alive. Each season needs to be sensed at its best expression, and I think we are experiencing the very essence of winter." After a few moments, Thomas called forward to the next seat, "Henry, where have you told your driver to take us?"

Henry turned and responded, "I thought we should go to our own estate first. I have invited Kitty to see it and she still has not been able to come." Henry turned and began talking to Kitty again.

Thomas resumed talking with Georgiana, "I have not had time to tell you about my acceptance of the library assistanceship at Cambridge. I shall be leaving in a week or so to start my first session."

"Oh, Thomas, I shall miss you so." She remained quiet for a minute and then continued, "My feelings are mixed about your departure. You will be gone for such long intervals that I fear we may become strangers. On the other hand, you will discover more books and poetry and will return a scholar."

Thomas was quiet for awhile and did not respond to her last statement. He then said, "Henry, I cannot see it, but we must be approaching Westbrook Estate."

"Indeed, Thomas, you are right. We shall be there in five minutes."

Westbrook Hall was a fine estate. The graceful outlining of it by the snow increased its grandeur. The group was greeted by the Earl and Countess and they were all soon stamping their feet in the entrance parlor.

Lord Westbrook declared, "I think I have already had enough of this bitter weather. I will stay here and the rest of you may go on."

Caroline Bingley looked at the Countess and said, "I

also am more fatigued than I anticipated. May I stay tonight and return to Pemberley in the morning?"

"Of course, my dear," the Countess' replied.

Hot coffee was brought out to the group. The conversation turned to a discussion of the clergy.

Kitty said, in a careless way, "I usually try to hide when a clergyman visits our house in Longbourn."

"Pray tell me why?" was Henry's response.

"I find them to be such bores. Or, as in the case of Mr. Collins, the rector of Hunsford Park, they are absolutely silly."

The room became very quiet since the other young people knew of Henry Westbrook's plan to become a clergyman. Henry became serious and asked, "Have you no interest in religion at all?"

"Very little. I rarely say my prayers. I try to avoid going to church as often as possible." Smiling a little, she added, "My cough always seems to get worse on Sunday mornings."

Georgiana was aghast at such irreverent expressions and the discomforture that her statements must be causing her potential suitor. It was clear to Georgiana's observation that Kitty was not aware of Henry Westbrook's professional plans; otherwise, she would have not spoken so bluntly.

Caroline Bingley looked sharply at Kitty. Georgiana looked at Thomas, who appeared amused by Kitty's honesty. Georgiana gave him a gentle elbow in his side and he instantly acquired a serious look.

Henry Westbrook rose and said, "Then this is what you think of the clergy? A silly, useless lot?"

Kitty's face began to evolve an expression that recognized she had committed a blunder. Uncertain of the exact insult, she tried to retreat by saying, "I am sure they perform vital functions. I was just giving my reaction to them."

Henry Westbrook coolly replied, "I also have had enough of a sleigh ride today." Turning to Thomas he said, "Mr. Staley, would you be so good as to accompany Miss Bennet and Miss Darcy back to Pemberley Hall tonight?"

"Of course, Henry. We probably better get going before the weather worsens."

Back in the sleigh, Thomas and Kitty were sitting on each side of one seat, with Georgiana in between. When they were well away from Westbrook Hall, Kitty asked Georgiana in an anxious voice, "What did I do wrong back there? Why did Henry react so strongly to my statements?"

Georgiana tried to reply as gently as possible, "Did you not know that Henry is preparing to become a clergyman? He will finish Cambridge this next year and take his holy orders shortly afterwards."

Despite the wintry weather, Kitty began crying. Between sobs, she said, "I am so foolish. . . Father always said my foolishness would hurt me someday. . . Mr. Henry Westbrook is the first man I felt I could really love; and now, I have destroyed any good opinion he may have had of me."

Returning to the parlor at Pemberley, Georgiana bid Thomas a friendly goodbye and turned her attention to the crisis confronting Kitty. The fireplaces were rejuvenated. Mrs. Bennet, Jane and Elizabeth came to where Kitty and Georgiana were sitting. Kitty looked up at her mother and said, "Oh, Mamma, I have been so stupid."

Her mother replied, "Oh! Kitty. Nothing can be so bad as this. Tell me about it."

"I insulted Mr. Henry Westbrook's profession. I did not know he planned to enter the clergy. I told him of my hiding from visiting clergymen and my lack of interest in church."

Her mother exclaimed, "Did you not learn anything from your dear sister, Lydia, about how to capture a husband?"

Kitty began crying again.

This behavior caused her mother to reply in a soothing tone, "There, there, my dear. I must agree your statement was rather silly, even for you."

"Mamma!" Elizabeth protested.

"Well, well. Young women will make their gaffes, and I suppose it was time for Kitty to expose herself."

"Mamma! You are not helping Kitty," Elizabeth rejoined.

"Now, Elizabeth, do not pretend you have acted towards men with perfect behavior. Kitty has made her mistake and must go on to some other gentleman."

Kitty continued to cry and between sobs said, "But I felt so strongly for Mr. Henry Westbrook. . . he is such a fine gentleman. . . it is clear I have been much too foolish. . .".

"Now, now, girl," Mrs. Bennet replied, "You just must be more clever next time."

"Mamma, you are not helping here," Elizabeth said. "Would you be so kind as to find father and let him know what has happened."

Mrs. Bennet looked coolly at Elizabeth, but felt the force of the request since her daughter was now mistress of Pemberley. She arose and walked out with as much dignity as possible.

When Kitty's sobs quieted down, Elizabeth looked at her younger sister and said lovingly, "Now, Kitty, you know Jane and I have tried to remonstrate with you about the careless, self-centered behavior you engaged in with your sister Lydia. Lydia has made a most uncomfortable existence for herself with Mr. Wickham. Do you want the same thing to happen to you?"

"No, but what can I do?"

"You can repent of your frivolousness and attempt some serious behavior in your life."

"What do you mean?"

"I mean stop being self-centered and start trying to help others."

"How can I do that?"

"For one thing, you can help me with sewing for the parish poorbox. We need to mend certain pieces and embroider a few special garments."

"But I know little about sewing."

"Well, it's time you became interested in learning." Elizabeth then referred to Georgiana, "Our sister, Georgiana, is active in visiting the less fortunate in the parish. Perhaps, you can find out from her what the visitation involves."

Kitty, Elizabeth and Jane then turned their attention to Georgiana, who replied, "Do not think I have always wanted to help others. I discovered myself to be vain and selfish when I was rescued from a foolish elopement with Mr. Wickham."

Kitty gasped, "He tried to deceive you also?"

Georgiana replied, "Yes, and it is to my shame that only 18 months ago he almost succeeded. Oh, do not worry, I did not love him at all. In retrospect, it was merely infatuation and the thrill of a first proposal. My feelings for him dissolved within hours of his dismissal by my brother; but then, a goodly period of mourning ensued about my foolish behavior. I repented of my faults and became more serious about our religion. I started to look for ways to spend my time more profitably; one way I discovered was to help the rector in his visitation of the poor."

Kitty responded warmly, "Thank you for telling your story. I was beginning to resent your perfect behavior and thought you were born that way. I see you have matured because of your experiences."

Elizabeth said, "Yes, it is true. Good judgement comes from experience, and experience comes from bad judgement."

Jane continued, "You must not allow this period of mortification to pass without making resolution for improving your behavior."

"I think you are right," Kitty replied. "I despair that Henry Westbrook will ever consider me again; however, I hope that when I meet another grand gentleman, I shall be mature and serious enough to warrant his consideration. Georgiana, even though you are a year younger than myself, I can see you are far ahead of me in the pilgrim's progress. What do you recommend to me?"

Georgiana thought for a moment and then replied, "I have found much strength in my daily prayers. You may join me for awhile and we can discuss the profit involved in such an activity. Secondly, you can begin visiting the parish poor with the rector, Rev. Wilson, and myself every Saturday. The needs are even greater in this wintry weather."

Kitty replied, "I should like very much to do those things. May I start tomorrow in the chapel and visit this week with the rector?"

Georgiana replied, "I should be delighted."

Jane said, "And, Kitty, you must start attending church more regularly."

"I will," Kitty replied. Kitty approached her older sisters and hugged them and thanked them for their longsuffering interest. She also hugged Georgiana and expressed gratitude to her by saying, "I have never wanted so badly to change my ways. I think if I stay around all of my dear sisters, I shall make it. Perhaps, eventually, I shall meet with another gentleman as fine as Mr. Henry Westbrook."

The next morning, after prayers and a chapel visit, Kitty sat down with all of the Bennet and Darcy women and received instruction about embroidering. With several months of instruction from Elizabeth, Georgiana was more of a beginner than anyone else; and, she was, therefore, often more helpful in answering Kitty's questions.

Elizabeth demonstrated the french knot stitch twice, but Kitty was still unable to make it small and close to the fabric.   Elizabeth looked across the room in frustration, "Mamma, you are very good with french knots, perhaps you could help Kitty--I seem to only be confusing her."

"I am happy that you realize I have some talent--after all, I taught you," Mrs. Bennet replied as she took Elizabeth's place beside Kitty. She spent several moments emphasizing the finer points of keeping the knot close to the fabric, and soon Kitty was able to do it reasonably well. In this subject, for once, Mrs. Bennet was of real help. She had taught both Elizabeth and Jane how to embroider and still could perform as well as, or better than, her daughters. She could not see as well, but sewing was the one time the girls could count on their mother being fairly agreeable.

Mr. and Mrs. Bennet, along with the Bingleys, had to leave Pemberley the following morning. Miss Caroline Bingley had achieved her desire of beginning to capture Lord Westbrook, the older son of the nearby estate. She was invited to stay at Westbrook Hall for another fortnight to become better acquainted with the Westbrooks.

The next day being Saturday, Georgiana and Kitty were taken by carriage, about a half mile, to the rectory. The sun had finally broken out. When combined with the reflection from the snow, the day was very bright.

During the carriage ride, Georgiana thought how much she trusted Reverend Wilson. He had presided over the funerals of her parents. From him, she had learned the hope of heaven. Reverend and Mrs. Wilson had treated her with such love and warmth that she felt they were like grandparents to her. As a result, it was only natural when Georgiana suffered her spiritual crisis, eighteen months earlier, that she went to them for counsel. When Rev. Wilson suggested she begin working in visitation with him for the parish, she was eager to be of service, but was reluctant because of her shyness. When Reverend Wilson reassured her that she would be required to say very little, other than greetings, she joyfully consented. Her desire to continue the work was reinforced when she saw the deep needs.

The rector, a gray-haired older man, who looked like a grandfather should, met them when the carriage stopped. He introduced himself to Kitty as she stepped down.

"How do you do? My name is Reverend Wilson. I understand yours is Catherine Bennet?"

"Everyone calls me Kitty."

"And so it shall be, or Miss Bennet as needed." Turning to Georgiana he continued, "How is Miss Darcy today?"

"Fine. Thank you, Reverend."

"I appreciate your coming today. As you know, Miss Darcy, since my wife died one year ago, I have relied on your assistance. Today, we shall visit a family in desperate need. I will tell you both about it as we walk down to the village. First, come inside and pick up the baskets of blankets and food we are going to take to them."

The girls complied and soon they were walking the short distance to the village. The four inches of wet snow made for good traction under their boots. Spots of bare ground were beginning to show. After five minutes, they reached a small cottage, probably better described as a hut, which was boarded up tightly. The rector knocked and a three year old girl gently opened the door and shyly stood behind it.

Reverend Wilson said, "May we come in, Lucy? Your mother knows about our visit."

Without saying anything, the girl opened the door completely and retreated. They entered the gray, cold twilight of the single room. The fire had only a few low-burning coals. The darkness was made worse by the sunshine being interrupted by clouds as they stood at the door. On a bed to the left of the fireplace lay an unkempt man and woman under a blanket. The man coughed and did not stir. The woman, her hair in disarray, turned in the bed and tried to give a weak smile as the Reverend approached.

He drew up a little stool and, before talking to her, looked at Georgiana and asked her to place some coals in the fireplace. Georgiana complied. Kitty stood behind the rector, appalled at the condition of the cottage and of the adults lying before her.

"Mrs. Smith, how are you today?"

She coughed and said in a hoarse voice, "I am sorry, Reverend Wilson, I cannot sit up to greet you. The fever appears to be gone this morning, but I am still quite weak. As you can see, my husband is quite dazed after drinking last night."

The rector replied, "I can see he has returned from the mills in Ashton. Did he bring anything home for you?"

"No, only his drunken body. He gambled away all of his earnings, except for some cheap whiskey, with which he became drunk. It does not seem right that the church should help us, since we have only ourselves to blame."

"Now, now," the rector replied soothingly, "you must not worry about your need. This is no time for a sermon. Once you are all well again, we can talk about the future. We have come to bring some blankets and food."

By this time, the fire was beginning to blaze again, filling the room with light. Georgiana sat at the table with Lucy. After a moment, Georgiana edged closer to the girl and whispered, "I have a little surprise for you."

Lucy's eyes shone through her dirty face as Georgiana pulled out a hand-sized doll and presented it to her. Lucy gave a little shriek and snatched the doll, then ran and hid it under her mattress.

Georgiana asked, "Lucy, why did you hide the doll?"

"Cause I want to keep it."

"No one is going to take it from you." With this reassurance, the girl went back to the bed and retrieved the doll. She began hopping around. Georgiana stood up and took her hands as they danced in a circle. Kitty began to approach, when a loud cry alerted the trio to another member of the family in the cottage. Kitty followed the wail to a little crib behind the mother's bed. She picked up the fussing infant. Cradling the babe in her arms, she began to rock the child back and forth. The baby soon settled down, but upon any cessation of motion began crying again. Kitty looked imploringly at Georgiana.

Georgiana said, "The baby is probably hungry."

They both looked at the mother who said, "I am too sick to let him feed."

Georgiana moved to the table and put some milk in a small sipping cup and gave it to Kitty. The six month old baby eagerly sipped and swallowed the milk. Kitty began humming as she sat down to feed the baby. Georgiana observed a look of compassion and pity on Kitty's face and felt that the effort to involve her new friend was worthwhile. Georgiana and Lucy came over and sat next to Kitty.

Lucy beamed, "I help feed Paul." Then her little face drooped, "We out of milk."

"You are a good big sister," Georgiana reassured Lucy. "We will leave this bottle of milk for you. Can you come with me to get some water for heating? Then we can clean your baby brother."

They soon returned with water and placed it over the fire. After it was warm, Lucy assisted her visitors with placing a clean blanket on the table so Kitty could wash the now contented baby. After the baby was bathed and dressed in clean clothes, Georgiana washed Lucy's face. Noting her dirty dress, she asked, "Lucy, do you have another dress to change into?"

Lucy moved her head side to side in a negative

response and Georgiana said, "I think Reverend Wilson was wise enough to bring a dress about your size." She pulled a solid blue dress out of the basket. Lucy began hopping up and down again. Georgiana helped Lucy slip off the dirty garment and washed her arms before the new one was put on. Georgiana also pulled out a sweater for the little girl, who continued to bounce even as Georgiana tried to help her on with the sweater.

Georgiana looked over to where Mrs. Smith and Reverend Wilson were smiling at Lucy's gaiety. Reverend Wilson then began to take leave by saying to Mrs. Smith, "We do not wish to tire you out. I was not aware that you are unable to cook for your family, and I will ask one of our committee women to come by and help with a meal and laundry today."

"Thank you, Reverend. God bless you," Mrs. Smith replied weakly.

As the threesome walked away from the cottage, Kitty commented, "I have never seen such wretchedness. It gave me a good feeling as we were leaving to see a fire warming the cottage, the baby sleeping and Lucy with a clean face and dress." Kitty moved to take Georgiana's arm and said to her, "Oh! Georgiana, how shall I ever thank you for helping to open my eyes!"

For the remaining six weeks of her stay, Kitty continued to visit the Smith cottage and other places of the poor, with Reverend Wilson and Georgiana. On two occasions, Georgiana was unable to attend, but this did not change Kitty's resolve to continue. Kitty also began attending church every Sunday with enthusiasm, since she had seen Reverend Wilson's practical love in action and was anxious to learn more from him. From such fertile soil, a soul may revive and become stronger.

Three weeks after Kitty had returned to Longbourn

from Pemberley, Georgiana received a letter which read:

> Dear Georgiana,
>   I want to thank you for your help at Pemberley. I have so enjoyed our time and work together.
>   I want to let you know that I have begun visiting the unfortunate here in our Longbourn parish. I do not enjoy it as much as when I am with you or Reverend Wilson. I miss visiting the Smiths, and in particular, holding Paul and seeing Lucy dance.
>   I must confess that sometimes I do not feel like visiting others. Does this ever happen to you? My own response is that visitation is a necessary duty that helps me as much or more than the people I visit, but I wonder what your reply would be to my inquiry. I am afraid I am still very selfish, but as to what to do about it I am quite at a loss.
>   Father has said I may return to Pemberley in two months. I look forward to seeing you again. Give my love to Elizabeth. I will write her soon.
>   Your friend,
>   Kitty

Georgiana was touched by her sister-in-law's letter. She had experienced the same feelings, but had not shared them with anyone else for fear of being told that she was selfish--a trait she was trying her best to forsake. After thinking awhile about it, she penned the following response:

> Dear Kitty,
>   I received your recent letter. I am

pleased that you are continuing your visitation in the parish of Longbourn. We miss your help here.

I must confess that I also, at times, find helping others to be obligation rather than desire. Our feelings may be very common. Perhaps this is what is meant by— "And let us not be weary in well doing: for in due season we shall reap, if we faint not."

I speak confidently for the entire Darcy family that we welcome your return at anytime to Pemberley.

Sincerely, Your Friend,
Georgiana

Chapter Six

For the first time in many years, Georgiana was at home during the month of April. She delighted in this time of the year more than any other. To enjoy the springtime appearance of Pemberley, she took a longer walk than usual. She strolled past the south garden and over the stone bridge, which was formed into a series of arches over the Derwent River that ran through the estate. The ground on both sides leading up to the bridge was carpeted with primroses and other spring flowers. As she stood in the middle of the bridge, a sweet fragrance wafted by her face. She wished the sun would shine, but at least the high clouds did not threaten rain.

She recalled the events of the last six months--how the family atmosphere at Pemberley had been revived! Elizabeth's lively presence stimulated a warmth and depth of personality in her brother which Georgiana never knew existed. The large party before Christmas would now be anticipated each year. Phillip brushed against her dress. She was glad that he recovered with only an occasional limp as evidence for his severe injury last winter.

The Bennets and Bingleys had been gone for a few months. Mr. and Mrs. Gardiner arrived yesterday and Georgiana thought of their first visit here last summer with Elizabeth. She suspected Elizabeth was special to her brother even then, but she did not appreciate the dramatic tension present because of Elizabeth's refusal of her brother's first proposal. While her brother and Elizabeth received the Gardiners with abundant gratitude, Georgiana was also thankful to them for bringing Elizabeth into her life.

Returning to the house, she saw the ponies being brought out for the long talked about ride around the perimeter of the estate. Mrs. Gardiner and Elizabeth came up to her as she returned from the walk. Elizabeth said, "Will you not go with us Georgiana?"

"Is there room in the phaeton for the three of us?"

Mrs. Gardiner said, "I think so if one of us can take the reins for the horses."

Georgiana said, "I will be happy to direct the horses. It has been many years since I have seen the ten mile course around the edge of the property."

Elizabeth said, "I have brought a snack. We may go as far as we wish or return as soon as we wish."

They settled into the open phaeton with their bonnets and riding dresses on. Elizabeth said to Georgiana, "I have not been able to make this tour yet. Please, do not hesitate to show me all the details of it."

The trio soon crossed the arched stone bridge. The carriage trail turned to the south and descended slowly as it turned into the broad and grassy river bank, which stood several feet above the level of the river. Beech trees were to the left on the hill. In the shady places, ferns were untucking themselves. Wild hyacinths could be seen in and among the ferns. The trail was not traveled frequently like the main road above them; as a result, it had grass growing in places. Sparrows were chirping from the trees and the sun was trying to emerge. It was a good day for riding and promised to become a beautiful affair. As they wound their way down the riverbed, Mrs. Gardiner asked Georgiana, "Do you miss London this season?"

Georgiana replied, "Not at all. The air is much better here in the country and the scenery is picturesque. With

Elizabeth here, Pemberley has become animated again."

They soon passed a cluster of tenant houses along the river. Some of the occupants came out to greet Elizabeth and her companions. After an additional hour of riding, they came to a pleasant meadow on a knoll above the river, where it was agreed they would stop, spread out their blanket, and have their snack. While they were sitting down Georgiana declared, "I do not think I shall ever voluntarily return to London for the season."

Elizabeth replied, "Oh, do not say so. A young woman of your age needs the social interaction. However, I am quite happy to have you stay here. Pemberley House seems so large for just Mr. Darcy and myself."

Georgiana said, "I feel so shy at times. The obligation of pretending to enjoy the company at St. James' court is distasteful to me. I should only want to go to London if you would accompany me, Elizabeth."

Elizabeth replied, "Now that I am married, I have very little reason to return to London except that Hertfordshire is on the way. I will want to visit Longbourn on occasion."

Georgiana said, "After the infamous remarks my aunt made to you, are we ever going to visit Rosing Park?"

Elizabeth replied, "Oh, I am not afraid of Lady Catherine. I have asked Mr. Darcy to write her and invite her to Pemberley. I can partly understand her reasons for not wanting me to marry Fitzwilliam, but she is Mr. Darcy's closest relation, and I do not believe that she will remain estranged forever."

"Do you think that she will ever condescend to visit the 'polluted' waters of Pemberley?" asked Mrs. Gardiner.

"I think she will withdraw her censure, since it is in her favor to relate with Mr. Darcy, but whether she will ever condescend to forgive me is another matter," Elizabeth laughed.

Finishing their lunch, they mounted back into the

phaeton and continued their trip. The road was now beginning to ascend slowly away from the riverbed and became increasingly rougher. The trees on the river bank gave way to green heather on each side of the road.

Georgiana said, "We are now almost halfway around the perimeter of Pemberley Manor."

Elizabeth put her hands on her lower stomach and said, "I am afraid I am not feeling well. Let me get out of the carriage and walk about."

As she was doing so, Mrs. Gardiner remarked, "Lizzy, you look pale. We must have gone too far today."

Elizabeth replied, "No, that cannot be the problem. I certainly should be able to ride this far without...." With this statement, she fell to the ground. Alarmed, Georgiana and Mrs. Gardiner dismounted. They ran to her prostrate body. Elizabeth was barely responsive. The best they could understand from her is that she had severe pain in her abdomen.

Mrs. Gardiner looked at Georgiana and said, "Take the phaeton and ride to Pemberley. I think it's best that you go since you would know the most direct route to the hall. I will stay here with Elizabeth."

Georgiana mounted the carriage and wished that she had spent more time at mastering the art of driving the phaeton in a fast manner. She urged the ponies to go as quickly as they could. The thirty minutes it took to reach Pemberley Hall seemed forever. Arriving in front of the entrance hall, she was short of breath and shaken.

Mrs. Reynolds hurriedly came down the steps and said, "Where are your companions? What has happened?" She helped her off the phaeton and guided her into the parlor. Seating her in the nearest chair, Mrs. Reynolds said in a calming voice, "Now catch your breath, my lady, and tell me what happened."

Georgiana was exhausted. It took several moments

before she could tell the bad news. Mrs. Reynolds called out, "Mr. Reynolds, there has been an emergency with Mrs. Darcy! Fetch a wagon with blankets. Bring it around front immediately! I will run and tell Mr. Darcy."

A few moments later, Mr. Darcy burst through the parlor door and strode up to Georgiana. "What is the matter with Elizabeth? Where is she?"

Georgiana told him of her collapse on the trail. "I left her in Mrs. Gardiner's care and rushed back here. They are halfway up the second hill past the western cottages."

"I know exactly where you mean. You have over-exerted yourself today. Stay here. I will bring Elizabeth back as soon as possible." He and Mr. Gardiner hurried out the door.

Mr. Reynolds was in front with the wagon. Georgiana stood to watch them race in the direction from which she had returned. As she turned from the window, she heard Mrs. Reynolds talking to a servant about going to Derby and bringing the surgeon from there as soon as possible. Only a few moments later, the horse's hooves were sounding in the southerly direction of the messenger.

Two hours later, the wagon pulled up in front of Pemberley. Men began shouting to each other. Servants gathered around the wagon. Georgiana walked down the steps as Mr. Darcy picked up Elizabeth's limp body. He gently carried her into the house. As he started up the stairs, Georgiana followed closely. She glimpsed the uncharacteristically white face of Elizabeth. Elizabeth tried to say something, but Georgiana could not make it out.

Finally, the great bedroom of Elizabeth and her brother was reached. Elizabeth was placed in bed and Georgiana, Mrs. Gardiner and Mrs. Reynolds remained. As he left the room, Mr. Darcy muttered in a questioning tone, "Where is the surgeon? Why is he taking so long to get here?"

Mrs. Reynolds looked at Georgiana and said, "Miss, you look awfully fatigued. We may need your help tonight and tomorrow. It is important that you get some rest and wash up. The surgeon should be here within the hour. We will bring you news of her condition at the earliest possible moment."

Mrs. Gardiner came over to Georgiana and, taking her hand, led her from the room.

Georgiana was both exhausted and anxious about her sister. She was fearful that something awful had happened to Elizabeth. It would break her heart if her dear sister should die. She went to her room to lie down for awhile. After resting, she arose to change dresses. While she was in her dressing room, a servant came to call her down to the parlor. The surgeon wanted to talk to the family.

Everyone watched the surgeon intently as he descended the staircase. He entered the parlor with a worried face. Addressing Mr. Darcy, he said, "I am afraid your wife is seriously ill."

"What is the matter?"

"She is 'flooding' and has lost a significant amount of blood." The surgeon paused to place some papers and a book into his bag.

Georgiana took the moment to ask Mrs. Gardiner in a whisper, "What does he mean by 'flooding'?"

She replied in a whisper, "It means she is bleeding from her female parts. The surgeon may use the term differently than what I am used to, but it usually means bleeding during pregnancy."

The surgeon finished with his bag, looked up grimly and said, "If the bleeding continues, I fear the worst; in such a case, the three of them would not survive."

Everyone raised their eyebrows and Mr. Darcy said, "The three of them?"

The surgeon said, "I have neglected to tell you that I can hear two different heartbeats in her lower stomach. It seems quite clear to me that she is carrying twins. The bleeding is occurring from some problem associated with this condition."

This was too much for Mr. Darcy. He sat down.

The others in the group murmured their subdued joy over Elizabeth being with child; but, the alarm of Elizabeth's illness was providing mixed emotions in the group.

Mr. Darcy asked, "What are her chances of living or dying?"

The surgeon continued, "The next twenty-four hours are critical. If the bleeding stops, there is hope she will survive. But, in her condition, I fear there is little chance for the babies. I have given her morphine and she is sleeping. Her situation is now in the hands of the Almighty." The surgeon then concluded, as he was putting on his coat, "I shall return tomorrow morning to see the patient. You must enforce absolute bedrest for her."

Mr. Darcy stood up after the surgeon was gone and began pacing the room. He muttered, "What can I do? What can I do? I feel so impotent with Elizabeth lying ill upstairs. Money, cleverness, and strength cannot rescue her."

Georgiana stood and walked upstairs to talk with Mrs. Reynolds. She begged for some time when she could watch Elizabeth. She saw that Elizabeth was no better. Mrs. Reynolds promised Georgiana sickroom duty for three to six hours after dinner.

Satisfied with this response, Georgiana turned and walked down the stairs. She turned down the hallway and entered the chapel. She began saying prayers for Elizabeth. Her heart was broken. She did not know what words she spoke, but she laid her heart open with earnest supplication. After about fifteen minutes, she heard the door open. Her brother, pale and visibly shaken, came in and sat next to her.

He began sobbing and attempted to pray with his sister. She felt a source of strength come into her heart. Putting her arm around her brother, she began speaking soft reassurances to him. After an hour or so, they returned to the subdued atmosphere in the parlor.

A servant arrived to ask what was to be done about supper. Georgiana had absolutely no appetite and realized she was being looked to as the household mistress. She turned to Mrs. Gardiner and asked what should be done.

Mrs. Gardiner said, "Well, by all means, we need to try to serve dinner. This may be a long ordeal. It is important that we keep our strength up in order to help Elizabeth."

Chapter Seven

The next morning the family gathered in the parlor. Georgiana was tired from watching Elizabeth until nearly midnight, when Mrs. Gardiner relieved her. During breakfast, the surgeon had come again and his report was eagerly awaited with a somber mood. Georgiana watched him come down the stairs. He seemed to be energetically descending the steps--perhaps this was a good sign.

"The news is better today," said the surgeon. "Her hemorrhage has stopped and her pulse has settled down."

"Thank God," said Mr. Darcy. "What can we do for her?"

"She will need strict bed rest. She cannot sit up for any reason or the bleeding may begin again and become fatal. You may prop her head with a pillow, but her body must remain flat."

"How long will this be necessary?" asked Mr. Darcy.

"If all goes well, she can expect to have her babies in about four months. When the time comes, there is an experienced mid-wife, Mrs. Cheshire, in Bakewell who has delivered numerous twins. You will need to have her begin attending your wife."

"How is Elizabeth now?"

"She is more awake today. I can see she is a strong, healthy woman. Many a weaker woman would have died from her problem yesterday." He paused for a moment and then continued, "If there are no further questions, I need to be heading back towards Derby. You can, of course, call me again, but Mrs. Cheshire will be of more help to you."

With that, the surgeon strode to the door and was gone. The previous atmosphere of tense anxiety had dissolved into one of quiet hope.

Georgiana and Mr. Darcy went up the staircase to Elizabeth's room. Upon opening the door, Mrs. Reynolds shushed them, but Elizabeth heard and turned her head to see who it was. She said weakly, "Mrs. Reynolds, let my husband and sister in."

"Yes, Ma'am."

Mr. Darcy walked quietly to the bed. He picked up her hand and leaned over to kiss his wife. Georgiana heard him say, "I am glad you are better. I was fearful of losing the light of my life."

"The doctor says I am to have twins."

"I am glad, however, I am more interested in you getting well."

"I will then, but I will also give you sons. Pemberley will be filled with the sounds of boys."

"Even when you are weak, you are lively," smiled Mr. Darcy. "I must go, so I do not sap your strength."

"Please visit me often for you are my tower of strength," Elizabeth said as she closed her eyes.

Three days later, Mr. and Mrs. Bingley arrived. Stepping out of the carriage, Mr. Bingley exclaimed, "Darcy, we came as soon as we heard the news about Elizabeth."

"How is she?" Jane asked breathlessly.

"She appears to be out of danger; however, she is quite weak from anemia and must lie absolutely flat. Come, let us go up to her room."

Mr. Darcy and Mr. Bingley waited in the hall as they let Jane enter the bedroom. Georgiana stood as Jane entered.

"Lizzy, my dearest Lizzy," Jane exclaimed, as she saw

her sister's head turn towards her. "How are you?"

"I am to have twins!"

"I am so happy for you, but did you have to announce it in such a dramatic way? You gave us a terrible fright." Jane took her sister's hand and smiled, "How are you taking the strict bed rest?"

"I feel most wretched having to lay still. My legs want to jump up and walk in the springtime air, and yet, I must remain a prisoner."

"Oh, Lizzy, it must be so difficult for someone like you who loves the outdoors. . . . I also have some news that only Mr. Bingley knows about. I am with child and the midwife says it will be six months from now."

Elizabeth smiled.

"Oh, Lizzy, did you not have any symptoms of your condition?"

"No."

"I am glad. I have had nausea almost every day. The coach ride here was quite distressing, but I would let nothing keep me from seeing you. . . . Enough of my troubles, I only want to be with you. It is my chance to repay you for your attention during my illness at Netherfield."

"My dearest Jane, your presence shall cheer and comfort me."

"What do you want most?"

"I would like most to be at the window looking out at Pemberley's springtime, but that is impossible."

"I will go talk to Mr. Darcy and Mr. Bingley to see if there is anything that can be done about your wish."

After a few minutes, Jane returned with some of her embroidery and joined Georgiana who was also involved with it, and sat by Elizabeth. Little was said for the next three hours until Mr. Darcy, Mr. Bingley and Mr. Reynolds came softly into the room.

Elizabeth looked up and said, "What is the

commotion about, Jane?"

"Your husband has a surprise for you."

"What can it be?"

Mr. Darcy came to her side and said quietly, "We have fashioned a pallet for you to lie on. We can then take it over to the bay window so you can look outside."

Elizabeth smiled and said quietly, "I should like that very much."

They placed the pallet on the bed. Georgiana and Jane helped Elizabeth slide onto it. The three men then took it over to the window and gently placed her down. Georgiana and Jane brought pillows from the bed.

Before leaving, Mr. Darcy leaned over, kissed her and said, "Anything for my dearest and loveliest."

When the women were alone, Georgiana pointed out the flowers blooming in the south garden.

"This will do much to soften my wretched condition. I shall be happy to have my children, but the wait will be quite a trial." A few moments later she continued, "I can also see the bridge over the river. Now I can see who is coming or going from the estate."

All of the events of the past few days had left a deep impression on Georgiana's mind. She now knew, in a more concrete manner, what was involved with marriage. The fairy tale, affectionate aspects of her romantic novels were being balanced with the duties and outcome of married love. She resolved that she should only marry with the greatest affection or stay a spinster for the rest of her life.

Chapter Eight

May arrived and with it, one evening, an unexpected guest. Mr. Darcy was listening to Georgiana play the pianoforte, when a servant came into the music room and announced, "The honorable Mr. Henry Westbrook."

Georgiana's fingers faltered over the keys and she quickly stopped. She observed that the visitor was not unexpected to her brother. They rose and greeted him. Without further elaboration, Mr. Westbrook followed Mr. Darcy into the study.

After an hour or so, the men returned to the parlor and stood about the fireplace.

"Well, my dear sister, how would you like to have Mr. Henry Westbrook as the new rector of Pemberley?"

She stood, "Oh! Henry, I am so pleased. I knew Reverend Wilson was retiring and I was quite concerned about who might replace him." Looking at her brother, she said, "Fitzwilliam, I wish you had let me in on the secret."

"I did not want to raise your hopes. Henry had numerous questions and I wanted the parish committee to speak to him before he made up his mind."

Georgiana asked Henry, "When will you take the position?"

"I graduate next week and take holy orders soon after. I will remain at home for a few days and then return to Cambridge." He then looked at Mr. Darcy and said, "Shall we make the first Sunday of July my inaugural time?"

"Good. Reverend Wilson said he would be available until the end of June."

Georgiana said, "I know we have been expecting your elevation to the clergy for some time; but I, at least, think 'Reverend Westbrook' will take some getting used to."

After a few more minutes of conversation, Mr. Westbrook took his leave.

Georgiana did not dwell upon Mr. Westbrook's position very long. The Bennet family was arriving the following day. Arrangements for the visit needed to be finished with Mrs. Reynolds. She was glad that Mr. Westbrook had missed Kitty, so as to avoid embarrassment to them both. Georgiana then went and watched Elizabeth for the evening.

The Bennets arrived after breakfast the next morning. Georgiana felt much more comfortable with them this time, particularly with Kitty. Her prior visit and their ongoing correspondence had made them good friends. Mary, the second youngest of Elizabeth's sisters and much plainer than the other Bennet girls, also came to Pemberley for her first visit.

In the middle of the afternoon, Mrs. Bennet, Kitty, Mary and Georgiana were sitting in the parlor discussing and working on their embroidery. They had already been in Elizabeth's room and after several hours had tired Mrs. Darcy out. Mrs. Reynolds had to chase them out of the master bedroom, and their retreat had led them back to the downstairs parlor.

All the women were surprised when a servant announced the attendance of Mr. Henry Westbrook. Georgiana, Mrs. Bennet and Mary looked at Kitty with dismay. Kitty hung her head and looked like she wanted to crawl away.

Mr. Westbrook walked tentatively into the room and

stood by the fireplace. He cleared his throat and remained silent for a moment as he surveyed the group. He then said, "You are probably wondering why I have come today."

No answer was forthcoming. Georgiana tried to think of something clever to say, but words escaped her.

Mr. Westbrook cleared his throat again and looked in Kitty's direction and said, "Miss Bennet, I have heard glowing reports of your work in this parish and in Meryton."

Georgiana looked at Kitty's tense body and saw it relax a little.

Mr. Westbrook continued, "No one here is going to make this easy on me, and this is only right since I am to blame for any discomfort being felt now."

Mrs. Bennet said, "You are welcome to visit us anytime."

"Thank you," he replied and continued, "As I was saying, Kitty, your works of charity and enthusiasm towards church have not gone unnoticed. Reverend Wilson speaks highly of you."

Kitty lifted her head showing a facial expression of mingled surprise and happiness. "Mr. Westbrook, your upbraiding last Christmas was something I needed. It helped me take a look at my shallow life. I believe the changes induced in me have helped me be less selfish."

"Miss Bennet, please call me Henry."

With this statement of Mr. Westbrook's, Kitty turned her head away and Henry looked in another direction, towards the window.

Georgiana finally rejoined, after several quiet moments and said, "Now, Henry, you should not think Kitty has done this in an attempt to impress you. She despaired of ever seeing you again."

"I know," was his soft reply. He cleared his throat again and looked at Mrs. Bennet and said, "Mrs. Bennet, would you and the other ladies be so kind as to allow me a few minutes alone with your daughter, Miss Catherine Bennet?"

"Certainly," was her quick reply. She rose and grabbed Mary, whose head was engrossed in a book, and prodded her into the adjoining assembly room. Miss Darcy retreated with them.

After fifteen minutes, Kitty came to find them. She rushed up to hug Georgiana, while saying, "I am so happy and it is all because of my sisters and you, Georgiana."

"What did he say?" Mrs. Bennet asked.

"We shared mutual apologies and he asked if he could begin courting me again. He made it clear that he was not yet asking for an engagement; but given our recent difficulties, he thought it best to approach me in an official way, so as to not give an impression that he was trifling with me. He has gone to find father and discuss this with him."

Mrs. Bennet said, "I believe you would do well to capture his affections."

Georgiana asked, "Is this what you want?"

"Yes. I never stopped liking Mr. Westbrook. That affection worked to change my ways. Apparently, Mr. Darcy encouraged Henry to reconsider me while they were discussing his possible position."

At this statement, Mrs. Bennet sat down and fanned herself. She exclaimed, "A fourth daughter to be married and all of them with encouragement by Mr. Darcy! Had I known he was cupid when I first met him, I should have fainted!"

"Mamma, I am not yet engaged."

"You are as good as in that blessed state. I doubt Mr. Westbrook will change his mind."

Georgiana then asked, "What else did Mr. Westbrook say? You were alone with him for fifteen minutes."

"He said he was blessed with courting a woman who

had already favorably impressed the parish with her work. He said it is seldom that a clergyman could start off on such a sound footing in his first position."

The time for dinner approached. Poor Mr. Darcy! He already was given the honor due his position, but now he was worshiped by Mrs. Bennet! Fortunately, her awe made her quiet, which facilitated the meal well. When Elizabeth was told, by Kitty, of the visit of Mr. Westbrook, she responded with warm congratulations to her sister.

Georgiana felt the well-deserved satisfaction that she had helped Kitty in an important matter.

Chapter Nine

The four months of Elizabeth's confinement wore on. A routine settled upon the household. Elizabeth endured this with her usual liveliness, particularly after a month, when her anemia began to improve. Georgiana observed that her sister would endure anything to have these babies. The difficult pregnancy served to strengthen felicitous bonds between Georgiana and Elizabeth. It helped Georgiana to show her love by helping Elizabeth. The acts of companionship and devotion helped bridge any remaining emotional gap that their five year age difference might have caused. In addition, the wait sharpened Georgiana's desire to have nephews or nieces. She felt a significant investment in her brother's and sister's children.

Mr. and Mrs. Bingley returned to Netherfield for Jane's advancing pregnancy. Charles had found an estate to purchase only 30 miles from Pemberley, in Yorkshire, but it was not going to become available until the fall. As a result, it was decided the Bingleys would settle in the north after the birth of their first child.

Finally, one day in early August, several weeks before Georgiana's seventeenth birthday, Elizabeth told Georgiana, "I have an unusual cramping pain that I have never felt before. It has lasted two minutes and is now wearing off. I hope and wonder if this is labor."

"I certainly have no experience with those symptoms," Georgiana smiled. "I will run and get Mrs. Reynolds."

She returned minutes later with Mrs. Reynolds. The older housekeeper soon turned and said, "It is, indeed, labor. Go and tell Mr. Darcy to send for Mrs. Cheshire from Bakewell as soon as possible."

Georgiana ran breathlessly downstairs to her brother. He commanded his best driver to go and fetch the midwife. They both watched moments later as the carriage raced away from the estate. When Georgiana and her brother entered the bedroom, Mr. Darcy rushed to Elizabeth's side. Mrs. Reynolds placed her hand on his shoulder. "Now sir, this is Mrs. Darcy's first labor. It will probably last twenty-four hours or more."

Indeed, Mrs. Reynolds was right. Mrs. Cheshire arrived in plenty of time to make arrangements for the delivery.

Georgiana felt as if her heart would break as she listened to Elizabeth's moans and saw how exhausted her sister looked. The night wore on. Georgiana dropped off to sleep as dawn approached and was awakened by a sound strange to her ear--the cry of a baby.

She jumped up. Mrs. Cheshire was holding a baby upside down. The midwife handed the newborn to Mrs. Reynolds for cleaning. She said, "The Lord be praised, Mrs. Darcy, you have a healthy baby boy; but wait, the other baby is coming quickly."

Georgiana watched intently as Mrs. Cheshire delivered a second boy. He also wailed, even more heartily than the first.

Mrs. Reynolds said, "Miss Darcy, pick up a blanket and take the second baby."

Mrs. Cheshire handed the second twin to Georgiana. She awkwardly but carefully held the tiny boy and dried him off. The little infant had blond hair and blue eyes. He was clearly not an identical twin since the first child had dark black hair like his father.

Mrs. Reynolds and Georgiana approached Elizabeth to place the now quiet little boys in her arms. She looked at them momentarily and said, "They shall be called Andrew and John." She then dozed off. Mrs. Reynolds picked up the blond-haired John. Georgiana took the other, named Andrew, and noted his abundant black hair and blue eyes. She imagined that her beloved brother looked like this when he was born. Andrew was quiet in contrast to his younger brother, John, who resumed announcing his arrival to the world with loud crying.

Mr. Darcy was called into the bedroom. As Georgiana handed him each child in turn, her heart swelled with love for the children he was so proud of. She sat down in a rocker. After a few minutes, Mr. Darcy relinquished the boys to her. He then sat speaking quietly with Elizabeth, while Georgiana rocked her new nephews. She could not imagine any handsomer babies--nor any happier parents. Georgiana wondered if she would ever love someone enough to marry and bear children.

The next morning, Georgiana was sitting by her sister's bed when Elizabeth's eyes opened. She heard Elizabeth exclaim, "Now I can sit up. Would you be so good as to help me with some pillows?"

Georgiana helped her to a sitting position.

"Now, where are my babies?" Elizabeth exclaimed.

"I will go get Mrs. Reynolds," Georgiana replied.

In a few moments, Mrs. Reynolds, Mr. Darcy and Georgiana came back into the bedroom. Mr. Darcy was holding the black haired Andrew, ever so gently, like a priceless heirloom; Mrs. Reynolds had the blond-haired John, who needed calming down for a moment before conversation could begin.

"Here is our oldest," Mr. Darcy said as he brought Andrew over.

"He looks just like you," Elizabeth told him as she settled the infant in one arm.

"And here is John," Mrs. Reynolds said, placing him on her other side. "He is more rambunctious than his brother."

"His hair and face remind me of my sister Jane," Elizabeth cooed.

After several minutes admiring her babies, Elizabeth relinquished them to Mrs. Reynolds who said, "Which nurse-maid shall we send the boys to for feeding? Mrs. Cheshire says there is a good, affectionate woman in Lampton."

"I had not thought of that before. Must I send them out?"

"My lady knows that the custom for gentle women is to not breast feed their own children, but to send them out to a nurse-maid," said Mrs. Reynolds kindly, but firmly.

Color came into Elizabeth's face as she said, "I will **not** send my sons out to a stranger. I did not endure the last four months in order to be spared of their company. I will suckle them myself, thank you very much!"

Mrs. Reynolds appealed to Mr. Darcy with a look. Mr. Darcy chuckled, "Since when has Mrs. Darcy been conventional? I see no wrong in her desire."

Georgiana was delighted. Whatever her thoughts about love and marriage, the birth of the twins had aroused a maternal instinct in their aunt. Despite the strong desire of Elizabeth to take care of her own children, Georgiana knew her sister would need help.

Section Two

October, 1815

Miss Georgiana Darcy

Chapter Ten

Georgiana was sitting on a bench in the south garden of Pemberley. Her nine year old nephews, Andrew and John, sat next to her. Her seven year old niece, Maria was beside John. "Thank you Andrew and John for bringing this bouquet of flowers you have picked. The daisies are so lovely. I enjoy looking at fall flowers."

"You have taught us so much, Aunt Georgiana," said the elder Andrew, "we thought of you when we were gathering them."

John looked embarrassed. "Next time I get in trouble, will you try to remember I helped pick the daisies?" he asked with a grin.

Tousling his blond hair, Georgiana replied, "I always keep your kindnesses in mind--that is why your parents are not informed of all your classroom antics."

The boys ran off to play a rudimentary game of cricket on the lawn in front of the bench. Maria moved closer to her aunt. Maria was average height for her age, with dark hair which was naturally curly. Her eyes sparkled and she had a lively disposition just like her mother. She looked at Georgiana and asked in a gentle, childlike tone, "Why are you not married, Auntie?"

Surprised, Georgiana looked at her niece and said, "I don't know. I am quite shy around strangers, particularly men, and I expect this is taken as being overly proud."

"What is shyness?"

"For me, it is being afraid to or not wanting to talk to people."

"You are not afraid when you talk to me or Mamma."

"I am perfectly comfortable talking to my family or friends. It is strangers, or those I have recently met, with whom I have difficulty speaking."

"Have you ever been engaged?"

"I was infatuated one time with a young man named Mr. Wickham. I almost eloped with him."

"What is in. . .fatted?"

"Infatuated, you mean. I am sorry for using such a big word. Being infatuated means you desire someone without a good foundation of esteem or respect."

"What happened?"

"Your father showed me the foolishness of my feelings and Mr. Wickham left. I knew this to be infatuation since my feelings were not hurt after his departure. If I had loved him, I should have been sorely wounded."

"Have you ever really been in love?"

"I think I might have been. It seems such a long time ago."

"Tell me about it."

"I was young and there was a friend that I had known for many years. He loved Phillip and made me feel very comfortable."

"What happened?"

"He went away to the University and then into the army. I have only seen him once, for a brief period, in the past nine years." Georgiana's voice trailed off as she finished, "I feel as though I let him slip away, but I am not quite sure how it happened."

"That's sad, auntie."

"I know. . .if I had been able to express myself better, perhaps we would be married today; but, no matter, I am quite content here at Pemberley with all that a woman could desire--your father and mother, your brothers," and then tickling Maria's side, "and especially you."

"What did we hear about someone getting married?" queried Rev. Henry Westbrook as he rounded the bushes with his wife, Kitty. Both he and Kitty had gained weight since becoming husband and wife eight years ago, making them look jolly.

"I am unaware that anything of the sort is about to happen to me," Georgiana said as she stood and continued, "I do not wish to excite any anticipation on your part."

"Marriage has turned out well for us," ventured Kitty, smiling at her husband.

"Yes, and to have the living of Pemberley is such a blessing," Henry finished.

"I am glad for your felicity," Georgiana said stiffly, not wishing to continue the talk about marriage. She called to the boys and asked Maria to accompany her back to the breakfast parlor. Reverend and Mrs. Westbrook wished her a good day and continued their walk.

In her bedroom that evening, Georgiana recalled the only time she had ever felt strong feelings of love towards a man.

Three years earlier, Mr. Thomas Staley had returned to Derbyshire for the first time since he left for college in Cambridge. At that point, he had completed four years of college, and two years as a teaching assistant. She heard from his father, Sir William Staley, of his return and looked forward to seeing her childhood friend at the annual Westbrook ball. Two new women, Miss Harpur and Miss Helena Harpur, from the opposite side of Westbrook Manor were in attendance. Miss Harpur's Christian name was Cassandra and she was mildly pretty at age two and twenty. Her younger sister was much better looking at age twenty. Both of the sisters were several inches shorter than Georgiana.

Mr. Thomas Staley and Sir William Staley were the last to arrive at the ball. The Staleys progressed down the reception line. It was evident to Georgiana that the Harpur sisters were delighted to meet Mr. Staley and told him directly in no uncertain terms. Thomas stopped in front of Georgiana, bowed and said, "Miss Darcy, how are you this evening?"

"Very well, Mr. Thomas Staley. Even though it has been six years since you deserted your childhood friend, you may still call me Georgiana."

He smiled, "Of course. I am uncertain why I reverted to formality with you. Perhaps it is the beauty of your face and the felicity caused by your presence that makes me wish to formalize my manner to you."

"Oh, Thomas, I have never known you to be a flatterer, but only honest and straightforward."

"And I still consider myself honest. Pray, do not be afraid to accept my compliments. May I, if you would be ever so good, engage you for the first two dances?"

"Of course. It shall be a pleasure."

Thomas then left to talk with some of the Westbrook family. Thomas did not have to endure the disdain of the Countess, since she had died in the six year interim. He was chatting with Reverend and Mrs. Westbrook until the call came for the first dance. He approached Georgiana and took her hand. During the dance, she asked, "Tell me, Thomas, why have you deprived Derbyshire of your presence for the past six years?"

"My absence has sprung from a willful desire to pay my own way at school, rather than burdening my poor father," he paused to complete his movement and then continued, "but seeing Staley Hall and you, I have been reminded of what good company I have been missing."

Georgiana smiled, "I am glad you enjoy your old friends here in Derbyshire; but, surely, Thomas, you need not be so concerned about supporting yourself?"

"Alas, and it is a true fault in my character. I must worry about my financial affairs, since no one else will. Growing up with little fortune has caused me to focus on it."

"Thomas, you should not be so worried about it."

"I do not mean to sound harsh, my dear friend, but those who grow up with great fortune may not understand those who do not."

The dance came to an end and Georgiana offered her hand to Thomas and said, "Please forgive me. Indeed, I do not understand your fixation about finances. . . . However, I am sure it is a just concern."

Thomas left to get some refreshments and the two Miss Harpurs came over to where Georgiana was seated. Miss Helena Harpur said in an excited whisper, "Miss Darcy, where have you been hiding this Mr. Thomas Staley? Is he not handsome and gallant?"

"He is a childhood friend who has been away at Cambridge for the past six years," Georgiana replied.

Miss Helena Harpur continued, "You will not monopolize his attentions this evening will you?"

"Sister!" the older Miss Harpur exclaimed.

Her younger sister said, "Do not try to quiet me. You would also like to dance with the new gentleman, would you not?"

Her older sister remained quiet, but a telltale blush gave her unspoken answer.

Thomas returned from the refreshment table with a cup for Georgiana. The four of them sat down and Miss Helena Harpur sighed, "There are so few gentlemen here this evening. I suppose I shall only watch the ball tonight."

Thomas looked at Georgiana, who gave him a look of permission. He then said, "I am engaged with Miss Darcy for the next dance, but if you would do me the favor of the following dance, I should count it as pleasure."

She blushed and said, "I shall be happy to dance with you."

During the second dance Georgiana had with Thomas, she found herself looking at Thomas in a new light. As she sat out the third dance and watched the younger Harpur sister dance with her long-time friend, she observed both Thomas and Miss Helena Harpur laughing and smiling. Georgiana could not understand their soft talk during the dance, but their gaiety was obvious. It was clear to Miss Darcy that Miss Harpur was flirting with Mr. Staley--and he seemed to be enjoying it. An idea began to awaken in Georgiana that Thomas was indeed a desirable man! While his face was not perfect, the effect of his strong muscular build, graceful movement and curly hair was one which began to stir feelings in her. These feelings were initiated because of the admiration for him among others at the ball! A childhood friend whom she had taken for granted--until others found him grand!

Before she would let her feelings build anymore, she would have to discover if his skepticism about religion remained. She waited until he came to her after dancing with both of the Harpur sisters. As they sat alone at the table, Georgiana ventured, "And what have you learned about Christianity at Cambridge?"

"I see you are still concerned about that. My journey has come a long way since I left, but may not be complete yet."

"What do you mean?"

"While a student at Cambridge, I met with a group of Wesleyan colleagues. Their discussion about the nature of

Christianity illuminated my soul. It has ignited a desire that my heart can be warmed with a relationship with the Almighty, rather than confining myself to a set of rules and rituals." He paused and hastened to add, "I now believe in the confession and church attendance. I hope that I can find the assurance that these Methodists speak of."

Georgiana had not heard the religious experience formulated in this way before. His present confession was, however, a great improvement over his prior skepticism! She could only say, "I trust you will find all that your heart desires."

"Thank you, my friend," was his reply. While Thomas was called to another table, Georgiana dated the start of her affection for him from that moment. He danced with her later in the evening and she savored every minute of it; but, because of her feelings, she said very little. She had never been shy around her friend before; however, with her deepening admiration and feelings for him, she felt reticent with him for the first time.

Thomas was home for one more week and returned to Pemberley a few days after the Westbrook ball. Arriving on horseback after breakfast, he dismounted to be greeted by the Darcy women.

Elizabeth said, "What is the reason for the pleasure of your visit, Mr. Staley?"

"My purpose is to see Pemberley once more before I leave again," as he glanced at Georgiana.

"For what cause are we to lose you this time?" Georgiana inquired anxiously, but in a warm tone of voice.

"I have friends who have procured me a commission in the army."

Georgiana was dismayed at the thought, but tried to keep an unchanged face as she asked, "When will you leave?"

"I report in one week to Essex to begin my training. Where I shall go after that I am not allowed to say."

Elizabeth said, "It will be a sore loss for us to see you leave Derbyshire again. Pray, Mr. Staley, will you excuse me so I may attend my children. . . . Georgiana, will you accompany Mr. Staley wherever he wishes?"

"Yes," Georgiana replied as Elizabeth turned to the entrance hall. Georgiana smiled at Thomas and asked, "Do you want to take a turn with me in the south gardens?"

"I should be delighted," was his response.

After a few steps, Georgiana said, "Have you seen the ah. . .ah. . . ," and she stopped with an embarrassed silence.

"Do you mean the Harpur sisters?" he grinned.

"I am sorry, Thomas. I uttered the question without thinking. You certainly have the right to see whom you please."

Here, he interrupted, "I am touched by your interest. No, I have not seen the Harpur sisters. I think them rather silly, if the truth be known. . . . I would rather visit you and Pemberley than anyone else in Derbyshire."

She turned her head away. What did this mean? Was this a prelude to his declaration of love? While she longed for this expression, she did not quite feel ready for it.

After a few more steps, he said, "I am eager to start my service. If I can in any way assist our country to defeat Napoleon, I am willing to help."

Georgiana did not quite expect the last statement and was perplexed how to turn the conversation to their relationship. She wanted to tell him how important he was, but her voice could not utter the words.

They finished walking the garden and went inside to the music room. Georgiana offered to play a song and performed with the utmost passion. She stood after finishing and tried to say something about her feelings to Thomas. The words froze on her tongue. She was glad he had not seen her expression and questioned her--Phillip had diverted his attention by jumping into his lap.

By the time of Thomas' departure, she tried once more, unsuccessfully, to express her feelings for him.

Indeed, she was uncertain if she understood her own metamorphosis over the past week. After he left, she was disappointed that she had not obtained a promise of writing or a knowledge of when he might return.

Her feelings for Thomas over the past three years had become wrapped in a thick cocoon of activities involving family, parish activities and her music. As she explored her memory of Thomas' last visit, she was now uncertain whether any affection remained. She was able to cherish the brief time he had spent back in Derbyshire with satisfaction, and only occasionally fretted over the lack of expressing her love to him. She was unsure whether Thomas returned that love; but she knew he remained a faithful friend. She would have to let the situation remain as it was and hope events should resolve her feelings one way or the other in the future. As a lady in a rural setting, there were not many eligible young gentlemen available to court her. Thus, her memory of Thomas was not diverted by any competition.

At the breakfast table the next morning, with all of the Darcy family seated, Mr. Darcy said, "We have received an invitation from Lady Catherine De Bourgh to visit Rosing Park in a fortnight."

The atmosphere in the breakfast room became somber and silent.

"Come, now, children, visiting Rosing Park is not all that bad," said Elizabeth.

"Oh, Mamma, our great aunt is so stiff and forbidding.

She always wants us to act formal," John complained.

"Why does she want us so soon?" Georgiana inquired of her brother.

"Apparently, the new Duke of Kent is to visit Lady Catherine and she wants us to meet him. I was aware Rosing Park was to be inherited by a distant relative but I have never met him. The new Duke of Kent is apparently the heir."

Elizabeth looked compassionately at Georgiana and said, "I am afraid she also wishes to discuss marriage, or the lack of it, with you."

Alarmed, Georgiana said, "Surely, not with this Duke of Kent?"

"No, I do not think that is her intent. I seem to remember, though I may be incorrect, this fellow is quite old."

Georgiana's mind pictured a white-haired man who needed a cane to walk. The dukes she had previously met looked ancient. She caught up with her next to last feeling and exclaimed, "Why is everyone all of a sudden worried about my marital status?"

Elizabeth calmly replied, "Be assured, we are not trying to play matchmaker. Your brother and I only want what you want; but, since you are only a year away from seven and twenty, people will increasingly inquire about your marital status as, somehow, the age has been identified with spinsterhood."

"I will never get married," declared Georgiana emphatically. "Why should I leave the grandest estate in Derbyshire or my dear family? I do not care if I become a spinster."

Elizabeth continued, "You are so dear to us, Georgiana. We are ambivalent about any change in your present status, since to marry would take you away from Pemberley and from our children who love you dearly."

Georgiana wished to turn the conversation from this

uncomfortable topic to one about the children and asked, "My dear brother, I believe we need to discuss the future education of my nephews and niece and **not** because I plan to leave Pemberley."

"Auntie, we do not want anyone but you to teach us," piped Maria.

"I love to teach you," she smiled, "but, in some subjects, such as French, your brothers are beginning to exceed my knowledge."

"Oh! You are the best music teacher in the whole world," boasted Maria as she stretched her arms out wide.

"I will continue teaching you music," Georgiana replied with a smile.

"We are finished with the meal," Elizabeth said. "Children, you may be excused to go play outside." John immediately stood and raced ahead of the others. When the children were gone, Elizabeth stood. "Shall we remove to the parlor to discuss their education?"

The three adults headed to the entrance parlor. Mr. Darcy stood by the mantel as he listened to Georgiana describe the areas in which the boys had exceeded her knowledge--particularly in mathematics and the languages in general, but French in particular.

"Then we must consider a tutor. The other option would be to send them to a private academy," replied Mr. Darcy.

"Let us **not** send them to a school. Children learn dreadful manners and rudeness at such places," Elizabeth said forcefully.

"My thoughts, exactly. I am glad to see we think alike, my dear Lizzy," replied Mr. Darcy.

"Now, then, where can we find a good tutor?" asked Elizabeth. "We must be very selective."

"Actually, I already have one in mind." Pulling a letter out of his pocket, he continued, "This letter is from Sir

William Staley regarding his son, Thomas. You know, the one we have not seen in years."

Georgiana's heart leapt involuntarily at the mention of Thomas' name. She tried to stay calm and to return her facial expression back to what it was prior to the name being uttered.

"Sir William gives us the news that Thomas was wounded in the war and is convalescing in a hospital in France."

"How badly is he hurt?" Georgiana interrupted with more concern in her voice than she wished to show.

"He suffered a shrapnel injury to his left leg. It appeared serious at first and the surgeons wanted to amputate, but Thomas refused and he is apparently doing better. However, we shall see his condition when he visits Pemberley."

"You never told us about this," Elizabeth and Georgiana chimed in reply.

"I took the liberty of inviting him here. I knew you would not mind seeing an old childhood friend, Georgiana. Sir William tells me that Thomas is looking for a teaching position, preferably at Cambridge; but with the war ending, many of the officers have claim to the college positions and it may be several years before one will open up. In the meantime, Thomas is looking for employment as a tutor."

Elizabeth smiled and said, "What a perfect opportunity for us. There is no substitute for personal knowledge of a teacher. My memory of Thomas is quite a favorable one. He is both sensible and amiable."

"But what if he has changed, Lizzy?" asked Georgiana.

"I should be surprised if his basic character has changed."

"I know he speaks excellent French, since his grandmother emigrated from the continent. His mother, Lady Marilyn, made him speak both French and English as a boy. But, what of his doubt concerning our beliefs?" Georgiana pressed on wishing to clear the candidate as soon as possible.

"We will see what his beliefs are when he visits. I doubt he will say anything that will disqualify himself," said Mr. Darcy. He continued, "Who knows, he may have several attractive offers. He seems quite qualified."

The next day a letter arrived for Mr. Darcy. He read it and passed it to Elizabeth and Georgiana. It read:

> Dear Mr. Darcy,
>
> Thank you for the inquiry about my future as a tutor. I should like very much to return to Pemberley and discuss this. Your house has many happy memories for me from the association of our families.
>
> My French is excellent and I have been serving as an interpreter for the battalion staff and now for the hospital.
>
> My leg is recovering and I am now walking without a cane. I fear I have a limp, but God be praised that my injury was allowed to be so slight. My discomfort has been minimal compared to the Heavy Price some of my friends have paid.
>
> My unit is to disembark next week. I should be at Staley Hall within a fortnight, and after a day or two, I will come to Pemberley.
>
> Give my regards to Mrs. and Miss Darcy.
> Sincerely,
> Thomas Staley

After reading the letter, Georgiana retired to her room. Her thoughts were quite happy as she recalled Thomas' praise of the Almighty in the letter. She wondered what his condition would be--both spiritual and physical.

How much damage had the injury caused? How weak would he be from the prolonged recovery? Were his shoulders still strong? Would his eyes still sparkle? Would his spirit be bitter? Would his leg be crippled? She recalled his tanned face as a young man--would it be a sickly white from laying in the hospital?

She thought, after a while--he may have a feminine attachment in Cambridge from his days there as a student. Georgiana decided she should guard her heart until answers were obtained to her questions. What were her feelings? Was Thomas worth risking her current position?

How could she know the difference between infatuation and love? Her mind kept revolving these subjects; she made little progress on answering any of her questions with certainty.

Chapter Eleven

The day of Thomas' visit finally dawned. A message had been sent the day before that he would arrive that morning. Georgiana spent the first hour after breakfast looking out the south window at the distant bridge to detect when he might come. Mr. and Mrs. Darcy were in the adjacent parlor trying to busy themselves with reading and embroidery, respectively. The word *trying* is used, since Andrew and John were having trouble entertaining themselves. Maria was attempting simple needlework next to her mother and was not contributing to the lively atmosphere her brothers were sponsoring.

Finally, Georgiana spied a tall man on a brown horse, trotting over the bridge. She guessed it to be Thomas and, as he approached, she recognized the man she had not seen for three years. His shoulders were as strong as ever, his brown curly hair unchanged and his face had the same healthy look she remembered.

Georgiana ran to the entrance hall door, with Andrew and John trailing her by five to ten feet. Thomas dismounted, gave the horse to the groom and began walking towards Georgiana. The only changed aspect was a slight limp, but it was barely noticeable. He was certainly not a cripple!

Phillip had been wagging his tail next to Georgiana, but now rushed out barking happily at Thomas. Thomas picked him up and walked to the door, whereupon he smiled at Georgiana and looked at her with his soft, friendly eyes. Upon reaching her, he let Phillip down and took her hand and kissed it, saying, "I am so glad to see you again, Georgiana. Your appearance is even more pleasing than the beauty I recall."

"You have changed very little, Thomas, except you appear to be even stronger than when you left. I was worried that you might have weakened during your convalescence."

"No, I was treated quite well. I tried to use my arms extensively while my leg was healing, so I would not have to recover them as well. . . . And, who are the young gentlemen hiding behind you, Miss Darcy?"

Urging them forward, she said, "Captain Staley, this is Andrew, my older nephew, and his brother, John." The boys bowed and followed Thomas and Georgiana as they moved into the parlor. Mr. and Mrs. Darcy greeted him and then urged him to sit down.

"How is your family, Thomas?"

"Very well, sir. Thank you. My father is in good health. My brother, George, is doing well in the West Indies. My father received a letter from him a fortnight ago."

As Thomas finished, Georgiana noticed Andrew tugging on his father's coat sleeve. Mr. Darcy leaned forward and allowed his son to whisper into his ear. After a moment, Mr. Darcy said out loud, "Andrew, go ask him yourself."

The boy began, "I suppose. . . ," and then stopped.

His mother interrupted, "Mr. Staley, you will have to tell us sooner or later and the boys clearly want it sooner."

Andrew approached Thomas and asked, "John and I are very curious about your war injury." John interrupted breathlessly, "Tell us about the battles you have been in."

"My injury is not really very much. I do not wish to fill your heads with false gallantry. As you know, I was part of a diplomatic unit serving as an aide de camp to Colonel Freemantle. We were closing in on Paris after the battle of Waterloo. Our unit had been moving between the French and Allied lines with messages concerning a truce and surrender. We were returning to the English section late one night; when apparently, a French guard mistook us for an attacking force and fired on our unit. I was wounded in the melee. It took us some time to convince them we were a diplomatic unit. What I remember most about that night is waking up in the field hospital with a terrific pain in my leg. Now, does that satisfy you, boys?"

"Wow, yes sir," they both replied in unison.

Andrew continued, "Does it still hurt?"

"Only a little at times, but I can now take extended walks with very little discomfort."

Mr. Darcy then said, "Boys, take Mr. Staley and your sister up to your classroom area next to the library and show him around."

Andrew and John each took a hand of Mr. Staley. They led him up the circular staircase behind the marching style of Maria. They appeared to have lost all shyness of Mr. Staley.

After the foursome was gone, Mr. Darcy said to the two remaining women, "Captain Staley is too modest. I have it, on General Maplethorpe's authority, that Thomas saved the Colonel's life in the melee. A soldier does not earn the regimental cross by simply being wounded; but like other veterans I know, he is reluctant to discuss his experience. I think he has the right amount of proper pride."

"He has my approbation," Elizabeth said, "I hoped he would not glorify the military; since, as a mother I would prefer not to see my sons head off into war unless it were absolutely necessary. I think he will make a fine teacher."

"His academic credentials are excellent. Sister, you have been their teacher for many years. What do you say?"

"I am also in hearty approbation. He appears little changed from the amiable Thomas we knew three years ago. By asking him, we avoid the discomfort of inviting a stranger into Pemberley."

"I agree, sister. I think we should ask him immediately, lest someone else lure him away."

Thomas returned a little time later, and Mrs. Reynolds took the children outside.

Mr. Darcy began, "Well, Mr. Thomas Staley, are you interested in tutoring our children?"

"Yes, sir, I am. They seem full of energy and curiosity--two good traits for scholars; however, I am uncertain about a time commitment."

"We can understand that. We do not expect you to be a tutor for life. When a fellowship opens up at the university, you may take it. Let us consider your position month to month. We offer the usual inducements and your salary will be nearly what the University fellowship would be."

"Thank you, sir. Then it is agreed," Thomas said as he stepped forward and shook Mr. Darcy's hand.

Georgiana noted Elizabeth's smile and found herself pleased about the arrangement.

Mr. Darcy turned to Elizabeth and said, "Now it is time to show Mr. Thomas Staley his home."

Elizabeth and Georgiana escorted Thomas to his room. Elizabeth remarked, "Mr. Darcy thought you might like the turret room. It is in the oldest part of the hall. It has a good measure of privacy. However, it is on the second floor of the turret and you may find it too arduous for climbing each day."

"No, Ma'am, I do not believe a second floor room will be too difficult for me."

"If this room is not what you like, we have several others to choose from here at Pemberley, so do not feel this is your only choice," replied Elizabeth.

After going through a maze of hallways which turned left and right on several occasions, they approached a room-sized vestibule which had stairs leading off in a spiral to the right. The stairs were only about four feet wide and made of stone. Elizabeth and Georgiana led the way up to the second floor room. As a very large, plain wooden door was pushed open, Thomas felt that he was being moved two hundred years back in history. The room had only three small windows. It was apparent the chamber had been recently cleaned. There was a large fireplace across from the entrance. A four-poster bed was present and a large desk was situated about eight feet in front of the fire. Bookshelves lined the walls to the right of the doorway. Thomas went to one of the windows and looked out upon the forest of Pemberley. He turned to Elizabeth and Georgiana and said, "I think this will be perfect. I appreciate the bookshelves. I have many books to study about the French Revolution."

"The servants will bring your luggage here in a few minutes. After you are settled in, you may wish to come down and visit us. Mr. Darcy likes to have supper directly at five o'clock."

Chapter Twelve

The next morning, when Thomas awakened, he noted a pitcher and bowl on his desk. Getting himself ready for the day, he left his room expecting that he could easily find his way to the dining parlor. However, after several turns in the hallways, he became uncertain which way was the true direction. He sat down for a few minutes and then heard the sound of young boys running. John turned the corner and said, "There you are, Mr. Thomas. Mamma was concerned that you might lose your way in the maze of the hallways on the west side of the house, and she sent us to reconnoiter your position. You made one mistake turning, which is all too common with our visitors on this side of the house."

They both took one of Thomas' hands and led him into the breakfast parlor, where the rest of the Darcys were waiting. As breakfast was served, Georgiana said, "Thomas, I shall be happy to show you where I left off teaching the boys and Maria. What will you try to teach them first?"

Thomas replied, "I shall want to see what their abilities are. I will give them a few questions in mathematics and the languages."

"I believe you will find the boys quite above average and Maria does well. The boys have advanced past my knowledge of the French language."

"They must be exceptional; since I know, from the three years you studied with my mother, your French is quite good," replied Thomas.

Mr. Darcy then said, "In two days we shall be leaving for Rosing Park to see Lady Catherine de Bourgh. Since you are here, Thomas, I believe I shall allow the children to stay at Pemberley and not force them to attend on this visit. While we are gone, I do not expect you to entertain them at all times. Mrs. Reynolds will see to their care. Your duties are scholastic, and you need merely to teach for a normal amount of time during the day."

The children's faces beamed at this pronouncement.

Georgiana said, "I hope you do not mind, Thomas, if I sit in the classroom and listen to some of your teaching. I still feel there is so much I do not know."

"I would be pleased to have you in the school room as often and as long as you would like," replied Thomas.

"If you have no objections, I should like to continue teaching the children music and art in the afternoon and you can teach them their studies in the morning."

"That is quite agreeable," replied Thomas.

After breakfast, the boys led Thomas, Georgiana and Maria up to the classroom. It was on the second floor in a westerly direction from the breakfast parlor. Upon entering the classroom, Thomas voiced his pleasure with its spaciousness. It measured 25 feet by 25 feet, with a one-foot step down around most of the room, about five feet away from the wall. There were several desks. Large windows on the western side of the room gave ample lighting. Thomas sat down with the two boys and wrote out several mathematical questions for them. He asked Maria to copy a poem. Georgiana sat about fifteen feet away from the three desks, watching the activities.

After copying the poem, Maria put her chin in her hand and stared at Mr. Staley. After several minutes she asked, "Are you married?"

Thomas appeared taken aback for a moment and

replied, "No."

"Are you engaged or promised to any woman?"

"Maria!" Georgiana said. "Mr. Thomas need not be asked those questions." Though secretly, in her heart, she was glad that the information was being discovered.

Thomas gently replied, "That is all right, Maria. No, I am not promised or engaged to any woman." Leaning over and winking at Maria, he said, "Perhaps you want me to court you?"

Maria giggled. "Oh, no sir. I just wanted to know."

Georgiana was glad, though a little embarrassed, that Maria asked such point blank questions. She had wondered, since Thomas' arrival, if he was attached to any other woman. She certainly possessed an answer now.

After several hours of assessment and questions, Thomas declared it was time to walk outside. Georgiana had watched the proceedings with interest. As they descended the circular staircase and went out into the south gardens, the boys took off for their make-shift cricket field and Thomas walked with Georgiana and Maria.

"Thomas, since you will have a part in religious instruction of the children, I wonder if your views are any different than they were three years ago."

As a warm smile spread across his face, Georgiana wondered if he knew the question had greater import than just for the children. He said, "I have come a long way since then. As you know from my visit three years ago, while at Cambridge, I attended class with several of my Methodist friends. We would frequently talk about views of the Christian doctrines or the Methodist approach to them. I found their passion most interesting and it seemed more and more probable to me that their account was true. However, it was not until after my leg injury, when I had hours to recuperate, that I felt my heart strangely warmed one night during attempts at prayer. I now understand that necessary personal experience that transforms the Christian life from 'duty and rules' to 'desire and relationship'."

"I am glad to hear your approbation of the Christian life," Georgiana replied.

At that moment, the two boys came over and took Thomas' hands to pull him over to the cricket field. They asked him if he would take his turn at bat. Maria and Georgiana sat down on the park bench to watch the three-man game take place. The boys were quite surprised that Thomas could hit the ball three times farther than they could. They were also soon amazed that he could run faster than either of them, despite his injury. After about fifteen minutes, the two boys finally jumped on Thomas and brought him to the ground where they wrestled in the grass.

Georgiana was pleased at what Thomas brought to Pemberley. His presence represented a fascinating improvement. She felt secure in Thomas' ability to teach and manage the boys. She was glad that he had answered questions in a favorable manner concerning the Christian faith--and his lack of feminine attachment.

That afternoon, Georgiana and Elizabeth escorted Thomas to the library of Pemberley. Showing him around, Georgiana remarked to Thomas, "I am a little reluctant to admit my favorite reading genre consists of novels."

"Tell me why?"

"The novels are held in low esteem and are criticized by those in society."

"Have you read Jane Austen's novels? I think you would find them on a higher plane," said Thomas.

"No, I have not," was Georgiana's response.

"I have a copy of Miss Austen's *Sense and Sensibility* if you would like to borrow it."

"May I?"

"When I return to my room I shall bring it to you."

Turning to another bookcase, she pointed out the

books which were in obvious disrepair. "These are the oldest books in our library."

"Indeed, Ma'am, may I look at one or two of these?"

Georgiana looked at Elizabeth, who replied, "I am sure Mr. Darcy would not mind."

Thomas gently lifted down a very large book, the binding of which was dissolving. The volume originally appeared to be three inches thick and the cover about twelve by nine inches; opening the cover, the group discovered it to be a very old family Bible. Turning the first few pages, Thomas remarked, "There is a Darcy family tree listed here."

The women crowded next to him as Georgiana stated, "Here is my mother, Lady Anne, listed as being married to my father, Arthur Darcy, on August 1, 1779."

Going up the converging genealogical lines, Elizabeth said, "Look here, Mr. Staley, the great grandmother of Mr. Darcy was named Mary Staley of Staley Hall!"

"I have never been told this!" Thomas exclaimed.

"Nor I," Georgiana replied. Smiling, she said, "That makes us distant relatives."

Closing the book, Thomas remarked in a soft tone, "I should like to repair these books. This one, however, is much too valuable to start with."

Elizabeth said, "Do you know how to bind books?"

"I was taught book repair during my library assistanceship at Cambridge. It has been three years since I have worked on books, but I know exactly how it is done. If you find me space to work and obtain the necessary materials, I should like to put new covers on these books to restore them."

"Let us know what you need since tomorrow we have to go to Rosing Park and can easily stop over in London."

Discussion ensued about the special leather and glue

needed. Thomas indicated he would send to Staley Hall for his tools. Georgiana thought there was a small room next to the library that might function well for his purpose. It took several tries to find the right door. It opened into a small room with a large window. A thick layer of dust blanketed everything. The room held little, save a large wooden table with two chairs. Thomas declared it perfect. Elizabeth said she would leave orders for the room to be cleaned.

Two days later, the Darcys headed down the road in a carriage. Georgiana was vexed at having to leave Pemberley. She felt Thomas Staley to be a most interesting addition to Pemberley and sorely wished that she did not have to go to Rosing Park at this particular time. On their way to Kent, they went through the northern aspect of London and picked up the bookbinding supplies Thomas needed.

As they approached Rosing Park, they could see Reverend and Mrs. Collins waiting for their arrival. Mr. Collins was Elizabeth's cousin on her father's side. He was the rector of Hunsford, but considered himself accountable only to his patroness, Lady Catherine de Bourgh. Mr. Collins rushed forward as the family stepped out of the carriage. "Ah, cousin Elizabeth, it is good to see you looking well. . . Georgiana, your beauty grows every day. . .Mr. Darcy, the honor of meeting you is increased with each visit."

The Darcys could tell that Mr. Collins was most pleased to escort them into the entrance hall, where they were informed that dinner would be served immediately.

After the very formal supper at Rosings, Lady Catherine de Bourgh held "court" in her drawing room, as usual. Georgiana was asked, in a not to be refused tone, to play for the assembled family. After doing so, she came and sat down by Mrs. Darcy.

"Now, let us get down to one of the reasons I invited

the Darcy family here. Georgiana, what plans have you made about marriage?"

"I am not interested in getting married," she replied resolutely.

"Nonsense, girl. You must get married."

Lady Catherine paused and Mr. Collins interjected, "Lady Catherine is right. You must enter that blessed state. A woman of your accomplishments and beauty would grace any estate and uplift her husband."

Lady Catherine interrupted, "I understand there is very little opportunity in rural Derbyshire; and thus, I think you must start attending court again in London."

"I do not wish to attend the season in London."

"Don't be impertinent. Of course you do!" Lowering her voice somewhat, she continued, "I need not remind you, Georgiana, that in a little less than a year, you will be seven and twenty years old--an age many consider to be the status of an old maid."

Georgiana's mind desperately searched for a compromise in her favor. If she did not make a counteroffer, she could visualize her aunt demanding a long stay in London until the desired result took place. She answered, "If I attend court for two months, will your ladyship release me from the duty of searching for a husband?"

"A beautiful, accomplished girl like you will have no trouble in attracting suitors, if she would only desire one."

"But, you forget, Ma'am, that Georgiana is quite shy around strangers," Elizabeth interjected.

"It is something she must get over, or she may end up as a lonely old woman like myself." Looking maudlin, she added, "It is terrible to be alone as I have been since my husband and daughter have died, God rest their souls."

Georgiana chose not to answer. She thought that marriage had not done much for Lady Catherine, but decided saying so would be unwise.

Turning the subject, Lady Catherine continued, "Tomorrow, the Duke of Kent will arrive. I hope you will receive him well. I am proud of you, Fitzwilliam, and our family. Georgiana, I am also proud of you and know that you will be a credit to your family."

The next morning, as the Darcys and the Collins finished breakfast with Lady Catherine, the arrival of the Duke of Kent was announced. The guests left the table and went into the parlor. A young man, who was somewhat shorter than Georgiana, entered the parlor. The Darcys looked behind him for the old man they expected. When the young man approached Lady Catherine, she curtsied to him and said, "Welcome, your Grace, the Duke of Kent!"

Lady Catherine then began the introductions. Along with the rest of her family, Georgiana was astonished. Her preconception of an elderly man was at variance with the youth before them. He had blond hair, a square jaw and refined, pleasing manners. He turned and looked at her with penetrating eyes. She felt like retreating but he approached and took her hand; after kissing it, he said, "I am glad Lady Catherine has introduced us. I have heard rumors about the *hidden jewel of Derbyshire*, but gave them no credence until now. Your tall beauty is wonderful to behold."

Georgiana reacted to the size reference with disapprobation. She was repelled that he was at least two inches shorter than herself. She also soon learned that he was only three and twenty.

Mr. Collins began to approach the Duke, but in doing so he became unsteady and staggered to a couch.

"Is he unwell?" Elizabeth cried as she saw Charlotte, his wife, attend to him.

"There is nothing wrong with him," Lady Catherine said. "He always does that when the highest peers come around."

Georgiana could hear him blithering, "I am in the presence of the Duke of Kent. . . sixth from the throne!"

The Duke turned to Georgiana and said, "I apologize. I am most uncomfortable with the reactions I cause in people since my assumption of the title one month ago. It is quite a change to ascend to such a title. You may continue to call me 'Lord Percy', rather than 'your Grace', since I am still much more familiar with the former title. "

Georgiana sensed this was said with an air of arrogance. It also began to occur to her that this meeting might be contrived by Lady Catherine de Bourgh for the sole purpose of introducing the Duke to her. She moved behind her brother, who asked, "Does your lordship enjoy fishing?"

"Yes, very much so."

"I had heard so. What kind of fish do you pursue?"

"Any sportfish will do."

"Then you must visit Pemberley sometime. We have trout in the streams and bass and perch in the lakes. I can show you all the best spots."

"That sounds like jolly good fun. I would come directly, but the season at London is beginning, and I plan on staying there for the winter."

Georgiana cringed. It even sounded like her brother was in the conspiracy; though, she knew he would never stoop to such efforts. She had heard him invite many friends for fishing in the past, so she would try not to be too concerned about the Duke's invitation being special. The fact that Derbyshire was so far north of London often prevented visitors. She certainly hoped this would cause the Duke to forget his invitation.

The Duke was shown the house by the assembled group. Mr. Collins continued his usual unctuous behavior to the lord, who was plainly irritated by his manner.

That evening, Lady Catherine prevailed upon Georgiana to play and sing. Georgiana excused herself from singing by mentioning a sore throat, though, she thought to herself, "If someone was here I really wanted to sing to, I could make the effort."

She did play the pianoforte, but only listlessly. Having the Duke stare at her during the performance made her feel like an art object at auction. While her shyness and withdrawing character could not confront her aunt directly, she could passively decide not to perform her best for the group.

His Grace, Duke of Kent

Chapter Thirteen

While it was always a relief to leave Rosing Park, Georgiana thought the departure most refreshing this time. She eagerly anticipated the approach to Pemberley.

The carriage pulled to a stop. As the family stepped out, the children came rushing forward to hug their mother and father. Maria came and grabbed Georgiana's hand. Phillip was also present with his barking. The boys were telling a jumble of events very excitedly when Elizabeth asked them to settle down and save their stories for dinner.

Georgiana looked at Thomas and was pleased with what she saw. He was watching the boys and seemed to be avoiding looking at her, in a shy sort of way. Maria took Georgiana over to Thomas. Maria said, "Thomas has involved us in some adventures. A loud noise has been heard around the house at night."

"Mamma, please do not let Maria tell our story," said Andrew. "I discovered it first with Thomas."

"Now, children, let us wait until supper to hear these wonderful events which have you so excited," cried Elizabeth.

Thomas asked, "Were you able to obtain the needed supplies for the library?"

"Yes," Georgiana said and pointed to the medium sized trunk. She turned to Mr. Reynolds to say, "Make sure the servants take that trunk to the library workshop." Turning back she resumed, "Thomas, you may want to supervise them doing so, since it is your material."

After dinner was served, Elizabeth turned to Andrew and said, "Now, tell me what you were so anxious to say when we arrived."

"John and I have divided things between us so we do not interrupt each other. I am to tell about the mysterious sound Mr. Staley and I heard one night, when we were in his turret room."

Elizabeth interrupted, "Thomas, you know you do not have to see the children outside their scholastic time."

"I know, ma'am, but I wanted to let the boys sleep in my room one at a time. Teaching is sometimes best accomplished outside the classroom."

Elizabeth continued, "I am sorry for interrupting you, my son, pray continue your story."

"The wind was blowing hard one night when we heard the most mournful cry."

"Do you think it is a ghost?" Maria asked excitedly.

"Now, sister, no one has said this sound comes from a ghost," Andrew said in a big brother fashion.

"Why not?" Georgiana laughed, "All the estates of Derbyshire seem to have their own ghosts, why not ours?"

Andrew continued, "Mr. Staley says we must try to study it since it is some sort of natural 'nomenon'."

Mr. Darcy said, "You mean 'phenomenon'. And yes, by all means, study it. I am sure Thomas, like myself, does not believe in ghosts. Sir William Staley and I have discussed the ethereal issue before. I have never been aware of unusual noises in the hall."

Thomas replied, "I believe it is centered in the older part of the house, where my turret is located. It is difficult to study, for it only occurs occasionally and usually on windy nights."

"There you have it--the wind must be causing it," Mr. Darcy said.

"That is my opinion also," Thomas continued, "However, the sound changes character rather frequently, making it quite curious."

With a tone of playfulness, Georgiana said, "Now that we have a real mystery at Pemberley, a delicious adventure may ensue. Pray, let us not solve it too quickly."

Andrew said, "We have not been able to solve it yet. When we approach the sound, it seems to move or disappear."

"Mr. Darcy, may the boys and I have permission to go onto the roof of Pemberley house?"

"You must include me in the request, Thomas," Georgiana said.

Thinking for a minute, Mr. Darcy replied, "I do not see any problem, as long as they are with you or Georgiana. Most of the pathways have ramparts and, thus, should be safe. Only, do not stay out if it is raining, since the footing can become treacherous."

"My turn," piped up John.

"Yes, Master John, you have shown remarkable patience in waiting," Mrs. Darcy said in an approving tone.

"Not really, Mother. I was listening to the story. I have had the rotten luck of not hearing any ghostly sounds when I stayed in the turret, but I wanted to tell you about the den of foxes we discovered across the river on our walk. If you wait on the bridge in the twilight, you can sometimes see the red foxes come out."

"Yes, Mamma, and Thomas has helped show us hares and squirrels," Maria beamed with her report.

Thomas and Maria left after supper to return to their respective rooms. The boys were excused and headed outside to check on the foxes.

Mr., Mrs., and Miss Darcy sat sipping their coffee.

"Can there be any doubt that Thomas is an excellent tutor?"

The women nodded in agreement.

"My approbation is complete. I have often felt guilty about the affairs that draw me away from home. Thomas has developed a felicitous presence here at Pemberley. We are obliged to him."

Georgiana was pleased that her brother expressed such approval. Thomas was becoming more and more interesting to her. He was rising in her esteem and the feelings of love she had, three years earlier, were beginning to warm her soul again. Little did she realize that her oft repeated intention to never marry was beginning to melt.

Chapter Fourteen

A fortnight later, Georgiana wandered into the school room to listen. The children were present, but Thomas had not yet arrived. She no longer was monitoring him, but enjoyed the atmosphere that Thomas created for the children in the room.

Thomas entered shortly and she watched as he approached his seat. He sat down and his facial expression became chagrined. John began shaking as he tried to stifle his laughter. Andrew and Maria looked puzzled. Georgiana noticed water dripping in all directions from Thomas' chair. Georgiana could not help but laugh; she put her hand over her mouth in an attempt to suppress her giggles. It was clear to her that the mischievous John had soaked Mr. Staley's seat cushion as a lone conspirator. He now observed his teacher with open merriment. Maria also began giggling; while their serious older brother, Andrew, appeared embarrassed. Georgiana was interested to see how Thomas would react.

Mr. Staley quickly regained his composure and acted as if nothing had happened. He said, "Andrew and John, I have a difficult mathematics test for each of you. The boy that finishes his test first, gets the rest of the morning off." Maria was told to read a story in her primer while the boys took their test. Competitive looks filled the faces of her nephews. Thomas rose from his seat and the dripping ceased. He handed the tests to the boys and told them to start. Mr. Staley dropped his pencil in front of John's desk and, unbeknownst to the concentrating young man, tied the lad's shoelaces together. After doing so, Mr. Staley returned to his seat and glanced towards Georgiana who gave a smile of approbation.

Andrew and John finished at nearly the same time. Mr. Staley came to their desks to pick up their tests. After a moment or two of looking at the answers he said, "It appears you have done equally well. I will give you both the morning off."

With a gleeful yelp, both boys stood up and Andrew began to run, only to see John fall forward. This time everyone else in the room saw what had caused his fall and began to laugh without restraint. Thomas knelt to help John turn over onto his back. By this time, John was smiling and said, "I think your trick was better than mine."

Mr. Staley replied, "Not at all. You just need to learn not to play tricks on an old Cambridge man. Every college student seems to learn more about pranks than he does about knowledge."

Thomas untied John's shoes and the children scampered off. He then stood and approached Georgiana. She said, "Thomas, you must tell me about these pranks at Cambridge. No one has ever told me such stories."

"Well, my lady, I have this need to change clothes. While in the army I had a wet uniform on many occasions, I see no need to continue that practice. If you will wait, I will return after visiting my room and tell you anything you like."

Twenty minutes later, he returned and moved to look out the window. Georgiana joined him and playfully said, "You must tell me of the most diverting prank that happened while you were at Cambridge."

"If you wish. . . to set the scene, we had one student on our floor who was always getting up before everyone else. He did his best to inform his fellow residents that he was an early riser by singing and slamming doors. Our floor conspired to fool him by arising quietly at 2:30 one winter morning. One fellow snuck into his room and moved his clock ahead three hours. As you know, there isn't any daylight at 5:30 a.m. in the winter. We then began banging doors and singing and several of us went by his room to ask him why he was not up with the rest of us. He woke up and looked panic stricken as he ran around getting ready. He rushed off the floor and hurried across campus. We then doused the lights. We corrected the time on his clock and retired to bed as if nothing had occurred. He returned a half hour later, and for some odd reason, was much more quiet in his early rising thereafter."

"Oh! Thomas, what a diversion! I am glad you are not too serious. John needs someone with your character around." They were silent for a minute.

"Excuse me, my lady, I am going down to the stable to take care of my horse. I usually tend to her while you are teaching music to the children."

"May I watch sometime?"

"Certainly," Thomas said as he turned to leave the room.

It would not surprise the reader that Georgiana found opportunity to visit the stable the following afternoon. She and Andrew approached Thomas as he was brushing down his mare. Thomas remarked, "Where are your other pupils, Georgiana?"

Andrew answered, "John threw some water on Maria and was sent to his room for reflection this afternoon. Maria was not feeling well before John attacked her and has been kept in for the sniffles."

Georgiana then asked, "Thomas, why do you not let the groomsmen take care of your horse? I am sure they will do a good job."

"Perhaps. But, after a horse like Jenny has carried you through thick and thin in the war, a man becomes very attached to his mount. In some ways, the horse becomes a part of oneself. Andrew, have you heard of the mythical centaur?"

"Yes, sir. A centaur was an animal that was half horse and half man."

"Good. Well, Andrew, when you have a favorite horse for a long time, you will begin to understand how the image may have been inspired. Another thing, Andrew, it is perfectly acceptable for a gentleman to groom his horse, particularly when he loves the animal."

Georgiana then said, "Thomas, why do you not come riding with us?"

"The weather does not look promising, my lady. The rains have been heavy to the north lately and it may rain here soon."

"Oh, come now, Thomas. You said you were wet many a time on the continent. You do not fear it now, do you?"

"Not at all. I was only thinking of the comfort of you and Master Andrew."

"A little water never hurt anyone."

With this said, Thomas gave orders for their horses to be brought out. He assisted Georgiana and Andrew onto their respective mounts. Their planned route was to circle the manor so the ride could be discontinued at any time without a long return.

As the horses turned right off the bridge, Thomas remarked, "The river is much higher than normal. The report of the rains in the north must be true."

Georgiana was thinking more about this being the route taken by Mrs. Gardiner, Elizabeth and herself on that infamous day nine years ago. Certainly no one in this party would suffer an obstetrical complication today!

After following the river downstream for a mile, rather than following up the hill, they elected to cross a small wooden bridge onto a wooded area called "The Island". The island derived its name from the fact that the river, divided into two parts, surrounded a bit of land. Once onto the island, they guided their horses to the southern aspect, where an old camp with an open-sided shelter was present. Here they dismounted, tied their horses and sat on logs in front of the shelter.

Andrew asked, "Mr. Staley, could we come camping here some time?"

"Yes."

Georgiana looked around and said, "I should come out here to do some sketching. The interplay of shadows would be challenging to capture." As she finished speaking, raindrops began to fall.

She got up to move under the roof, as Thomas chuckled, "I thought you said you would not mind getting wet!"

"Not if I can avoid it."

As the rain became heavier, Thomas and Andrew also moved under the shelter.

After several minutes, Georgiana saw Thomas's troubled look. "Thomas, what is the matter?"

"The sound of the river is changing." He stood and moved away from the shelter, towards the river. He returned breathless and soaked with water. "My lady, the river is rising very fast. I think we should seek higher ground immediately. This area may soon be flooded."

They all moved to their horses, mounted and began to retrace their trail to the northern part of the quarter mile island. Emerging from the trees, they could see the small bridge they had crossed was underwater. The noise of the rain required that Georgiana shout to Thomas, "What shall we do? Should we return to the shelter?"

"No. I fear it will soon be underwater also. We need to dismount."

Georgiana and Andrew obeyed. Andrew huddled next to his aunt. The rain continued to pour down. Thomas shouted, "We. . .must let your horses go. They will have a better chance of survival without a rider. We will all get on my horse and try to cross the shorter aspect of the river to the eastern bank."

"Why not the western bank, so we can return to Pemberley?"

"I fear the uncertain footing of the fen [swamp] and wide current." Thomas took out a rope and tied it around each of their waists with ample slackness in between.

Andrew asked, "Mr. Staley, why are you tying us together?"

"In case one of us is swept away, the others can pull him to safety." Thomas put Andrew up on his horse, mounted himself and pulled Georgiana up. He coaxed his horse into the current and then let loose of her reins. "Jenny will be able to find her own way better." With water at their waists, Georgiana held on tightly to Thomas. She clasped her hands around his waist. Her face was pressed against his back. The feel of his broad and muscular shoulders was reassuring to her. Despite the water dripping down her face, she could see they were making progress towards the southeast hill. After several attempts, the horse finally pulled itself out of the flooded river. A little more climbing brought them to the main road. They began the return to Pemberley. Approaching the stone bridge to Pemberley, they saw the flood waters had enveloped it.

Thomas turned his head and said, "I do not think we should attempt it."

"Let us go to the rectory and see if we can stay with the Westbrooks."

The rain poured as they headed one half mile to the east. Arriving in front of the parsonage, Thomas lowered Andrew down and then dismounted himself and cut the ropes. He helped Georgiana down and said, "Take Andrew inside while I take care of Jenny."

Kitty Westbrook met them at the door of the parsonage and remarked, "Georgiana, you are completely soaked and Master Andrew, too. Please come inside quickly."

Once inside, Kitty continued, "You will need to take the wet clothes off. I have some clothes for you, Georgiana, though they will probably be baggy on your figure; and, Andrew, I have clothes to fit you, because of our surprise announcement!!"

"What do you mean?" Georgiana queried.

"I will explain once you are dry and warm in front of the fire."

Minutes later, Georgiana, Kitty and Andrew were sitting in front of the fire sipping tea. Thomas finally entered with Reverend Westbrook. Georgiana said, "Thomas, what has taken you so long?"

"I needed to dry and take care of Jenny. A horse that has saved my life time and time again is more important than my own comfort."

Kitty said, "I have some clothes of Henry's laid out in the next room. They may be a little loose on you, but at least they are dry."

Thomas soon returned with a change of clothing and went to the window where Henry Westbrook was standing. Henry remarked, "The deluge appears to be ending. However, from your description, I doubt if the river will be passable into Pemberley until tomorrow. You are, of course, welcome to spend the night here."

"Thank you for your hospitality," Thomas replied.

Georgiana said, "I wish there were some means of getting a message to Pemberley that we are all safe."

"I am afraid not tonight, Georgiana. We can send a messenger first thing in the morning," Henry replied.

Thomas nodded in assent with the reverend.

Georgiana said, "Kitty, you told us about a surprise announcement."

Kitty fidgeted with her dress and replied, "You know, Georgiana, that Henry and I have been unable to have any children in our eight years of marriage. You also are aware that Mrs. Smith died last month, leaving Lucy and Paul as orphans." Her voice took on a joyful tone as she announced, "The legalities are finally finished. We have officially adopted Lucy and Paul as our children!"

"I am so happy for you," was Georgiana's reply as she rose and sat next to Kitty, putting her arm around her.

Kitty continued, "I am so obliged to you, Georgiana, for introducing me to the parish work here and the little baby Paul. He is just as sweet at age nine as he has been all the years I have watched him grow. Lucy and Paul have seen us so much they had already begun to call us Aunt and Uncle; so, the excitement is mutual for the adults and children."

Thomas asked, "Well, Henry, how will it feel to be called Papa?"

"I do not expect any different. In some ways, adoption is better than natural birth, since you can choose your own children."

Kitty interjected, "This is why we have clothing for Andrew to borrow. We are getting ready for the children to arrive from the orphanage."

After dinner that evening, Andrew was sent to bed and the four adults sat around the fire.

Henry began, "Thomas, it is good to see you coming to the parish church every Sunday. Tell me what you think."

"Henry, we have known each other since we were children. If I did not like the service and your sermon, I would not come; still, I wish you would talk more about the relationship with our heavenly Father than you do."

"Pray, Thomas, tell me what you mean. I know you

are honest and will not dissemble with me."

"Henry, I think you spend too much time explaining the Thirty-nine Articles of Faith."

"Thomas, would you trifle with these foundational statements of the church?"

"They are well and good, but only go so far."

"You puzzle me."

"The Christian life consists of rules, rituals and relationship. The rules and rituals help to foster our relationship with God, but exercising or reciting the doctrines puts one only at the rules level; and if one stays there, the religion can easily become one of choking legalism."

"What do you mean?"

"The rules and rituals exist for the possibility of delight. Performing them is like people digging channels in a waterless land so, when the water comes, it may find them ready."

"You would not have our religion be one of emotional frenzy, would you?"

"Not at all. A relationship consists of commitment and a love awareness. No one can be emotional about it at all times; however, those who never have any emotions are missing out on what the Christian religion may impart best-peace and joy, in a right relationship with God."

"Is it wrong, then, to consider our duty towards God?"

"Not at all. The difference between duty and loving devotion is desire. When one begins to desire something, the sense of duty disappears and loving devotion takes over."

"Your words are high sounding, but I am uncertain of their meaning."

"This concept, more than any other, kept me from believing in Christianity. As soon as my heart desired peace and joy, the doctrines ceased to be a duty."

"I like your statement, Thomas. I am not sure I comprehend it fully. At the least, your thoughts have brought you back to the church."

Georgiana listened to the conversation between her two long-time acquaintances carefully. Thomas had a way of perplexing her at times. She often thought that much of her religious activity was duty. She sometimes felt compelled to attend her daily prayers, rather than desiring them. Thomas' words were both wonderful and puzzling.

As the men continued to talk, and Kitty was checking on Andrew, Georgiana snatched the opportunity to continue looking at Thomas. His gallantry, strength and amiability made her admire him as she never had before.

In the morning, the Westbrooks had their carriage take Miss Darcy and Master Andrew back to Pemberley, while Mr. Staley accompanied them on his horse. The river had subsided to below the stone bridge, allowing passage back to Pemberley.

Mr. and Mrs. Darcy, along with John, greeted them in front of the hall. Elizabeth said to Georgiana as she was stepping out of the carriage, "We are very relieved to see you well. We were quite worried last night when you did not return. Our worry deepened when two of your horses returned alone."

As Andrew stepped out, he exclaimed, "Oh, Mamma. We were caught in the flood, but Mr. Staley knew just what to do. He and his horse took us to safety!"

His mother replied, "Andrew, I shall want to hear all about it in a moment."

Mr. Darcy came up to Mr. Staley as he dismounted and thanked him for saving his family. He asked the details of the flood as they walked the horse towards the stable. Elizabeth escorted them into the entrance hall and asked Georgiana, "Are you feeling well?"

"Yes, of course. As you know, we stayed at the

rectory."

"Yes, it was such a relief to receive the message first thing this morning that you were safe."

"I am thankful that Thomas was with us. His courage and presence of mind during the emergency helped me not to be so frightened."

Chapter Fifteen

A month passed, when at dinner, Elizabeth remarked, "We only have six weeks before you go to court, Georgiana. We must get you a new wardrobe. Do you want to go to London or shall we have a dressmaker come to Pemberley?"

"Please, if you will, have one come to Pemberley. I wish to spend as little time in London as possible."

"Mr. Darcy, may we do so?"

"By all means." After a moment, Mr. Darcy continued, "My dear, Lizzy, you may want to have more dresses made for yourself, as well." Turning to the boys he asked, "What has been happening with our strange sound or the lack of it?"

John piped up, "I finally got to hear it father. It sounds like a low moan that sometimes screeches!" As he raised his hands for emphasis, Georgiana involuntarily shuddered. "But, rotten luck! Mr. Thomas and I crept onto the roof from the third floor of the turret, and the sound died away. We were not even certain whether we were investigating in the right direction."

"Investigating? Where have you learned such a big word?" asked Elizabeth wrily.

"Mr. Thomas uses it when we are trying to figure something out."

"And do you know where the sound is coming from yet?" his mother queried.

"Not yet. I think it sounds like an old lady moaning,

but we don't have any old ladies here now."

Mr. Darcy interrupted, "And I can assure you there are no ghosts here. All of our ancestors to my knowledge, died honorably and peaceably."

Turning the conversation, Georgiana inquired, "Thomas, why do you go out on the north trail so often?"

"Why do you not come with me and the boys tomorrow after our morning lessons?"

"Yes, Auntie, come with us!" Andrew said eagerly.

"I shall be happy to come," responded Georgiana with a smile. However, she began to feel a little vexed--it occurred to her that her nephews were almost always with Thomas in the morning, with herself in the afternoon, and with him again after dinner for an evening walk. Would she ever get time to be alone with Thomas? She tried to put this thought aside, since it evoked ambivalent feelings.

The next morning she went to the Pemberley classroom with the children.

Maria was beginning to read her French lesson and needed help from Thomas, who said, "'Au contraire' means 'on the contrary'." A few moments later, Thomas said, "'Mon amour' means 'my love' or 'my friend' depending on the context of the conversation. The French do not have 'like' and 'love' as we English do. They must make the same word perform double duty."

After their French lessons, Thomas read them a story about a woman married to a cruel husband, who made her life miserable. Daily, the husband would list extra work she should do to "earn her keep". Her life was one of drudgery and slavish duty. Eventually, her husband died.

Later, she fell in love with a kindly man who treated her like a lady. They were soon married, and she began to keep house for him. One day she ran across a burdensome schedule that had been outlined for her by her former husband. Checking the list, she discovered she had done everything on the list that very day. What a change! What once had been mere drudgery, was now a labor of love for the man who loved her so much!

"Now then class, what is the story trying to teach us?"

"Doing things for those we love is much easier than for those we do not," said Maria.

"Well said," Thomas replied and continued, "In the first case, the woman did her duty, but it was a heavy burden."

Andrew interrupted "And in the second case, she desired to help her loving husband."

"What areas of our life does this apply to?" Thomas continued.

"In a marriage, like Mother and Father's," Maria said.

"Very good, Maria. Of course."

The boys and Maria were quiet for awhile, but they could tell Thomas wished more.

An insight touched Georgiana who unconsciously stood and said, "The story also stands for our relationship with God. The moment desire and love enter in, the sense of duty disappears."

Thomas looked at her and smiled. "Your aunt has said it better than I could." He closed his book and said, "Enough book work for today. Let us take to our trail." Turning to Georgiana he asked, "Will Phillip be able to come with you?"

"No, I think not. At eleven years of age, he does not move very fast and seems to prefer to stay inside."

The group walked out together into the November sunshine. Out the south door, around Pemberley Hall, the trail ran past the lake and into the low lying wooded hills beyond. After a mile, they reached the top of one large hill where they could see the horizon. Several large boulders and logs were present, inviting them to sit down.

Thomas said to Georgiana, "Do you see why I like to come here now? My father always referred to this area as Becker's point."

As she looked north, she saw the grounds of Staley Hall. "Is that the roof of Staley Hall in the distance?" she inquired.

"Yes. What you see in the foreground are the Inglenook cottages and the Moorgate tenant farm."

"This is beautiful and picturesque," Georgiana replied. "How far is it to Staley Hall?"

Thomas replied, "About half a mile."

"That makes it much closer than by road. I always traveled to Staley Hall in a carriage as a child. I did not realize it was so close by trail."

John pulled on Georgiana's hand and said, "Let me show you the reason I like to come up here." As soon as Georgiana began to move, John dropped her hand and raced forward with Andrew and Maria. "Follow me," John shouted. They went down the hill a short distance to a spot behind a large boulder.

"Auntie, see the tree just beyond this boulder?"

"Yes."

"Look at the hole in it above the third limb. Can you see the entrance to the squirrels' nest?"

"Yes."

"We watch to see squirrels bringing in their treasures for the winter."

Georgiana liked the earnest interest her nephews and niece were showing in their observation. Thomas was truly an exceptional teacher. She wished she had such a tutor while growing up.

As the group returned to the top of Becker's point, Georgiana asked, "May we walk over to Staley Hall? I have not been there for many years."

"I am afraid, my lady, it has sadly deteriorated since

you last laid eyes on it," Thomas said.

"It does not matter. I have fond memories of your mother beginning my music lessons there."

The children declared their wish to go; and, after assuring Thomas they could walk that far, he consented.

They descended the northern aspect of the hill, leaving the view of Pemberley behind them. At the bottom of the hill, they crossed a small bridge and embarked upon a fairly straight and flat trail leading up to the Elizabethan house. Passing the Inglenook cottages, Georgiana noticed they had been boarded up.

As Thomas opened the gate to the yard in front of the "E" shaped building, Georgiana was shocked to see the exterior condition of Staley Hall. Chimney smoke had blackened the walls in some areas, and patches of paint were peeling off in other spots. The gardens on each side, which used to greet visitors with an assortment of colors and fragrances, were now unkempt and overgrown with weeds. A broken down wagon was over to the right of the main building.

Thomas said apologetically, "I am sorry you have to see Staley Hall in such poor condition. My father has only one servant inside and one outside; but even if we had the labor to fix it up, we do not have the money to do so."

"Oh! Thomas, you should ask my brother for help! He would be happy to assist Staley Hall to regain the beauty I knew as a child!"

"My lady, Father and I appreciate your offer, but we do not wish your charity."

"Why must it be considered charity, when it is between two gentle families of ancient ties?" She observed that Thomas sighed, so she turned the subject, "When was Staley Hall constructed?"

"It appears this site has had some type of structure since the tenth century. The present building was begun during Queen Elizabeth's reign and was constructed in an 'E' shape in her honor."

John ran ahead to harass a lone goose wandering the yard. After a few moments of surprise, the goose began chasing John, nipping at his heels. The group began laughing and Maria asked, "May we go inside, Mr. Staley?"

"Of course. If you are disappointed with the outside, you will be dismayed inside; however, whatever hospitality we have, we are happy to offer."

John was perched on the only safe spot in the yard, the old wagon which listlessly occupied one corner. Thomas went and shooed the bird away and John dismounted, awed at the influence of his tutor.

Entering the front door, a stooped, elderly man greeted them. "Good day, Master Tom. Your father sends his regrets, he will be unable to meet with your group."

"Why not?"

"His stomach is bothering him and he has taken to bed."

"Is it serious?"

"I expect not. He says it is his dyspepsia again and not to worry." Looking at Georgiana, he exclaimed, "Is that you Miss Darcy? What a wonderful surprise! It has been much too long since we have seen you here. How long has it been?"

"Fifteen years, I think."

The servant continued, "You look very much like your beautiful mother, Lady Anne. I am afraid we have not been able to keep the house up to the standard you remember."

Thomas said, "I am sorry, Giles, that I have forgotten my manners. You will not know the Darcy children. This is Andrew, John and Maria."

The boys bowed and Maria curtsied.

Thomas turned to Georgiana and said, "Would you

like some tea?"

Georgiana glanced at the children who indicated their approbation. Sitting down in the entrance parlor, awaiting the tea, Georgiana looked around. The furniture was the same as she remembered, but very faded and somewhat dusty. She looked across the room. The pianoforte had a layer of dust. A cobweb dangled from the ceiling above it. Despite the deteriorated condition of the room, she felt voices and music coming from the walls--the laughter and singing of the now gone Lady Marilyn, as she encouraged Georgiana in her music. She recalled her own halting attempts at playing the pianoforte and the love she so desperately needed, and received, from Thomas' mother after her own mother, Lady Anne, died and the wretched feelings she had three years later when Lady Marilyn died. Her thoughts were bittersweet; but the sweet feelings began to predominate as she sensed what she had felt most in the room as a child. . .a feeling of love. Unconditional love, from a woman who sang from her heart and filled Staley Hall with music.

She saw Thomas talking to her nephews and, for the first time, emotionally connected his mother with him. For some unknown reason, Thomas had not been around during her lessons with his mother; but now, she saw the same kind and gentle spirit in him. This reconnection made her love for him grow all the more.

Finishing the tea, they rose to leave. On the return to Pemberley, Georgiana observed that Thomas appeared sad and, possibly, even ashamed about his home. He was very quiet on the return to Becker's point, but his spirits seemed to rise to his usual countenance as they descended down the Pemberley side of the hill.

Georgiana was also quiet during the walk. She now feared Thomas would consider the humble state of his father's home, and thus his background, to be a barrier between them. She longed to walk next to him, grasp his hand, and tell him she did not care about his family's wealth or the lack of it.

Chapter Sixteen

Nearly six weeks passed, when, after the morning lessons, Maria took Thomas' hand and led him away. "I have something to show you, Mr. Staley." Taking him into the east wing, she opened a door and brought him into a sparsely decorated dressing room. Georgiana was standing on a table one foot high with the dressmaker making adjustments.

"I am sorry, ma'am. Maria brought me here, I did not know you were dressing."

"Do not leave, Thomas. I am only getting a fitting on this gown."

"Will your ladyship please be still? I need your cooperation. You have only two days before you leave for London and I must make these final adjustments."

Thomas looked at the light yellow gown Georgiana was wearing and began to have feelings come to his consciousness that he had not recognized before. Georgiana was made to look the other direction by the dressmaker, allowing Thomas to continue staring at her.

"Is she the most beautiful woman you have ever seen, Mr. Staley?" Maria asked in a whisper.

"Of course," Thomas replied in a low voice. His continued look made him aware he was more in love with her than he realized. He decided it best to withdraw, lest he say something to betray himself.

Thomas retreated to his workroom off the library and began repairing another book. An hour later, Georgiana knocked at the door and entered. She left the door open, "I hope I did not scare you away."

Looking at his work, he replied, "Not at all."

"I wish I were not obliged to go to court in London."

"Why?"

"The social life and conversation seem so artificial. I would prefer staying at Pemberley."

Thomas suspected the last statement might be directed at him. Still avoiding eye contact, he asked, "You said you were obliged?"

"Yes, my aunt, Lady Catherine de Bourgh, made me promise to attend court one more time. She is quite concerned I will become an old maid."

Thomas did not reply to the last statement; instead, he showed her a book that he was nearly finished rebinding.

"Oh, Thomas, this is beautiful." She turned and cried to Elizabeth in the library, "Lizzy, come here and see the Bible Thomas has finished."

Elizabeth came. Georgiana pointed to the large book with a new brown leather cover, with gold lettering. "Mr. Staley, this is exquisite."

"Some of the lettering needs to be finished, but the binding is complete." Thomas replied.

"May I show it to Mr. Darcy this evening?"

"Yes, of course."

Georgiana and Elizabeth took the volume into the library. Thomas was not only a scholar who loved books, but an artisan as well. His esteem rose further in the mind of Georgiana. She thought how perfectly matched they were.

As the family began to sit down for dinner that evening, Andrew volunteered, "The wind has been gusting quite strongly this afternoon. Do you think, Mr. Thomas, we might hear the moaning tonight?"

"It is quite probable that we will," Thomas replied.

"Then, what is your plan for discovering it?"

Georgiana inquired.

"Bring the boys and meet me outside my room in the tower at nine o'clock tonight. Hopefully, we can find out more about this sound."

The boys looked gleefully at each other and at Georgiana.

After supper, in the parlor, Elizabeth and Georgiana showed Mr. Darcy the antique family Bible. He was effusive in his praise.

"Now, you must fill in your names to complete the genealogy," Thomas said.

Mr. Darcy asked, "And how shall we ever repay you for your kindness?"

"I have an idea, brother," Georgiana interrupted. "Shall I make a sketch of Thomas? Would that be agreeable?"

Thomas was going to politely object, but Mr. Darcy said, "Excellent idea, my sister. We need a visual record of the man who has helped us so much here at Pemberley House."

Georgiana seated Thomas in one of the high backed chairs and began sketching his face. She started over two times before becoming satisfied as to its likeness. She had the further pleasure of being able to look at him, while he was forced to look over her shoulder. His face grew more handsome in her mind the longer she drew his likeness. She finished an hour after she began, with the family praising her for the true representation.

As the hour drew near to eight o'clock, Thomas excused himself to return to his room. The boys and Georgiana watched out the parlor window. Dark clouds intermittently covered the full moon. The south garden would change every few moments from being bathed in light to utter darkness. The wind continued to gust strongly.

"Can we go yet, Auntie?" John said impatiently.

"No, Thomas said to meet him outside his room at nine o'clock. We must wait a little longer."

Finally, the hour arrived. The boys took Georgiana's hands and led her towards the western part of the house. Reaching the base of the turret, the wind began howling again and a loud long moaning was to be heard. The group stopped at the base of the stairs and the boys huddled closer to their aunt.

"John, are you afraid?" Andrew asked.

"Of course not."

In truth, Georgiana felt uneasy. She thought the sound most unusual. Was it even of this world?

A blast of cold air came down the stairway as they began walking up. When they reached Thomas' doorway, he was not to be seen. Despite the shawl Georgiana had put on over her dress, she was quite cold.

She knocked at Thomas' door. With no answer, she pushed the door a little and it opened easily. The room was inviting. A fire roared in the fireplace. Thomas' desk was illuminated by several candles. The boys jumped on the smaller bed, which they were accustomed to sleeping on when they stayed with Thomas. Georgiana sat at the desk. Waiting a few minutes, she glanced at the papers on his desk and one caught her eye because of her own name. She nudged it out a little and read a poem in the style of Cowper:

Georgiana

I have known you since childhood. You were my
best friend, my confidant, we played our own
games, invented worlds. Now I can only sigh
inwardly. . . I love you. My life's on loan

now to you. . . You have become everything
to me. When you walk into a room I
can hear your music. . . your playing, singing
transports me to heaven. I can only cry

now--the years have separated us. Wars,
finances, our station in life. . . I dream
of you nightly. . . I see you at the doors
of all the world's ballrooms. Without you I seem

empty. . . it is cold and silent. I'm
incomplete without you. . . I'm lost in time
unworthy of you, a song without a rhyme.

Can you see how I feel,
or do you care at all?

Georgiana blushed after reading the poem. Her heart
swelled with happiness that Thomas reflected the love she
had for him. She felt a little guilty about invading his privacy
and feared Thomas might discover her at his desk. Would he
surmise that she had seen the letter, or did he intentionally
leave the poem so that she would see it tonight? Certainly,
he could have no assurance that she would see it; however,
the idea that he might be somewhat shy to introduce his
thoughts helped her feel closer than ever to him.

Why was Thomas late? She thought it best to replace
the paper to its former position. She did so, then moved over
to another chair.

The wind gusted more fiercely. The eerie moaning
began again. The boys got off the bed and spontaneously
came over to her, with a look of mild fright in their eyes.

A few minutes later, they heard boot steps on the
stairs. The heavy door to the room opened with a gust of
wind, bringing Thomas into the room. "I am sorry, my lady,
that I am late for our appointment. The sound stayed
constant for a prolonged period and I pursued it, thinking I
could detect it easily; however, the direction of sound on the
roof can be confused."

The boys reflected renewed confidence upon the
entrance of their tutor. They grabbed his hands. Georgiana

rose and Thomas said, "You may become quite cold with just the shawl. Here let me put one of my coats over it, to make sure of your comfort."

She was warmed by his gallantry, and enjoyed his placement of the coat about her. For a moment she caught his glance and smiled. They proceeded out the door and crept up a dozen stairs. Georgiana felt as though they were hunters pursuing prey. Were they afraid a ghost might see them and flee?

A door was encountered that opened out upon the roof with a long creak. The wind had temporarily died down and the moon had come from behind the clouds, revealing a bright moonlit scene before them.

"The sound seems to be coming from the eastern side of the house. Let us go and position ourselves there."

They went along a rampart briefly and then started through a series of older rooftops that, being built over centuries, had created a maze. Finally, when they could see the lake on the eastern side of the house, they became certain of their position. Spotting an overlapping roof, which created a lean-to, Thomas guided Georgiana to it and they sat down to wait. In a few moments, the wind began again and the moaning sound, though much more musical now, recurred very loudly.

They all stood up and looked at a short chimney near them. The sound was emanating from it. A few bricks were missing in the side of it, not too far from the top. They walked closer and spotted several wires across the empty space.

"This must be an aeolian harp," Thomas exclaimed, "I have never seen one, have you?"

Georgiana replied, "Only once. The one I saw was held in a window, but the design is roughly similar."

The sound died and restarted twice. Thomas picked up a loose roof tile and placed it over the opening during the sound, causing it to cease. Andrew and John had to each repeat the exercise before they were satisfied that the mystery had been solved.

"The bricks appear to have fallen out as the mortar decayed," Georgiana ventured.

"I would agree with that observation. That would explain why the sound has only been heard recently."

At that moment, a strong gust with pelting raindrops hit the group causing a retreat to the lean to. The rain was intermittent, lasting only ten to fifteen seconds at a time. Andrew and John edged over to a rampart on their knees to watch the lake in the sporadic moonlight. Georgiana looked at Thomas and felt, for the first time in her life, that she was truly in love with him. She wished she could say something to fix his interest on her. After all, he stated he was uncertain of her feelings! She felt herself blush and was ashamed that words failed her. She put out her right hand to straighten her dress and it bumped Thomas' left hand.

He turned, looked into her face, and gently grasped her hand. He did not let it go. She saw his eyes full of love for her and she smiled in response. She knew he was unlikely to say anything, due to the inhibiting presence of the boys.

Her heart was full of requited love. She wished she could always stay here. It seemed so cozy. She felt so safe and secure sitting next to him. She realized how strong his hand and arm felt, yet how gently he held her hand.

The boys were preoccupied with peering over the rampart. She was confident in the faded moonlight that, when they looked back in the storm, they could not see the details of the clasped hands. In her remembrances later, Georgiana felt the time lasted for hours; but, she knew in reality, it lasted only ten minutes, when Thomas said, "Much as I regret it, we better return before the storm worsens."

The boys concurred, though Georgiana was in no hurry. They rose and retraced their steps to the landing outside Thomas' door. The boys continued to go down the stairs leaving Thomas to gaze in the dim light, once more, into her face and touch her hand. She returned the gaze with the best expression of love she could muster.

"Come on, auntie," Andrew shouted after he had walked down enough stairs to be out of her sight. She reluctantly took one last look at Thomas, let go of his hand and went down the stairs.

Mr. Thomas Staley

Chapter Seventeen

The next morning, Georgiana awoke with strongly mixed feelings. She was vexed that her last day at Pemberley would be consumed with final preparations for the trip to London. She was irritated at having consented to Lady Catherine's wishes to attend court once more, yet glad her promise was limited to two months--two months! an eternity away from Pemberley, with Thomas here. Oh, that she had refused Lady Catherine! She could still stand up and refuse to go to London, and send her regrets; but then she would need a reason for doing so. She was not ready to make any announcement nor did she wish to risk any fledgling love with Thomas by trying to hurry their relationship along. No, as disappointing as it was, she would have to abide by her word as a gentlewoman and go. Duty would take priority over desire.

Her positive feelings were those of a woman in love. She recalled the hand caresses from the night before and enjoyed the passion they evoked. Her eyebrows furrowed as she thought again of the statement in his poem about feeling unworthy of her; perhaps, he would slip away during her two month absence! Maybe she would never see him again! What if he should leave for another three years? Surely not; the letter was written before last night. He must now be much more certain that her love reflected his.

She got up, determined to do her work for the trip as quickly as possible. She and Thomas did not say much during the breakfast time. She was at a loss how to encourage him, until midmorning, as she was packing her new yellow gown. She decided to put it on and visit the schoolroom. Her maid complained of the slowness of packing as she helped her dress. Georgiana left the dressing room feeling very elegant as she walked down the corridor with her ball gown on. She nudged the door to the school room open. Maria spotted her, ran and brought her into the room, saying in a loud voice, "Introducing Lady Darcy from Pemberley Hall!"

Thomas looked up, stood, and smiled. Georgiana saw his smile and focused on his face as she entered.

Maria came over to Thomas and said in a lower voice, "Is she not the most elegant woman you have ever seen, Mr. Staley?"

"Yes, Maria, without a contest," he replied.

"I knew I would interrupt your teaching, but I came anyway to show you my best gown for London."

"I am delighted that you came," replied Thomas.

"Come, Miss Darcy," her maid chided from the doorway, "we need to finish getting you ready."

Maria observed that Thomas seemed distracted for the rest of the day. He dismissed school somewhat early.

Dinner came. Again, Thomas and Georgiana were very quiet. After dinner, Georgiana played several numbers on the harp. Even though the whole family was present, she played only for Thomas, who remained focused on her during the entire performance.

Chapter Eighteen

The next morning Georgiana felt nervous and anxious about leaving. Mr. and Mrs. Darcy came out to the coach along with Thomas and the children. Adieus and promises of being missed by the Darcy family were made.

Thomas handed her into the carriage. As it drove away with Georgiana and her maid, Georgiana looked back and saw Thomas gazing at her intently. She fixed her eyes on him as long as possible. She was delighted that he met and responded to her gaze. When he faded from view, she suddenly realized that she had failed to obtain or give any promise about letter writing from Thomas. Since they had not yet used the word "love", it might have been broached in a letter! As a lady, she could not write him first; no, she would have to wait. She could write her nephews in a tone, or with references, that would cause them to show the letter to Thomas. Perhaps that would stimulate him to write her; if not, communicating by proxy would be better than no word at all.

Her thoughts wandered to his letter again. Why does Thomas feel unworthy towards me? He has nothing to be ashamed of as a scholar and gentleman. He is the second son of a baronet--a position not as high as the Darcy family held--but still a decent, respectable standing for a gentleman; certainly, nothing that would cause embarrassment for him or her should they become more serious. His Christian faith was no longer a barrier between them; in fact, she felt he understood many aspects of living a Christian life better than she. Perhaps he was concerned because he limped with his left leg on occasion. Georgiana knew that men were quite proud about their physical abilities. Thomas had compensated by developing unusually strong shoulders and she felt very secure around him. After all, her beloved Phillip limped on occasion and she loved Phillip all the more for it; she would do the same for Thomas.

No, it must be that he was substantially poorer than she. Though Staley Hall had never been as grand as Pemberley, its fortune had rapidly declined over the past sixteen years. Perhaps he felt the sting of "having to work" to make his way in life and help his father; but what was wrong with being a tutor and eventually a teacher at Cambridge? Since he would not inherit Staley Hall, his income was forecast to be modest. She did not care about the character of his wealth, but the wealth of his character. She concluded by accepting the thought that Thomas felt unworthy because of his lack of riches. She would have to think how to address the issue without offending him. Indeed, she would be quite happy to exist on a modest income with a loving man of such good character. These thoughts occupied Georgiana's mind for the remainder of the trip.

The following day would bring her to the Darcy home in London. It had been almost ten years since she had stayed regularly in London. She missed it very little. Between the pea-soup fog that smelled of horses, coal and other harsh smells, and the requisite social visitation that was almost as obnoxious as the air at times, she had little cause to rejoice.

Nevertheless, she would fulfill her agreement to her aunt once and for all. Lady Catherine was also planning to stay at the Darcy home in London. Georgiana looked with trepidation to interaction with her aunt, particularly without the presence of Elizabeth to shield her.

Her heart was sheltered and protected by her certain love of Thomas. Lady Catherine might introduce her to princes or dukes, but she would not worry about losing her heart. Thomas already possessed her affection.

She arrived at the home on Grosvenor Street and was shown into Lady Catherine's presence. "It is good of you to attend the season in London with me. I am so proud of my niece--I shall display you everywhere!"

Georgiana had not expected such a warm welcome from her usually dictatorial aunt. Her elderly relative appeared unusually tired and less regal than normal. "Thank you, Lady Catherine I have come to stay the two months as agreed."

"You need stay no longer than your promise; but, I daresay, when you become involved again, you may decide life at court is not so bad after all."

Georgiana chose not to respond directly to the last statement, looked around and asked, "Is the pianoforte I used to play still here?"

"Yes, it is behind you. I had it tuned for your visit." Lady Catherine resumed, "As you know, the large ball is to be at St. James' court in three days. I have taken the liberty to obtain box seats at the theater tomorrow evening. I hope you will feel well enough to go?"

Georgiana was intrigued by the theater, since it appealed to her artistic interest and usually involved very little social conversation. She asked, "What is the title of the performance?"

"Romeo and Juliet. Will you go?"

The play was well known to her, of course. The subject might offer a vicarious expression of her own feelings and, perhaps, lessen the trapped sensation she felt in London.

"Yes, I think I shall go."

Arriving at the theater the following evening,

Georgiana was impressed at the deference shown her aunt as they were escorted to their box. She had forgotten how esteemed Lady Catherine was in society. Her aunt took every opportunity of introducing her niece. Georgiana was thankful that she merely had to curtsey many times and was not required to say anything beyond greetings. The looks of reverence, in those she was introduced to, made her increasingly uncomfortable. On her last prolonged stay in London, ten years ago with her aunt, she did not appreciate the social station of the de Bourgh's.

Upon entering their box, the Earl of Westbrook (formerly Lord Alfred Westbrook) and his wife the Countess (the former Caroline Bingley) rose to greet them. The Countess asked, "Georgiana, how is your family and that sly brother of yours, Mr. Darcy?"

After the expected answers and inquiries, they sat down to watch the play. Georgiana thought about Caroline's intensity with social climbing. Despite recognizing the former son of the Earl as a fop, Miss Bingley inclined herself to marry him--particularly when it became obvious that the Earl, his father, would soon die. The focus on marrying to obtain a title was repugnant to Georgiana. She was so glad her brother had chosen Elizabeth, rather than be ensnared by Miss Bingley.

The performance was excellent. Georgiana's heart soared during the lovers' vows in scene two, and fell with the final tragedy.

The next morning, Georgiana awoke thinking about the play. She was glad to imagine that her family would not oppose marriage to Thomas, should their love progress that far. Her principle guardian, even though she was now of age, was still her brother; and he only wished what she wanted. Lady Catherine might have something to say, but her ultimate protection would be under Mr. and Mrs. Darcy.

"Miss Darcy, you are wanted by Lady Catherine in

the breakfast parlor--it is already mid-morning," her maid said.

Arriving at the table, her aunt said, "Come and sit down. You must have something to eat before we go shopping. We shall *Londonize* ourselves."

Georgiana was astonished that her aunt would go shopping, even with her niece, and replied, "I have never seen you go shopping. I assumed that the salesmen came to you."

"That is not always the case. We have fine shops here on Oxford Street and a lot of time can be saved by going to them. We must have the latest fashion."

The shopping expedition surprised and pleased Georgiana. Her aunt seemed quite pleasant when focused on objects, rather than controlling people. She would, however, sometimes cause the shopkeepers to cringe with her matriarchal stare.

In examining shoes, Georgiana favored a pair of low cut slippers with willow green lace around the instep and ankle.

"The shoes are elegant, my dear niece," Lady Catherine said. "With the fashionable hemline for women your age being above the ankles, we must find embroidered white stockings as well." Glancing over the selection, she held up a pair, "Will these do?"

Georgiana took them and smiled in assent.

"Now, let us pick out a bonnet that will reflect your beauty. You said your dress was a light yellow, did you not?"

"Yes."

"Show us some yellow bonnets," her aunt ordered (she seldom asked) the salesman. After looking at six or seven, Georgiana focused on the Jonquil colored hat for a minute.

"Is that what you want?" her aunt asked.

"It is the most beautiful bonnet I have ever seen,"

cried Georgiana.

"Then it is yours. You must have the best clothes for the ball tomorrow night. I want the whole world to see the beauty of my niece."

As they continued shopping, her aunt helped select a Kashmir shawl, long gloves, a reticule (which matched her shoes) and, of course, a fan.

Returning home, Lady Catherine said, "Please come to my room." Once there, her aunt opened a jewelry box and pulled out an exquisite diamond necklace. "This was my mother's, and her mother's before that. I want to give it to you."

Georgiana gasped and said, "I shall be happy to wear it tomorrow night, but you must not give it to me! It is too precious!"

"No, family heirlooms must stay in the family. I shall not be happy unless you say you will keep it and pass it on to your daughter or relative."

Georgiana was genuinely moved with the generous gift on top of all she had received that day. For the first time in her life, she moved forward and hugged her aunt.

Falling asleep that night, she wondered if she had misjudged the character of her aunt.

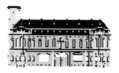

Chapter Nineteen

The next afternoon, Georgiana wrote a letter to Mr. and Mrs. Darcy. She enclosed a separate note to their children that read:

Dear Andrew, John and Maria,
I am enjoying London better than I anticipated. Lady Catherine is in an unexpected amiable mood. Your great aunt and I went shopping yesterday. She obtained beautiful shoes and accessories for me, which I will show you later.
Our first evening out, we attended *Romeo and Juliet* at the national theater. The most interesting scene for you would have been in Act II. Show Mr. Staley this letter and he will explain the scene to you.
I miss you. Everyone at Pemberley must write me or I shall be most lonely here.
Sincerely yours,
Aunt Georgiana

Georgiana thought her last sentence would give Thomas a clue to write her, without going beyond the bounds of propriety.
The following afternoon, she began to prepare for the ball. As she was dressing, her hands began to shake a little

and her stomach felt nauseated. It dawned on her that she was anxious over the ball that night; hers was not a happy anxiety, looking forward to a wonderful event, but a dread of the evening! She felt an increasing reluctance to converse in strange circles. She had an ever-present fear of appearing awkward in dance or elegant movement. After all, it had been ten years since she attended St. James' Court. She had been so happy to stay at Pemberley and live the country life with her family in Derbyshire.

Evening came. Lady Catherine led Georgiana into one of the most magnificent carriages she had ever seen. The bright red line on the black carriage matched the red and black livery of the footmen.

"How do you feel now that we are approaching St. James'?" Lady Catherine inquired of her niece.

"To be honest, I am quite nervous."

"Nonsense. I have no doubt you shall give the Darcy name honor. Your gown is magnificent and the accessories we selected enhance your natural beauty."

The coach stopped. As Georgiana stepped out behind her aunt, she saw many elegant carriages. Splendid scarlet clad cavalry paraded by atop jet black horses. Trumpets sounded! They were escorted by footmen, who walked with a synchronized cadence, up the stairs to the entrance of the grand hall. Georgiana could hear soft orchestra music. She was also greeted with a pleasant mixture of fragrances, perfume and prepared food, as she ascended the stairs to the magnificent doorway.

At the top of the stairs, Georgiana saw three hundred or more gaily dressed people. Suddenly, she heard a shout, "Lady Catherine de Bourgh of Kent!" Conversation became hushed in the hall as many of the crowd turned to watch her aunt descend the stairs before her. Georgiana was so engrossed with the awed response of the crowd to her aunt, that she was startled when a voice near her cried, "Miss

Darcy from Derbyshire!"

Georgiana took a deep breath and began walking down the stairs, about ten feet behind her aunt. Reaching the bottom of the fifteen stairs, her aunt began introducing Georgiana to lords and ladies. They soon came upon the Countess of Westbrook who said, "Miss Darcy, you look simply astonishing tonight. How are you doing?"

"Fine. Thank you."

"It is so important that you meet the right people," Lady Catherine said to her niece.

"I could not agree more," replied Lady Westbrook and continued, "You have been hiding too long at Pemberley."

They were interrupted by the announcement of, "His Grace, the Duke of Kent!" followed by, "the Honorable Samuel Moore of Kent!"

Georgiana turned and saw the Duke, whom she recognized, being followed by a taller young man with black hair.

"Who is Mr. Moore?" Georgiana inquired of her aunt.

"He is the second son of the Earl of Sussex. He is often in the company of the Duke. Do not pay attention to him, you need to greet the Duke."

Lord Percy began coming down the long reception line. It was clear that many of the ladies were enthralled with him and, particularly those who were unmarried, greeted him with the greatest amount of delight their voices could feign.

Lord Percy stopped for a few moments in the group next to them; Georgiana could hear a sweet, feminine voice utter, "Pray tell, your Grace, do you know how to flirt a fan?" as she snapped her fan open.

He paused for a moment, took her fan and began fanning her as he reparteed, "No, but I do know how to fan a flirt!" Laughter erupted from the group.

The Duke then approached Lady Catherine's party. He walked up, took Georgiana's hand and bowed to kiss it.

"I am delighted to see you. You are the brightest jewel in the hall tonight."

Georgiana had not expected such a declaration and found herself blushing.

"Would you honor me with the first two dances?" the Duke inquired of Georgiana.

With both Lady Catherine and Lady Westbrook looking intently at herself, Georgiana knew she had no recourse but to stammer, "Yes--Yes, I will."

"Delightful," was the Duke's reply. He continued, "Allow me to introduce my companion, Mr. Samuel Moore. This is Lady Catherine, Lady Westbrook, and Miss Darcy."

"How do you do," was his reply as the women curtsied.

The Duke and Mr. Moore moved away. Miss Darcy stepped back from the line to take a few breaths, as her aunt and Lady Westbrook continued to greet other arrivals.

To think that the Duke asked her for the first dance! This was far more than Georgiana expected. She felt a certain pride and rise in self-esteem, since she knew many other ladies present would be thrilled to have the Duke ask them to dance!

While she felt her heart protected with Thomas, it would still be a benefit to associate with the Duke. He and others would help her learn the art of conversation; this would make her more engaging with Thomas when she returned to Pemberley. Lately, she had become aware of the handicap of her shyness, particularly when she wanted to keep Thomas' attention in conversation.

She decided to respond to the Duke without giving him any particular encouragement.

After a few minutes, the two ladies walked with

Georgiana to the beverage table. Lady Catherine advised, "Georgiana, you must be charming and entertaining tonight. Treat the Duke well."

"How am I to do that?"

"Use your arts and allurement, girl."

"What do you mean?"

"With your shyness, you have leverage in not being openly flirtatious as the other women are. Use it to your advantage."

Lady Westbrook interjected, "What your aunt means is, do not look at him much; answer questions briefly. A man in the Duke's position will either become fascinated or lose interest; in any case, outright flirtation is not working, and few women in the court will attempt the 'disinterested' approach. Your behavior will come naturally."

Georgiana was relieved they were not asking her to act out of character; however, she had never considered her weakness as something in her favor!

The host of the evening came to where Georgiana was standing and asked if she and Lord Percy would be the lead couple to open the dance.

She was incredulous as the Duke came to take her hand. He led her to the base of the stairs, where the dance was to begin. She felt awkward since all the eyes in the ballroom were fixed on her and the Duke. The uncomfortable feeling continued until several other couples joined in the dance. Later, her aunt praised her facile movement during those moments.

"How is your family, Miss Darcy?" the Duke inquired during the latter half of the first dance.

"Fine."

"I want to visit Pemberley to take up your brother's invitation to fish there. Tell me, is your brother quite a sport at fishing?"

"Yes, indeed."

Small talk continued until the middle of the second dance when the Duke looked at her and said, "Your beauty and accomplishments must have brought you many offers of marriage."

She blushed and said, "Only once." Realizing he expected more, she continued, "When I was young and naive."

"Well, then, the men of Derbyshire must either be few or fools for that to be the case." The Duke appeared to understand that he had embarrassed Georgiana, and he spoke no more during the second dance.

After Miss Darcy had rested a dance, Mr. Samuel Moore came over and asked her hand for one movement. At the beginning of it, he said, "I have heard of your accomplishments with the pianoforte and the harp. Is this true?"

"Yes."

"And you sketch?"

"Not nearly so well."

"I have never been to Derbyshire. Tell me about it."

"It is quite difficult to give you short answers on that subject."

"I see, you are quite right."

Mr. Moore spoke in a much more amiable manner than his friend. The Duke spoke as to an audience, Mr. Moore as to one person.

Georgiana retired to the table of ladies where her aunt and Lady Caroline were seated. The emotional and physical performance required of her was quite exhausting. For the remainder of the evening, she listened to the court talk and turned down requests for dancing from several other gentlemen. Her party returned home at 2 a.m.

Chapter Twenty

Two days later, Georgiana was sitting alone in the parlor after breakfast. She was surprised to have the servant announce "The Honorable Samuel Moore of Sussex."

He came in with a bow.

"Please be seated, Mr. Moore."

"You are likely wondering why I have stopped by. I came to discuss my friend, the Duke. You may need enlightenment on him."

"Why?"

"Because you puzzled me the other night. . . ."

"I do not apprehend your point."

"I have not decided if you are virtuous or innocent."

Georgiana blushed and looked away.

Mr. Moore continued, "A virtuous woman has been tempted with evil desire and has triumphed; an innocent one has never been tempted. Many women delude themselves thinking they are virtuous when they are merely innocent."

"What have you concluded?"

"I do not know yet. If you are virtuous, you need fear nothing. If you are innocent, he may prove to be too strong a temptation. Quite frankly, Miss Darcy, he has broken many hearts." He paused for a few moments and then stood.

"I can assure you my heart is safe from him."

"Good." He walked to the door and paused before leaving, "If I can be of any service to you while in London, do not hesitate to call on me."

After the door closed, Georgiana returned to the parlor feeling bewildered about the caller. Lady Catherine entered the room and said, "That impertinent young man. Sticking his head into our house."

"But he came to give me a friendly warning," Georgiana replied.

"What does he know in his young life about character?"

"He appears to be a long-time companion of the Duke."

"Do not worry about what he has said. I knew the Duke's parents for more than twenty-five years; they were some of the finest people in the kingdom."

Georgiana wondered how her aunt knew what Mr. Moore had spoken about. Did she eavesdrop, or assume the report would be negative?   Attempting to maintain composure, Georgiana went to the pianoforte and began playing. This always seemed to placate and settle her aunt down.

After she played for nearly an hour, the servant came again and announced "His Grace, Duke of Kent."

He came in with a bow to the ladies. Georgiana rose from her pianoforte bench and came over to greet him. Lady Catherine excused herself upon some business and left the room.

Georgiana felt deserted by her aunt. "Please, sit down, my lord," Georgiana said, trying to be as gracious as possible.

"How are you today?" the Duke inquired.

"Quite well, thank you."

"I imagine you are missing the fine air and scenery of Derbyshire. I have only been to Derbyshire once myself, and that was as a child. I recall it being quite picturesque."

"It is as you say."

"My purpose in calling on you today is to extend an

invitation for you to go riding with my friend, Mr. Moore, and myself in Hyde Park. It will give you some morning air, and we shall cross the park to an exhibition of Gainsborough's paintings being held in Kensington. I understand you are an artist, and this may be something you would enjoy."

"I am only an amateur sketch maker. I should like very much to see the Gainsborough exhibit--however, I have no horses for myself and my maid."

He stood and walked to the fireplace and replied, "Not to worry. My family has six horses in town and we have two gentle mares for your use."

Georgiana was vexed and confused. She did not wish to encourage the Duke's attention, but she would like to ride and see the exhibition. She could undoubtably see the art display on her own. Lord Percy would be easier to turn down by note than in person.

"I will need to discuss this with my aunt and look at our engagements. I will send a reply to you later today."

"You are most gracious," replied the Duke as he bowed. "I will anxiously await your reply." He then left the room and Lady Catherine entered.

"My dear, what did Lord Percy have to say?" inquired Lady Catherine.

"He invited me to go riding in Hyde Park and then to view the exhibition of paintings in Kensington."

She sat down, looked at Georgiana, and finally said, "Well? Come, come girl! What was your answer?"

"I told him I needed to consult with you. Really, madam, I have not the least interest in riding with him. I believe my reply will be in the negative."

"Oh! Surely not, Georgiana! You are taking this disinterested approach too far. An invitation like this **must** be accepted."

"You do not understand. I am not interested in

encouraging His Grace."

"And why not? He is the most eligible peer in the land." With her voice increasing in volume and emphasis she continued, "All the dukes and princes above him are married. He is sixth from the throne."

Seeing Georgiana cringe, the matriarch fell silent for a minute. She continued, "He will inherit Rosing Park when I am gone. I should wish to see a near relation, like my beloved niece, inhabit its fine space."

Georgiana bowed her head and said, "My heart is elsewhere." She looked up again and saw the sneering countenance of her aunt surface. It was a facial expression that Georgiana had seen many times before, but which had been curiously absent during this visit.

Her aunt returned to a loud voice, "So, the rumors are true! I suppose you like that poor second son of a baronet, what's his name?"

"Thomas," Georgiana bowed her head again.

"Look, young lady, a woman has a duty to better herself by marriage whenever possible. You would be elevating the Darcy name and wealth by marrying the Duke of Kent."

Georgiana chose not to reply to the last statement. After a few moments she looked at her aunt again and noticed the return of the calm expression.

Her aunt said sweetly, with a crooked smile, "Humor your old aunt. Please accept the Duke's invitation, and I shall be most happy. I will not ask you to accept a second request."

Georgiana stood and walked across the room to the pianoforte and plucked a simple melody. She felt a quiet sense of victory. Finally, she had made her feelings known about Thomas. With this fact being secure, she was not disinclined to accept the riding invitation and would even look forward to the exhibition; further, she would no longer be obliged to her aunt, at least in terms of the Duke. She then replied, "I think I shall accept the invitation."

"Excellent, my dear! You please your old aunt very much. Let us send him a note promptly."

Chapter Twenty-One

The next morning, as Georgiana and her maid were escorted downstairs into a carriage, she was pleased to note the sunshine and unusually clear air. While they traveled the short distance to the riding stables, she felt a sense of confidence; a feeling that she was controlling her destiny, rather than having others determine her actions. The company was not special to her, but the ride and exhibition would be interesting. She was greeted at the stables by Mr. Moore and taken to the door of the livery. There she saw Lord Percy mounted atop a black, spirited stallion.

A groomsman had control of the horse's head. As the horse stamped its hooves, the servant pled, "Your Grace, the bit is too tight for him; he may be difficult to control."

Lord Percy cursed, "Do not talk to me that way! Do you believe me ignorant of horses? Leave it be. The way I placed it, he will respond to my slightest command."

The horse began settling down a bit, and the Duke looked up and saw Georgiana. As she approached he said, "Fine horses, such as this, need careful control."

Mr. Moore added, for Georgiana's sake, "You need not worry about your mounts. They are gentle mares." He then showed them a calm pair of horses; one of which was gray and the other brown. Mr. Moore assisted Georgiana and her maid into their saddles and then mounted his own.

"We will go through the center of Hyde Park," Mr. Moore said as he followed behind Georgiana and her maid.

"Lord Percy will lead the way for us."

Georgiana could observe the Duke tipping his hat to several ladies. They passed several stands of trees and the center fountain. At times, the group had to stop while the Duke asserted control over his nervous steed.

Mr. Moore's horse was beside her own. He asked, "Are you looking forward to the exhibition?"

"Yes, indeed," she replied. "I believe there are several paintings by Gainsborough, my favorite artist."

"I have heard the same," was his reply.

Some time later, Georgiana's horse came in close behind the Duke's. They had passed the center fountain by a furlong. Suddenly, the Duke's horse, amid curses of its rider, reared completely. As the Duke fought for control, it backed into Georgiana's horse. Georgiana's horse tried to backup; but, then lurched forward several feet. As the lead horse reared again, her mount began to rear a few inches. In the confusion, the black stallion backed up again. It pushed into Georgiana's horse. Both horses reared again. The stallion then fell into Georgiana's mare, causing both horses to fall over. The stallion immediately regained its feet and raced, riderless, across the park. Lord Percy stood in a daze. He did not pursue his mount.

Georgiana laid still. Her mount finally regained its feet after several attempts. Mr. Moore and the maid quickly dismounted and ran to where Georgiana lay. Lord Percy came over in a frightened stupor and asked, "Is she dead?"

Mr. Moore replied, "No, but her pulse is thready. Run and summon a wagon for help. We will stay here and watch."

The Duke seemed roused by the need of action. He mounted Mr. Moore's horse and galloped back towards the livery. The maid carefully lifted her mistress' head onto her lap. Mr. Moore stood and collected the two remaining horses and tied their reins down. He asked the gathering crowd to stand back. The open wagon soon came with a bed of hay. Mr. Moore and Lord Percy, along with two accompanying groomsmen, carefully lifted her body into the wagon. The maid climbed into the back of the wagon to insure a safe ride for her mistress.

Arriving at the Grosvenor street residence, Lady Catherine heard the commotion and hurried down the stairs, meeting the group at the door. She shouted, "What happened?"

"A grievous injury to your niece while riding," Mr. Moore replied and continued, "May we bring her inside?"

"Yes, of course. Take her up to her room, my servant will show you the way."

Lady Catherine could easily ascertain that her niece was unconscious and that the Duke appeared guilt-stricken.

Georgiana was placed in bed. Outside the room, Mr. Moore related the story of the accident to Lady Catherine. "I think she struck her head. There is a bruise over her left temple which extends a little over her jaw."

Lady Catherine turned to a manservant. "Hurry to Mr. Perry, the doctor. Now! Tell him it is an emergency."

An hour later, Mr. Perry emerged from Georgiana's bedroom and said, "She is unconscious. She probably has a concussion; fortunately, her neurological examination is normal. I have not dealt with many cases of this type, so my prognosis may not be accurate."

"Should we engage a consultant?"

"Indeed, I would recommend Dr. Parkinson, here in London. He is one of the best practitioners in England."

"I will stop at nothing for the welfare of my niece."

"I will send my man to Shoreditch to get him."

In the evening, Dr. Parkinson came to Lady Catherine and spoke. "Your niece has begun to awaken. She finally opened her eyes and spoke to me. As expected, she has a terrific headache. She remembers going to the livery this morning, but nothing after that. She does have a concussion, but I expect her to recover fully."

"How long will she be indisposed?" Lady Catherine inquired.

"It may take a month or more for the headaches to completely resolve, but they may recur periodically for a few months."

"What should be her care?"

"She must be confined to bed until this current headache resolves. Also, she should not attend social functions for at least one month."

"We will see that these things are done," Lady Catherine replied.

Chapter Twenty-Two

Four days later, as Georgiana was sitting up in the downstairs parlor for the first time since her accident, Lady Catherine entered the room and inquired after her health. "My dear, how are you feeling?"

"My headache is gone now. I am a little dizzy, but it feels good to sit instead of laying in bed."

"You may not know, but Lord Percy has visited every day to inquire about you. He appears quite guilt-stricken."

"Tell him I shall be well and not to worry."

"Do you wish to see him when he comes today?"

"No!"

"Why not?"

"I am not interested in him."

"Georgiana, you should realize the accident gives you a special hold on him. You now have his complete attention. With a little effort, you could evoke his entire tenderness."

At this point, the servant announced the arrival of Mr. and Mrs. Darcy. Lady Catherine rose to greet them. Georgiana remained sitting.

"We came as soon as possible once we received the news. Have we interrupted anything?" Mr. Darcy inquired.

"I have been trying to tell our aunt that I have no wish to encourage the attentions of Lord Percy."

"But, nephew, Lord Percy is so interested in your sister. Think of it!"

"My dear aunt," he interrupted, "I have always tried

to abide by my sister's wishes. If she does not wish to further Lord Percy's interest, then I must firmly ask you to leave the situation alone."

"As you wish," Lady Catherine replied in a haughty tone.

Mr. Darcy continued, "Georgiana, we have come to escort you back to Pemberley."

"What?! Absolutely not!" yelped Lady Catherine. She then continued in a softer voice, "I doubt she will be well for some time; further, she needs to finish the time of promise."

Mr. Darcy began pacing in front of the fireplace and said, "It seems quite clear to me that the latter promise has been fulfilled; Georgiana shall only return to London if and when she so chooses. As to her medical condition, when you notified us about Dr. Parkinson's evaluation, I took the liberty of contacting him by express. I have his written approval for the plan of our transportation. He felt the country air would effect a quicker recovery."

Lady Catherine, clearly agitated, but suppressing any irritation in her voice, asked Georgiana, "Is this what you wish?"

"Yes."

"I see. Nephew, when do you plan to return?"

"We will set out tomorrow morning. I have engaged a private coach, one that even has a foldout bed if we need it."

Elizabeth had been silent during the clash of her husband and Lady Catherine. She walked over to Georgiana during it, knelt and clasped her hand. She then said softly, "The bruise on your temple and upper jaw looks like your injury was quite painful."

Georgiana looked tenderly at her beloved sister-in-law. "I do not recall the accident itself. The only pain I have had was a headache for a few days. I am going to get well."

To show acquiescence to her family from Pemberley, Lady Catherine tried to talk pleasantly the remainder of the day.

The following day found Georgiana's brother and sister riding with her back to Derbyshire. To make the journey as smooth as possible, the trip was made in two full days, rather than the usual one day and four hours.

Chapter Twenty-Three

Upon arrival at Pemberley, the Darcys were greeted by their children and Mr. Thomas Staley.

"Oh! Auntie, we are so glad you are back," cried Andrew. "We have missed you so!"

"I have only been gone a fortnight."

"But, it seems like forever," Maria exclaimed.

Mr. Darcy interrupted, "Your aunt has had a recurrence of her headache during the trip; so, she needs strict bed rest."

While her brother was talking to the children, Georgiana eagerly looked at the expression on Thomas' face. She appreciated his friendly smile and happy countenance. If no one else had been present, she might have gone over and hugged him! Alas, the presence of the children and her family acted to restrain her. Despite her headache, she was glad to be home again at Pemberley.

Two afternoons later, Maria slipped quietly into Georgiana's room and said, "Mr. Staley and I wanted to know how you are doing, Auntie."

"My headache is almost gone."

"Oh, Auntie. The bruise on the side of your face is black and blue!"

"It looks worse than it feels." She smiled weakly at her niece, "I think I am ready to walk to the window. Help me pull the covers back." Maria did so and Georgiana walked to the window.

"Tell your teacher that I hope to be in the library tomorrow morning after breakfast. As you go, tell my maid in the dressing room to come see me. I must get my hair washed and fixed."

Indeed, Georgiana felt nearly well the next morning. She had her maid fix her hair while she had breakfast in her room. Soon after, Elizabeth and Maria came to escort her to the library. Elizabeth stayed a few minutes; then, for peace and quiet, she left Georgiana alone and took Maria downstairs.

Georgiana looked up eagerly, from her seat at the bay window, at the sound of a person entering. Thomas came in and sat in a chair across from her. She said, as she turned her face away, "I hope the bruise on my face does not change your opinion of me."

"What opinion does my lady think I have of her?" Thomas smiled.

Looking at him again, she replied, "I must confess. The night we waited for you in your room, I accidently discovered a paper with my name on it and read it before I could lay it down."

Thomas was taken back for a moment, but replied, "Nothing that was written in that note has changed. I did not miss your hidden meaning in the letter from London. If I am right, you referred to the lovers' vows that were in the play." He stood, came over to the window and sat down by her. Taking her hand, he continued, "I do love you. I will love you always."

Georgiana felt her heart would burst with happiness as she responded, "Oh! Thomas, I, too, will love you always." Georgiana felt enraptured as Thomas looked into her face.

After a few minutes of endearing conversation, Thomas sighed, "There are some things I need to resolve before we make an open declaration. Will you keep our love secret for a little while longer?"

"I shall, of course, be happy to keep our delicious secret," she replied with a smile.

The door opened and Andrew entered, closely followed by John. "Did I hear the word 'secret'?" Andrew asked.

"Never mind," Thomas replied and continued, "Are you boys already done with your reading assignment?"

"Yes, sir."

"Never a moment's rest," Thomas said as he winked at Georgiana. "However, your aunt does need rest and we should leave her alone." He and the boys bowed to a smiling Georgiana and exited the library.

Yes! Georgiana felt the ecstasy that only a lover can feel when the word "love" is exchanged between a couple for the first time. The extended time needed for maturity of her love, and the persistent steadfastness required of her in London, made the culmination only sweeter. She was so happy that she cried for awhile. She felt every muscle in her body relax, and the minor headache disappear.

She eventually returned to her room. For the first time since leaving London, Georgiana slept soundly, late into the next morning. She awakened refreshed; she had not a trace of a headache. She went downstairs and started eating as the rest of the family and Thomas were finishing breakfast. She assured the family that she was feeling well; indeed, no one who saw her radiant face could suspect otherwise.

After breakfast, she was sitting in the parlor with Mr. and Mrs. Darcy, when the servant announced, "Lady Catherine de Bourgh is arriving."

"Good Lord," Mr. Darcy cried as he stood. "I was hoping I would not have to see my aunt for some time. She can induce a headache even if one has not had an accident!"

A few moments later, after being ushered in, Lady Catherine said, "My dearest nephew, how are you?"

"Lady Catherine, you look pale." He earnestly inquired, "Are you certain you should have traveled so far?"

"I have come to see to the welfare of my dearest niece." Turning to Georgiana and sitting down next to her, she asked, "How are you doing, Georgiana?"

"My headache is gone for now." Her smile faded as she began to fear what her aunt might demand of her. She would never, willingly, leave Thomas again.

"And your strength?"

"I am stronger each day."

"Good."

"How long will your ladyship stay?" Elizabeth interjected.

"Hopefully, I plan no more than four days. I trust I am welcome."

"Of course," Elizabeth replied.

Between the tutoring of the children by Thomas, her frequent rests, and the obligate presence of Lady Catherine, for the next two days, Georgiana was able to see Thomas only at the family meals. Little secret talk could take place at a family meal, especially when Lady Catherine was present!

Chapter Twenty-Four

On the third evening of Lady Catherine's visit, Mr. Darcy, with a grave tone of voice, said, "Something has arisen which requires a family meeting. As soon as dinner is finished, the children are to go upstairs to play, while the rest of us gather in the parlor." He also requested the presence of Thomas.

When the time arrived, Mrs. Darcy, Lady Catherine, Georgiana and Thomas went into the parlor and sat down. Mr. Darcy followed the group, but remained standing and said, "I have business of a most serious nature for us to consider tonight." Turning to Mrs. Reynolds he said, "Bring the servant girl and her friend in; then, please wait in the hall in case we need you again."

In walked a young woman with long black hair. She wore a servant's uniform and appeared about two and twenty years old. Her face would have been lovely, if not filled with anxiety and distress. A tall, strongly built man, a few years older than the woman, accompanied her. His scowling face would always appear unhandsome.

Mr. Darcy addressed the servant girl. "Hannah, tell this group what you told Lady Catherine and myself this afternoon."

"My lord and ladies," she stammered and paused. She looked down and said, "I am with child." She stopped.

Mr. Darcy said, "Pray, continue."

She glanced at her friend, and at his nod, said, "The

father of this child is Mr. Thomas Staley."

Elizabeth and Georgiana gasped. Georgiana dropped her head and covered her mouth with a handkerchief. Elizabeth asked, "Is it certain you are with child?"

"Yes, ma'am. Mrs. Cheshire examined me this morning. She said I was about four months along."

"What is my lord going to do about this?" the tall male companion demanded angrily.

Mr. Darcy held up his hand to stop the man's speech and turned to Mr. Staley, who appeared grave, and asked, "What do you have to say about this, Mr. Staley? Are you responsible for this child?"

Thomas looked into Mr. Darcy's face and replied quietly, but resolutely, "I am not."

"There you have it," Mr. Darcy replied. "How are we to get at the truth?"

Lady Catherine interrupted by tapping her cane repeatedly against the floor. "Nephew," she snapped, "I have often seen young gentlemen fall into this fault." Glaring at Thomas she said, "Do you deny that four months ago you went to this woman's room on two occasions?"

"I do not," Thomas replied.

"See, there you have it, Fitzwilliam," Lady Catherine said triumphantly.

Thomas continued, "But it was not for the wickedness you think. Hannah asked that I translate some items written in French, which she received from her friends on the continent."

"A likely story," Lady Catherine scoffed.

The entire family looked at Hannah and she began stammering, "Not true, my lord. I will not say he forced himself on me, but he **is** the father of the child."

Elizabeth then said, "Please excuse us, Thomas. Hannah, you and your friend may leave."

After a minute or two of silence, during which Mr.

Darcy was pacing, he said, "What are we to do? How are we to obtain the truth, unless one party confesses they are lying?"

Elizabeth responded, "Let us interview Mrs. Reynolds, since she supervises the female servants."

While they were waiting for Mrs. Reynolds, Lady Catherine pressed in a prosecuting tone, "Fitzwilliam, you must do something. The honor of Pemberley Hall is at stake. We must not let the world think Pemberley Hall is full of licentiousness!"

"You can be assured we will consider our honor in the present situation," he replied.

Mrs. Reynolds rejoined them and said, "Half of the servants are in an uproar and feel Mr. Staley must go. The other half like him and want to be loyal to the Darcys despite the allegation."

"What of this woman, named Hannah?" Elizabeth asked.

"She has caused us little difficulty. In fact, my lady, she came from Rosing Park two years ago. I have never had occasion to catch her in a falsehood, but I have seen very little of her."

Lady Catherine interrupted, "We never had any problem with this girl while she was at Rosing Park."

The group turned again to Mrs. Reynolds, who continued, "I am inclined to believe the young gentleman, Mr. Staley."

Mr. Darcy replied, "And there you have it, the word of a gentleman against the word of a servant girl. Honor requires that we notice this. Thank you, Mrs. Reynolds, you are excused."

Georgiana was stunned by the initial events of the evening. She could not formulate a reply. Her head began throbbing again and she felt that, before she would faint or create an embarrassing scene, she must retreat to her room.

She stood up and cried, "This cannot be true of Mr. Staley," and walked quickly out of the room.

Now that Georgiana was gone, Mr. Darcy turned to his aunt, "Would you excuse us, Lady Catherine. This is a decision for the master and mistress of Pemberley Hall."

"As you please," Lady Catherine replied stiffly and exited the room, leaving Elizabeth and her husband alone.

After a minute more of pacing, Mr. Darcy said, "Shades of Mr. Wickham! I thought I would never have to encounter this dilemma again. This is most vexing." Looking at his wife, Mr. Darcy said, "Is it our responsibility to expose Mr. Staley's activity to the world?"

"There is insufficient evidence, Fitzwilliam. This case differs from Mr. Wickham's; since, in the prior instance, we were certain of his egregious character."

"How can we be certain in the current case? I suppose we can wait until the child is born and examine likenesses; however, waiting another five months is intolerable."

"And, if the charge against Mr. Staley be untrue, then any action against him would be grievous indeed," Elizabeth replied.

"There is also another substantial difference between this case and Mr. Wickham's. Mr. Staley's character has not belied any other weakness of temperament; in the former case of Mr. Wickham, we saw multiple character failings."

"And yet, if we fail to take some action, we may lose half of our servants. With the current labor shortage, replacing them with good people may be nearly impossible."

"Perhaps a compromise may be worked out," Mr. Darcy mused after a few minutes of silence.

"Pray, give me your meaning," his wife inquired.

"It seems obvious that neither party can stay at Pemberley House. We will offer a £100 severance to Hannah for her to leave. That would be more than six times her annual pay. Rather than force Thomas to quit, under questionable circumstances, I will find him another tutoring position. I have a recent letter in my study from the Earl of Devonshire; who, as it happens, is looking for a tutor. I could explain the situation, ask him to be watched and, after some time of exemplary conduct, we could absolve Thomas from any weakness of character."

"Your plan has merit. It would be preferable to know the truth; unfortunately, while the Almighty knows what really happened, we cannot," she replied.

"Before I consider my plan complete, I am obliged to travel to Staley Hall and discuss the difficulty with Sir William. I will do this first thing in the morning."

Morning came, and besides the children, only Lady Catherine attended the 10 a.m. breakfast. Appetites were otherwise non-existent in Pemberley House.

Mr. Darcy returned from his trip to his northern neighbor. He assembled Elizabeth, Thomas Staley and Lady Catherine in the parlor. Mr. Darcy addressed Thomas and said, "I have returned from Staley Hall, where I discuseed this matter with your father; he is in agreement with my plan. We have made a settlement with the servant and now propose something for you. It grieves me to have to do anything. You have become a part of our family, Thomas, and if we did not have to consider the household of servants, I believe we should accept your word and ignore the consequences; however, such is not my luxury. I am proposing to find you another position as a tutor. It so happens that the Earl of Devonshire is looking for one and you would be ideally suited for him. He will know of the allegations, but I am sure this will not matter in his opinion; this way, there can be no substantiation of gossip that you were dismissed from Pemberley Hall."

"You are most gracious, Mr. Darcy. I am

uncomfortable remaining here with this black cloud hanging over me. I will leave today. Will you give me a letter I can take to Devonshire?"

"I will compose it at once," Mr. Darcy replied. He went to the writing table nearby and penned the following note:

> Dear Lord Elgin,
>   In reply to your letter of 15 January 1816, I am sending Mr. Thomas Staley, with my recommendation for his skills as a tutor. An unfortunate incident has arisen here at Pemberly Hall, which necessitates his absence from us. I shall expand on this issue in a separate letter. Be assured, however, that you will find him to be an excellent teacher.
>   Yours Truly,
>   Fitzwilliam Darcy

Mr. Darcy read the note out loud to Thomas, folded it, placed his seal on the wax, and handed it to Thomas, who left the room.

Later that afternoon, Georgiana felt well enough to come down to the parlor. She anxiously inquired about the resolution concerning Thomas. She arrived in time to see Lady Catherine departing at the entrance door.

Her aunt said, "Fitzwilliam, I believe you have acted wisely in regards to this scandalous affair with the tutor. I am sorry I cannot stay longer, but my wretched health bids me return to Rosings."

"I understand, and I hope you will feel better," was his reply as he escorted their aunt to the carriage.

When he returned to the parlor and sat down next to Elizabeth, Georgiana asked with anxiety in her voice, "What have you decided to do regarding the situation with

Mr. Staley?"

Her brother replied, "His father and I have decided to find him another position as a tutor. I have given him a letter of recommendation to the Earl of Devonshire. . .".

He was interrupted by Georgiana's exclamation, "So far away!"

This remark raised the eyebrows of both Mr. and Mrs. Darcy, but Mr. Darcy continued, "The maidservant has been given a settlement, and she and her fiancé are to be married tomorrow. They are leaving Pemberley today."

"So, you do not trust Thomas!" Georgiana said.

"I do not know the truth in this case; if I disbelieved him entirely, I should not have assisted him in procuring another position."

He paused for a minute and Elizabeth said gently, "This incident was a vexing dilemma for us. Is Mr. Thomas Staley another Mr. Wickham--all goodness on the surface and vile underneath? Or, have we made a grievous misjudgement of an excellent man? We are still torn between the two."

Georgiana replied, "I wish I had felt better yesterday and stayed to defend him. There are things you do not know about him."

"It is a moot point now, since he is leaving," her brother replied.

"May I talk to him before he leaves?"

"Certainly. Perhaps you can soften the blow, which I fear may be more severe than he deserves."

Georgiana turned and walked hurriedly out of the room and down the hall towards the turret room. She encountered Andrew, John and Maria on the way and they asked why she was walking fast. "Mr. Staley is going to leave Pemberley Hall today. I must say goodbye."

"Where is he going?" asked Andrew.

Before she could answer, John inquired, "How long

will he be gone?"

She could only reply shakily, "I do not know."

"Can we come too?" Andrew asked.

"Yes, but I need some time alone with him."

"We understand," Andrew replied.

As she began walking up the stairs to his room, she had to stop for a minute to catch her breath. With the recent episodes of prolonged bed rest, she was not conditioned to walking this fast. Her emotional state further aggravated her breathlessness. After pausing for several minutes, she and the children continued climbing the stairs to his door. She knocked once. She knocked again. No answer. She lifted the latch and peeked inside. "Thomas. Are you there?"

Still no answer came. She walked into an empty room. His books and clothes were gone. An envelope was sealed on the desk. She broke the seal, unfolded the note, and read the letter while standing, so the children could not read it over her shoulder. It was the poem she had read the night they discovered the aeolian harp! She sat down and wept. She did not care what her nephews and niece might think. Thomas had left without saying goodbye. What did this mean? The phrase from the note, "I feel unworthy of her," kept revolving in her mind.

Could it be that Thomas was guilty of the charge levied against him and lied merely to avoid unpleasant consequences? Was this the reason for his feeling of low esteem? Was this why he wanted to keep their love secret? Her mind told her it was not so, but her heart remained torn with wretched feelings.

After a few minutes, she began to compose herself. Andrew approached her, with John and Maria behind him on each side, and asked, "Dear Auntie, what is the matter?"

"Thomas has left and did not say goodbye," she said with a tear stained face.

"Why would Mr. Staley do that?"

"I do not know."

The three children moved over by the bed and began crying. Georgiana joined them in their behavior. In a minute, Andrew turned to his aunt and exclaimed, "Was it because we were not good students? Sometimes, I failed to study and learn as I should have. It is my fault he has left."

John cried, "No, Andrew, it is I who did not always obey him. It is my fault he is angry and gone away."

Georgiana gathered the children in her arms and reassured them that Thomas was not displeased with them. She told them of the high opinion he had for them, a regard he had expressed on many occasions.

Andrew brightened a little and asked, "Where did he go? Will he ever come back?"

"He has apparently gone to Devonshire for awhile," Georgiana replied. She did not wish to tell them it was for another teaching position, for fear it would cause further unhappy feelings. "I do not know if he will ever come to Pemberley again. His family home is Staley Hall, of course, and he will surely visit it again. I have an address in Devonshire. Perhaps we can write him when we are more composed."

A state of depression settled over Pemberley Hall for the next few days, a forlorn feeling, from the lowest servant all the way to Mr. Darcy. Even the servants who had taken the side of Hannah, did not rejoice at the absence of the tutor.

Section Three

February, 1816

Chapter Twenty-Five

In the evening, four days after the departure of Thomas, a servant announced to the Darcy adults gathered in the parlor, "Reverend Westbrook is calling."

"Show him in," Mr. Darcy said. "Please be seated, Reverend."

"The purpose of my visit is to verify the rumors about Mr. Thomas Staley," Henry Westbrook began. "I hope you do not think me presumptuous."

"Not at all. These things are never able to be kept as secret as we should like."

"Is it true that Mr. Staley left Pemberley under a cloud of suspicion?"

Mr. Darcy replied, "It grieves us to confirm your report. Since you are the rector, you should be fully informed. One of our servants alleged that Mr. Staley was the father of her baby. He denied it, of course. However, it placed us in the most uncomfortable predicament. My aunt and some of the servants demanded that something be done. Uncertain about the truth of the allegation, we compromised and found him another position where he could be monitored."

Reverend Westbrook turned to Georgiana and asked, "Was this done with your consent?"

She bowed her head and said, "I am ashamed I did not defend him more vigorously, but I am still not well from my accident."

Mr. Darcy intervened, "Georgiana had very little to do with our decision."

Reverend Westbrook continued looking at Georgiana, who lifted her eyes to meet his. He said, "Thomas has his faults, such as worrying about his financial affairs, but dishonesty is not one of them. I have never known a more truthful man. Do you not remember, Georgiana, when we were all little and the three of us broke the expensive vase in the sculpture room? The only one of our trio who told the truth was Thomas. He took his punishment without implicating us." The room became uncomfortably silent and tears began streaming down Georgiana's face. The reverend continued, "I am sorry to grieve you, but I felt Thomas must have a defender. As Alexander Pope said, 'An honest man is the noblest work of God.' If this places me in jeopardy, then so be it."

Mr. Darcy replied contritely, "Do not fear, Reverend. My desire is always to find the truth and adjust my life to it. Your reminder is quite appropriate. Would you mind leaving us so we can discuss this matter further among ourselves?"

Reverend Westbrook stood, bowed and exited the house quietly. Mr. Darcy began pacing in front of the fireplace and said, "Reverend Westbrook confirms the troublesome feelings persisting in my soul. I fear we have been mistaken in this affair with Mr. Staley."

"Your feelings echo mine," Elizabeth said pensively.

Georgiana was lifted, knowing her kind and generous brother and sister reflected her own feelings.

Mr. Darcy continued, "The more I evaluate and recall the evening of the accusation, I cannot help but feel a grievous injustice was done to Mr. Staley."

"What is to be done?" Elizabeth asked.

"Perhaps we can recall him after one or two months of exile are finished. That way his honor, and ours, will have been restored."

"That is an excellent idea," Georgiana exclaimed. She had not yet been able to steady her feelings enough to write Thomas. The plan of requesting a recall was resolved upon. The letter would be written on the morrow.

After breakfast the next morning, the post arrived with two letters to Mr. Darcy. The first from the Earl of Devonshire read:

> Dear Fitzwilliam,
>   The tutor, Mr. Thomas Staley, has not yet arrived. Is he still detained at Pemberley? When shall we expect him?
>   Yours truly,
>   Lord Elgin

The second letter was opened and read:

> Dear Mr. Darcy,
>   I am compelled to write you and thank you for your effort in securing me another position. I can understand your dilemma of last week. However, my word and honor are the same; and, as such, I feel unable to continue in your service or that of your friend. I have decided against going to Devonshire. I am informing you of this so as to not embarrass you in further communication with the Earl.
>   Sincerely,
>   Thomas Staley

After Georgiana read the letter, she experienced overwhelming fear that Thomas was slipping away as he did three years earlier. Until the letter arrived, she at least knew where he was located. She raised her voice courageously and told her brother, "We must find out where he is so we can recall him. He does not yet know our plan."

"I will have a servant take a note over to Staley Hall today. Perhaps, Sir William knows the whereabouts of his son; surely, he has informed his father."

Chapter Twenty-Six

The following day at the end of breakfast, Mrs. Reynolds came to the table and announced, "I have just seen an ornate carriage pass over the bridge, with four elegantly dressed footmen and a horseman before and after! Who can it be, Mr. Darcy?"

The family rose and went out to the front steps as the procession arrived. The day was cloudy and dreary. The lead horseman dismounted and came to Mr. Darcy proclaiming, "His Grace, Duke of Kent, to visit Pemberley Hall!"

The footman opened the door to the carriage and Lord Percy stepped down with a certain step and surveyed the Darcy family. After bowing, he said, "I am sorry to barge in on you without any notice, Mr. Darcy; however, I had some business in Manchester. I trust your sporting invitation for angling still stands!"

"Yes, indeed," Mr. Darcy replied.

"To be truthful, I planned to come to see you and your family, but was uncertain as to the day. I did not want you to make any fuss on my account."

He turned to Georgiana and said, "I cannot forget your beauty. I hope you are feeling better?"

She curtsied, "I am, thank you, my lord." Phillip began to growl softly. Georgiana knelt beside her pet and stroked him in reassurance. She had mixed feelings about the Duke's surprise visit. She had thought, without remorse, to never see him again. As she stood, she suspected that his visit was only to see her. She was pleased that a man of such elevation would exhibit interest in herself and Pemberley Hall. On the other hand, she still felt loyal to Thomas despite the uncertainty surrounding his location and what his true feelings towards her and Pemberley Hall were.

The Darcy family escorted the Duke into the parlor. After they all sat down, he turned to Georgiana and said, "I must heartily apologize for my part in causing the accident and your injury. I am most anxious that you should recover and not think ill of me."

She replied, "Do not be obliged, my lord. Spirited horses cannot always be controlled, even by the best of horsemen."

"Looking at you now, the fading bruise on the side of your head sends a stave through my heart as to my willful irresponsibility. How can you forgive me so easily?"

"I have never resented you for the accident," Georgiana truthfully replied. The Duke signaled to a footman, who brought a large, shallow package forward.

"Take it to Miss Darcy," Lord Percy said. "I have brought an olive branch to you--a token of my respect for the Darcy family."

The children crowded around their aunt as she removed the elegant wrapping. A large two by three foot country painting in an ornate golden frame, was uncovered.

"It. . . cannot. . . be," she gasped. "A country scene by Gainsborough! This is nearly priceless. You should not have gone to the trouble of giving this."

"No trouble is too great for you and your family. Since I could not see you safely to the art exhibit, I thought I would bring the best of the exhibit to you!"

Georgiana blushed and sat back quietly as the children asked to be excused, since it was 'just a painting' in their language.

Elizabeth spoke up, "We thank you, Lord Percy, for

your generosity and your kind attention to us. We shall find a prominent place for a painting by such a celebrated artist."

Mr. Darcy said to Lord Percy, "If you would like to settle in the red bedroom, let us not waste any time we may spend fishing. I will see the equipment is made ready."

"I shall be dressed as soon as possible," was the Duke's reply as he stood and left the room with Mr. Darcy.

When they were gone, Elizabeth said, "Georgiana, I expect you knew about this."

"Not at all. It is a surprise to me."

"Do you not think he seems genuinely interested in you?"

"I pray that he is not. I do not wish to encourage his attentions."

"Why not? He bestows a great honor with his visit and attention."

"I am simply not interested."

"Whatever you wish, my dear sister. We do not want to force any decision, or person, upon you," was Elizabeth's puzzled reply.

That evening, after dinner, Mr. Darcy asked his sister, "Do you feel well enough to play your pianoforte for us and our visitor?"

She had not played since her accident three weeks earlier. She did not have a headache now. Her brother was so kind to her, that she felt it was her duty to play--despite the absence of any desire to perform. She begged off from singing and played several numbers, tolerably well, for her audience. She noted numerous mistakes during her songs and felt her performance was wretched. During the last song, she caught the admiring look in the Duke's face and wished that he would not stare at her so.

The following day, Lord Percy and Mr. Darcy were gone all morning fishing. In the afternoon, Georgiana was asked by her brother to lead a tour of Pemberley Hall for

Lord Percy. Hiding her reluctance, she agreed to do so. She led the Duke, Mrs. Darcy and the children from the entrance hall down to the chapel. Entering its doorway, the quiet chapel caused all to be contemplative. With the early afternoon sun, the stained glass caused more shadows than it would have in the morning.

Georgiana said, "This is where I pray each morning. My brother and sister join me on Sunday mornings before we attend the parish church."

"Such devotion is quite commendable," said the Duke in a tone of approbation.

After leaving the chapel and returning towards the circular staircase in the entrance hall, Andrew and John began arguing over an issue not apparent to the adults.

"Yes, you did!" Andrew said.

"Did not!"

"Did too!"

"Did not!"

"Boys," Elizabeth cried, "let us not vex our guest with an argument!"

"May we go outside?" John implored of his mother.

"Yes, you may; but, please, do not argue anymore."

"Yes, Ma'am," Andrew replied as the boys left and Maria followed.

"Boys that age can be quite obnoxious," said the Duke with a scowl, as they ascended the stairs.

Georgiana tried to ignore his remark, lest she be unable to continue in the hospitable manner required of her.

The large door to the library was opened. Georgiana wanted to see the effect the beautiful room would have on her visitor. He said shortly, "Quite a large room for a library. The view out the windows is magnificent. I, however, do not need such a large library since I read very little."

Not much encouragement was needed for

Georgiana to dislike Lord Percy. His disparaging remark about her nephews and his lack of enthusiasm for reading, formed objective reasons which solidified her disapprobation of him.

After the tour, the threesome returned to the entrance parlor where Mr. Darcy was sitting down and reading. A servant entered and delivered a letter to Mr. Darcy.

"It is from Sir William Staley," he said after he opened it. He looked hopeful for a moment, but then his countenance darkened. He handed it to Georgiana and said, "Apparently, Sir William does not know where his son is."

Her heart sank.

Lord Percy said in an innocuous tone, "Is this Mr. Thomas Staley, you speak of? Lady Catherine de Bourgh told me of his peccadillo. Young men often fall prey to that temptation."

Georgiana saw that Lord Percy looked surprised at the grave faces around him. He apparently surmised that his statement was unpopular, and he moved quickly to praise Pemberley Hall. The conversation moved to other topics which did not interest Georgiana. With a tumult of feelings, she excused herself from the company after an hour and hastened to her room.

What was she to think or feel now? No one knew where Thomas had gone. What did this mean? Was this an admission of guilt or breaking of the love vow by Thomas? The utter frustration of the question caused her to weep for awhile. At least the headache did not return with the change in emotion; and, fortunately, the headaches were becoming less frequent and less severe.

Her mind was full of doubts, but her heart whispered that Thomas was true. If she could only get some word to, or from him! She even fantasized about being bold and leaving Pemberley Hall to go search for Thomas. Perhaps he was only at Cambridge.

Yes, it would be distinctly out of character, and certainly frowned upon by society, for her to search for the man she loved. After some dreaming about being bold, she felt anxious about the role reversal and reluctantly let the dream go.

Chapter Twenty-Seven

The following evening, the entire Darcy family and Lord Percy were present in the state music room listening to Georgiana play the harp. After she finished two songs, Lord Percy approached her and said, "Indeed, I am not surprised that you play the harp so well, for you appear to me as an angel."

She blushed and did not reply. Seeking to escape, she joined Elizabeth on a couch.

He approached her again, took her hand and said, "I realize this may be sudden and unusual, but I would like to propose for your hand in marriage."

Georgiana was shocked. She could only whisper in reply, "Tell me it is not so."

"I must tell you how long I have admired and ardently desired you to be my wife. Your accomplishments and virtue will adorn the royal court of England and the Percy Castle in Kent."

Georgiana looked to her brother and sister for help, but they merely gave an encouraging smile.

"You must ask my brother for permission," she stammered.

"Your brother has already given permission for me to ask you."

Georgiana looked at her brother, who said, "I only want you to do what you desire."

The Duke continued, "I know it is irregular for me to

ask for your hand in front of your family, but you are difficult to find alone, and I understand how much your family means to you."

At this statement, Andrew and John joined hands, danced a merry-go-round and began singing in a chant, "Auntie's going to be married. Auntie's going to be married." Maria stood in disbelief.

Elizabeth said in a commanding voice, "Now children, your aunt has not yet consented to Lord Percy."

The family and the lord then all turned again to Georgiana, who replied, "This is all so sudden. I do not wish to excite your hope, nor to give any pain to you." She paused and then after a few moments continued, "My immediate response is to say no, but I wish to give some thought to it. I do not understand all that it would do to change my life."

She saw the Duke's face fill with surprise. He, obviously, did not expect any answer other than an affirmative one. He quickly recovered and said, "It shall be magnificent! The wedding would occur at Canterbury Cathedral in Kent. The archbishop of Canterbury would preside and all the royal court would attend, including the Prince Regent himself! Only someone like yourself should be destined to become an elegant duchess."

The room became quiet for a minute as those present waited for Georgiana's response.

"I am sensible of the honor of your proposal, but I must warn you that my inclination is to refuse it."

"Is this your final answer?" the Duke inquired, as his neck began to redden.

"No," she smiled slightly, to lessen his discomfort. "I need to consider it. You have caught me quite by surprise."

"Then may I beg a favor of you?"

"Yes."

"May I have a meeting with you alone, tomorrow

morning after breakfast?"

"I can see no harm in such a meeting," replied Georgiana.

Alone that night, Georgiana became quite anxious. Her heart and mind joined in doubting that she ever had any feelings for Thomas! She had not heard from him and despaired of ever meeting him again. If only he were here, or at Staley Hall, then she could be near him and have her love reinforced.

She could easily understand that a man of honor could consider himself released from any vow after the exile he had received from Pemberley Hall. She felt it only reasonable to free Thomas from his promise of love. Her feelings for Thomas remained sufficient, despite the emotional storm, for her to still believe in him. However, her belief was weakening each day he failed to contact her.

On the other side of the coin, what a grand life she would have as a duchess! A royal marriage in the Canterbury Cathedral! Even strangers would hang on her every word! Why, she would be even more respected than Lady Catherine de Bourgh--she would never have to feel intimidated by such a woman again! If she had a son, it was even remotely possible, as sixth in line, that he could become king! Think of that! She, Georgiana, the mother of a monarch! What a chance to influence the country for goodness!

While she was thinking thus, Mrs. Reynolds came into her room, "Is there anything you want before I retire for the night?"

"Only advice. . . what do you think of the Duke's proposal to me?"

"I think it is an honor quite befitting you. I have known you since you were born. It has always seemed to me you were destined for grandeur. . . and. . .".

"Please, continue."

"I think your mother would have endorsed his proposal."

Georgiana was stunned. She mumbled, "Thank you. Good night, Mrs. Reynolds."

After the housekeeper left, Georgiana felt as though a dagger had emerged from the shadows of the night. Suddenly, the compulsion to fulfill the wishes of her dear departed mother was intruding upon her thoughts. The death of her mother when Georgiana was age six had left her with an emotional reverence for her mother rather than an intellectual understanding; as such, Georgiana would have great difficulty in reasoning her position away from a perceived wish of her mother.

Oh! that Mrs. Reynolds had never uttered a word! While earlier she had toyed with the idea of being a duchess, now the chasm of obedient duty made the decision process awful. She shrank from the vision of the duties that life would entail. She would be constantly required to entertain and to be a clever conversationalist. These were activities that she had to force herself to perform. A shy woman should not be a duchess! She had long ago given up the notion that she could change her behavior toward strangers. Family and longtime friends were another matter--it was effortless to be at ease with them.

Finally, the Duke himself. What kind of man was he? A man that a near friend would warn her about? Certainly, he was a man of good breeding, but what was his true disposition? He was generous as demonstrated by his gift of the Gainsborough painting. However, she became uneasy when she remembered the treatment of his horse in London and his irritation towards the Darcy children. She thought that any fault perceived now should be magnified at least ten times.

Two thoughts were now crystal clear to her. Her unrequited desire for Thomas was sharpened. Her duty to marry the Duke was looming as the one decision she must submit herself to accepting. Her mother would have wanted it so!

The conjunction of these ideas made Georgiana turn in bed and weep for a long time.

The next morning, after breakfast, Georgiana and Lord Percy retired alone to the music room.

He gently inquired, "Have you any further decision as to my request last evening?"

"I am still undecided. You must forgive me, this is all so sudden."

"I can comprehend that it is so. I cannot perceive that you are one of those women who hope to increase a suitor's desire by forestalling a decision. No, you are all goodness; and thus, your equivocation must be honest. Your sweetness of disposition baffles all comparison."

Georgiana was quiet and he continued, "I may have acted hasty in the offer. It is customary for gentlemen in my position to take a three to six month Grand Tour of the continent to complete our education in society. Given your indecision, I intend to leave for Kent today and depart for France shortly. I need to test my feelings to see if they are constant. My offer of marriage still stands, but I may withdraw it at any time without loss of honor, unless you accept it first. . . . How long do you think you will need for a decision?"

Georgiana had not anticipated such a patient and gracious response. The Duke seemed like a man who would demand everyone to immediately fall in with his plans. She wanted ample time to consider her situation and replied, "Would my lord be displeased with a request for sixty days?"

"Not at all--better to be certain. Be assured that your answer, unless I withdraw first, will be honored. If it is negative, I promise not to persist in this matter and would then hope to remain your constant friend."

The Duke rose and began pacing in front of the fireplace and finished, "My steward at Percy Castle will know my location on the continent at all times. Send your reply to him." With this statement, he took her hand and leaned to kiss it. He turned and strode from the room. She did not see him again before he left for Kent that afternoon.

Georgiana flew to the south garden to be alone. She must become accustomed to thinking about a life with the Duke of Kent and let go of her love for Thomas! This was much easier stated than accomplished. Perhaps, her love could grow for the Duke like Marianne's affection did for Colonel Brandon.

At this moment, she wished she had never been born! She did not want to leave Derbyshire, let alone Pemberley. She did not want to let go of Thomas. She was miserable. But, then, this is what made her decision a duty! If she had any desire for what must be her final decision, then the sense of duty would be greatly softened.

After some time walking in the garden, she returned to the portrait hall and sat down in front of the painting of her mother. She spoke to the painting, "If only you were here to tell me your wishes. . . . Do you want me to marry Lord Percy or continue to hope for Thomas? Do you want me to be a duchess and reunite the family? Your desire would help me make a decision."

Chapter Twenty-Eight

Three days later, Elizabeth found Georgiana alone in the library, and quietly sat down across from her. After a minute of silence, Georgiana said, "I suppose it is natural for you to be curious about my thoughts concerning Lord Percy's proposal."

"Of course. However, your brother does not, in any way, wish to influence your decision. It must be yours and yours alone. My only purpose in coming to you is that you may wish to talk it over with another woman."

"I am sorry if my reluctance to converse with you has created a barrier between us. I have needed time to sort out my feelings." Georgiana paused and observed the look of compassion on her sister's face, "I am afraid it is my duty to accept Lord Percy's proposal."

Elizabeth replied, "It alarms me to hear you speak of duty. Is not your heart inclined in this matter?"

"To be honest, I have very little affection for Lord Percy."

"Then, why would you consider marriage to him?"

"I feel it is my duty. I think it is something mother would have desired."

"And how do you know this?"

"Mrs. Reynolds suggested my mother's preference. It makes sense to me that my mother would want to reunite her daughter with a distant relative of her own family."

"My dear sister, while it is true I did not know your

mother, from everything Mr. Darcy has told me, I sincerely doubt your mother would want you to marry without affection. With your permission, may I go and bring your brother here and solicit his opinion?"

"Oh! please do!"

After ten minutes, Elizabeth returned with Mr. Darcy, who strode into the room and sat down next to his sister. Elizabeth sat across from them. He took Georgiana's hand and gently said, "Elizabeth told me you are troubled this morning about what our mother may have thought. My heart has almost burst watching your downcast countenance the past few days."

"Dear brother, I think our mother would want me to marry Lord Percy despite having little affection for him. In doing so, it would reunite our family's influence."

"Is this what frets my little sister? You should have spoken sooner." He looked away for a moment and sighed before continuing, "You were so young when mother died. . . I was only eighteen at the time. Nonetheless, I do not think mother would want you to marry without solid love and respect for your partner."

"What makes you think so?"

"Mother and father simply adored each other. Their marriage was not one of property or design, but of love and loyalty. . . . Why do you think I searched for a woman so long? Among so many proffered women of status, I wanted someone I could love and respect as I do your dear sister, Elizabeth."

"Did Mother not promise you to our cousin, Miss de Bourgh?"

"Yes and no," he smiled. "Shortly before mother died, our aunt told me of Mother's intent regarding our cousin. When I asked Mother about it, she said her sister, Lady Catherine, should not have spoken the secret. Mother said the idea, for the most part, was promoted by her sister rather than herself. Mother, realizing my opposition to such a plan, and the sickly nature of our cousin, released me from any obligation in the matter."

Georgiana quietly asked, "Do you know if Mother wanted me to marry anyone?"

"If she did, she kept it a secret from me."

Georgiana began sobbing. Mr. Darcy put his arm around his sister. After several minutes, she pulled back a little, and drying her tears with his handkerchief, she said, "My dear brother, thank you for your concern and wisdom. Would you excuse us? There are some other things I want to discuss with Elizabeth."

Mr. Darcy stood, "Of course. Only, in the future if you wonder about what you think our mother would have wanted, please discuss it with me."

"Thank you."

The room was quiet for a minute after Mr. Darcy exited. Elizabeth ventured, "Perhaps, there is some secret which you are reluctant to divulge?"

"Oh, Lizzy," she twisted the handkerchief around her fingers. "Yes, you are right. I ask that you do not tell my brother--it would distress him so." She paused and continued, "Despite all that has happened, I think I still love Mr. Thomas Staley. We vowed our love for each other shortly before the accusation; but now, I despair of whether he will keep his vow after the way he has been treated."

"What a blockhead I have been!" exclaimed Elizabeth. "I did not think I was so far away from young love, at my age of one and thirty, to have missed the signs entirely. Your statement makes a good deal of sense in explaining your actions."

"My heart is still not clear. I wonder that the fundamental question vexing me is whether I am comfortable with the possibility of remaining unmarried. It is one thing to rashly declare one will be an old maid, when there are no suitors; but, when there are handsome men vying for my affections. . . ." She sighed, "It is just the lack of communication from Thomas, and my occasional fear about the accusation, that haunts me."

"My dear sister, there is little I can do to console you. My sister Jane is visiting next week and has quite a story to tell about waiting."

"I desire to hear it. I never thought about what happened from her point of view. Oh! do tell me."

"No, I think it best that you hear it from her own lips."

One week later, on the morning they expected Charles and Jane Bingley, a letter arrived after breakfast and was given to Georgiana. It read:

> My dearest niece, Georgiana,
>
> The news has arrived about Lord Percy's proposal to you. This is simply wonderful!
>
> I am confused by reports that you have not accepted it. Do not leave such a grand person in suspense for long! I understand the proposal may have come as a surprise.
>
> Do not worry if you lack rapturous feelings of love for him. Too much emphasis is given to such ideas nowadays. Consider it an honor to receive his proposal. It is every woman's *duty* to improve her status through marriage! Since Lord Percy is the highest ranking bachelor in the land, you can do no better.
>
> You will make your aunt quite happy if you hasten to accept his proposal. Then I can

feel that Rosing Park is staying in the family.
Sincerely,
Aunt Catherine

Georgiana was amused and vexed at the presumptive tone in her aunt's letter. She handed it to Elizabeth and watched Mrs. Darcy's face begin to color.

Elizabeth said, "As you know, Georgiana, I have also had to resist the will of your aunt." They hugged each other and began to move to the parlor, when the servant announced the arrival of the Bingleys. Mr. Darcy joined them in welcoming Mr. and Mrs. Bingley and their two daughters, Laura and Sarah. Laura was a pretty nine year old girl, with long blond hair, who looked very much like her beautiful mother. Sarah was seven years old, with brown hair and a very slender body. Sarah was quiet and rarely spoke, while Laura was always talking.

Once they were all in the parlor, Elizabeth said, "Do you girls want to go out to the south lawn? Andrew, John and Maria are playing there now." With this, the girls scampered off.

Mr. Darcy said, "Charles, I have two new magnificent horses to show you. Let us go to the stables."

This arrangement suited the three remaining women, since they had much to discuss.

"My dear Jane," started Elizabeth. "We have so much to talk about. Georgiana and you are my two dearest feminine companions. You must give us your opinion of Georgiana's dilemma; and, most of all, tell the story of how long you were uncertain about Charles."

"Do you really wish to hear about such a difficult time in my life?" replied Jane.

"Yes, because it will help Georgiana; but, first let us tell you about her situation. Georgiana, do you wish to tell what has transpired with Lord Percy, or shall I?"

"Please, Elizabeth, will you do so?"

Elizabeth proceeded to tell the story of the Duke's arrival and proposal. Jane was already familiar with Georgiana's accident in London. She listened with amazement on her face as the story was told. As it ended she said, "Oh! I do not know why I should be surprised that such an offer came to one so accomplished! It is, indeed, a high honor! What are your inclinations in the matter?"

"I have doubts about his character and cannot seem to work up anything more than a small amount of affection for him. Perhaps, I could eventually resolve these issues, but I think I am in love with another man." Georgiana proceeded then to tell Jane about Mr. Thomas Staley.

After finishing her version of events, Jane looked at her sister, Elizabeth, who was frowning and said, "My dearest Lizzy, did you really think these things of Thomas?"

"Oh! Jane, you who always see the best in everyone and suspect them of nothing! It was not pleasant to do what we did, but it was done on consultation with both Mr. Darcy and Sir William Staley. Nonetheless, I am uneasy about the matter and the effect it has had on our beloved Georgiana." The group was quiet for a few moments and Elizabeth continued, "Georgiana has now waited more than three weeks without hearing from Thomas."

"It feels like three months since I have heard," sighed Georgiana, "nor do I know where he is located."

Elizabeth looked at Jane and said, "This is why I want you to tell the story of your separation from Mr. Bingley and the despair it caused."

"Lizzy is right. I can see similarities and differences. Charles left Netherfield suddenly for London one day without explanation. I felt that he loved me, but we had not made any commitment. Weeks turned into months and his sister, Caroline, led me to believe he no longer cared for me.

I tried to convince myself I no longer cared for him, but when he returned unexpectedly, nearly a year later, all of my real feelings for him surfaced again. It turned out he had never stopped loving me, though his family had been trying to dissuade him from me. Eventually, his family accepted me."

"Did you hear from him during the separation?"

"No. The lack of communication led me to doubt my love. I tried valiantly to put him out of my thinking, but in retrospect, I do not believe I was ever successful at doing it."

"Almost one year!" replied Georgiana. "I could endure such a time for Thomas, if only I knew he would return. Part of my problem is this cloud of accusation which made him depart. I am afraid he will never come back."

Jane said, "If it is meant to be, he will reappear."

Georgiana thoughtfully replied, "I am now certain that I shall be forever in love with Thomas. It may be unrequited; in such a case, I shall be happy as a so-called 'old maid'. Only in this way, can my heart have happiness and hope."

Elizabeth spoke, "Your statement sounds wise to me. Shall we form a letter of reply to the Duke of Kent, giving your gentle, but certain, refusal?"

"Lizzy, would you help me write the letter?"

"Certainly."

The following morning, as they were composing the letter, a note arrived from London addressed to Mrs. Darcy.

Dear Elizabeth,

Knowing of the proposal between Lord Percy and your sister-in-law, we felt it imperative that we notify you of news from our nephew in Paris. This is information which cannot be doubted. It appears that Lord Percy is keeping a mistress with him during his stay in France. My nephew has seen this with his own eyes and several others have confirmed it. Unfortunately, this is all too common among the aristocracy here, and there is, apparently, little disapprobation of it.

Your uncle and I leave it to your discretion as to how, or if, you will reveal this to Miss Darcy."

Warmest Regards,
Your Aunt Gardiner

Elizabeth immediately handed the note to Georgiana, whose face alternated between shades of crimson and paleness as she read it. Georgiana passed the note on to Jane and said, "This is shocking and shameful. To think I even considered his proposal."

Georgiana sat down and Jane said, "Georgiana, this shows you have good understanding of character. You formulated your refusal without knowing of his licentiousness."

Elizabeth agreed and then said, "My poor Georgiana, to be exposed to the likes of both Wickham and Percy."

"Do not pine, Lizzy," replied Georgiana, "I was quickly over my infatuation with Mr. Wickham and with your help, avoided Lord Percy."

While Jane and Elizabeth looked compassionately at her, she paused for a minute and then sighed, "Is this libertine behavior common to all men? I cannot believe it of Thomas; however, this report of the Duke makes me worry about all men."

Elizabeth replied, "Do not fret so. I hope and pray, with all my heart, that you will find a man like your brother, who is not guilty of that fault."

"Or one like my Charles," replied Jane.

"Is there no way to prove the innocence of Thomas?" asked Georgiana.

Elizabeth replied, "I have given much thought to it. I have heard of phrenologists who examine bodies and cranial features to determine relatedness and ancestry."

"How would that help us?" Georgiana asked in a puzzled manner.

"If the science or art is as good as it is purported to be, perhaps, when this alleged baby of his is born, it can be determined with some certainty whether Thomas is the father."

"Oh, Lizzy, you give me some hope; however, we will have to wait another four months before the baby will be born."

"I can think of no other way; can you, Jane?"

"I cannot."

Georgiana said in a resigned tone, "If this be the case, then I must prepare my heart to wait. I hope the outcome will be as good as yours was, Jane."

After supper, when Mr. Darcy and Mr. Bingley were given the letter, Mr. Darcy exclaimed, "What a foul villain Lord Percy is!" Similar other epithets were violently expressed by both gentlemen. Georgiana could not recall ever seeing her brother exhibit more righteous indignation, nor had she ever heard Mr. Bingley express such disapprobation.

Mr. Darcy continued, "If I ever meet the wretch again, I shall tell him what I think of him. This libertine behavior may be winked at in some circles, but not in ours!" After pacing for another minute or two, he said, "Not that I doubt our beloved aunt and uncle, Lizzy, but I will seek one more confirmation of this report. If I find support, I shall inform my peers of this and he will never obtain the hand of a virtuous woman."

Georgiana blushed at the description of herself. She was glad that her entire family felt the same way about the Duke. What had previously been quiet and unspoken support for her to consider the Duke, became uniform condemnation of him. At least one part of her tri-lemma had been resolved. Now, where was Thomas and did he still love her?

Chapter Twenty-Nine

The next two months were uneventful for Georgiana and her family at Pemberley Hall. Elizabeth knew of her sister's hope and sorrow while they both kept the secret of her love from Mr. Darcy, to avoid giving him additional pain. Georgiana realized her only hope lay in the examination of the alleged baby, and tried to console herself that the time period would eventually end, despite it feeling like an eternity. With all traces of headaches having resolved more than a month ago, she could sleep reasonably well most nights. Occasionally, however, she would be restless at night with fears that Thomas was truly guilty of the offense; in her nightmares, he would laugh at her naivete.

One morning, after such a night, an urgent post arrived for her family. Her brother opened it and then handed it to Elizabeth and Georgiana who read it together.

Dear Mr., Mrs. and Miss Darcy,
      Your aunt, the great Lady Catherine de Bourgh, is ill. The doctors do not give much hope of recovery. She begs your immediate presence in Kent.
                              Sincerely yours,
                              Reverend Collins

Georgiana did not look forward with pleasure to the return trip to Rosings. Her aunt's antagonism towards her beloved sister, Elizabeth, and the contrived introduction to the despicable Duke made her feel less than charitable towards Lady Catherine. Even though Catherine de Bourgh's daughter, Miss de Bourgh, died five years earlier, her aunt still resented that Mr. Darcy did not marry the sickly girl, but chose Elizabeth instead. With each meeting, Georgiana could still detect hostility in her elderly relative towards Elizabeth. Lady Catherine usually would cover her disapprobation with good breeding; but, the attitude would erupt on occasion.

At the time of Georgiana's ill-fated visit to London, four months earlier, she had only vaguely felt her aunt's manipulation of the affair with the Duke. Now, in retrospect, she thought she completely understood the overt role Lady Catherine had played in it. In addition to these justified, yet uncharitable feelings, Georgiana sensed a revival of her former fear towards her aunt.

This would be her first visit to Rosings since the dissolution of, what many considered to be, a highly promising relationship to the Duke. While Georgiana was relieved that the Duke declared himself in another direction, she expected to be berated by her aunt for not being more vigorous in trying to capture him. Upon their arrival at Rosings, Mr. and Mrs. Collins greeted Mr. and Mrs. Darcy and Georgiana as they stepped from the coach.

"Mr. Darcy, what a great honor it is to have you visit us," said Mr. Collins in his usual obsequious manner.

"Thank you," replied Mr. Darcy curtly.

"And how is my cousin Elizabeth?" Mr. Collins asked, then immediately turned to Georgiana and said, "I am afraid you look a bit pale, Miss Darcy. I trust you did not find the trip too arduous."

Mr. Collins stepped back one pace and said solemnly. "I am afraid I have very bad news for you. Lady Catherine de Bourgh has worsened and has been ordered to bed by the doctors. She left word that she would like to see Miss Darcy upon her arrival."

Mr. and Mrs. Collins led the way through the large welcoming hall, up the elegant and straight staircase, to Lady Catherine's bedroom. During the procession, Georgiana whispered into Elizabeth's ear, "I do not want to see her alone. Please, Lizzy, come with me and give me strength. You are one of the few people who can withstand her displeasure."

"Yes, my dear sister, I shall come. However, my resistance to our aunt is never with pleasure," replied Elizabeth.

Mr. Collins opened the door. Georgiana and Elizabeth stepped in to see a pale, sickly looking Lady Catherine in bed.

"I did not ask **you** to come, Mrs. Darcy."

"Miss Darcy has asked me to accompany her," Elizabeth answered quietly. "I shall remain."

"You have always been impertinent! I suppose you shall always remain so. . . then by all means, stay," Lady Catherine replied.

Two chairs were brought near the bed by Lady Catherine's maid, and the visitors sat down.

"Georgiana, I have called you here to express my disappointment that the Duke did not become engaged to you. You must be heartbroken. I am greatly distressed that one of my near relatives could not have been installed in the Rosing Park estate. As it is, since I have no heir, Rosings shall revert to the Duke's family and I shall not have the pleasure of seeing you become a part of it."

"I am reconciled to the situation, Ma'am," Georgiana replied honestly.

Lady Catherine continued, "I hope you know that I did everything possible to forward your match with the Duke and to discourage your foolish infatuation with that tutor."

Georgiana did not know what to make of this last statement. What had Lady Catherine done other than introduce her to the Duke?

Elizabeth seemed to comprehend the import and her face began coloring; she started speaking her thoughts out loud, "Now it is making sense--why the accusation came against the tutor at the worst time. . . why the departing servants were able to buy a house and land. Further, I recall those servants were here at Rosings before coming to Pemberley."

"What are you rattling about?" rasped Lady Catherine.

"I see your hand in this matter with Mr. Staley." With a firm, prosecuting voice Elizabeth said, "Did you or did you not, Lady Catherine, influence or bribe those servants to give false testimony against the tutor?"

"You are one of the few people who would dare talk to me like that," replied Lady Catherine with a little color entering her otherwise pasty white face. Energy began coming into her body as she sat up.

"Once, Lady Catherine, you adjured me to tell the truth about my engagement to your nephew, Mr. Darcy. For the sake of the lifelong happiness of your niece, Georgiana, I now adjure you to tell us if you suborned false testimony against Mr. Staley!"

Georgiana saw her defiant sister looking straight at Lady Catherine, who was hatefully glaring back at Elizabeth.

"What have I to lose?" answered Lady Catherine as she laid back down. "I knew that threatening Georgiana with the loss of my favor would not influence her. She has been around you too long, Elizabeth, for that method to work. I admit to caring about the status of my niece and the purchase of testimony against the tutor. The interloper was a detestable dissenter anyway."

During the last sentence, Georgiana began to cry. She

stood and ran from the room, past her brother at the doorway, down the hall to her usual bedroom at Rosings, and closed the door.

Elizabeth then inquired, "And what of Lord Percy, was he in on the lie?"

"No. He was not part of the accusation. He did, however, respond to my encouragement."

Elizabeth stood and said, "Once again, Lady Catherine, you have wronged a loved one of mine; only now, I do not see how this evil can be undone. My opinion of you matters little, but I hope God will take notice of you with mercy on your soul." Saying so, she left the room, closing the door behind her. She saw her husband pacing, with furrowed eyebrows and a worried look. He stopped when he saw his wife and spoke, "Something is wrong. I saw my sister running to her room looking very wretched. Pray, tell me. What is going on?"

Elizabeth told him of the conversation between herself and Lady Catherine. She also told him that Georgiana had loved Thomas before the accusation. Mr. Darcy's worried look turned into one of anger. He began pacing with deliberate steps. While doing so, he emitted short sentences, "I have been a fool. . . .I suspected something wrong at the time. . . .This one is much more grievous to bear than her last insult to me, since it is directed at my precious sister. . . What am I to do?"

Elizabeth thought it best not to answer immediately. Indeed, her own heart was in the same turmoil. "Mr. Darcy, I am more to blame. I should have vigorously defended Thomas. I fancied myself having better judgement, after failing in my prejudices of you and Mr. Wickham. I persist in being a weak judge of character."

"I am equally, if not worse, a poor judge of character. Please, go and see what my sister's disappointment is and what I can do."

Elizabeth went to the door of Georgiana's room. She no longer heard crying, so she gently knocked at the door. Not hearing a reply, she slowly opened the door. She went and sat at her sister's bedside. After several minutes, Elizabeth ventured, "Your brother and I were very stupid in our actions towards Thomas. Had we known of your partiality to him at the time, we may have acted with greater courage. Our compromise between the two testimonies was a greater evil than completely believing or disbelieving Mr. Staley."

With tear-stained eyes, she lifted her head to Elizabeth, "My dear sister, do not blame yourself or my brother. I should have defended him with all my strength, and I did not. The admission of the lie against Thomas makes me love him even more. It is one thing to read a novel and another to be in a like situation. . . my situation has little hope of a happy ending. In one sense, it is a great relief to hear him vindicated; on the other hand, I despair of ever seeing him again."

"What can we do?" asked Elizabeth.

Attempting to dry her eyes with a handkerchief, Georgiana ventured, "Could my brother possibly find Thomas and repent of our family's grievous mistake?"

"If anyone can, your brother can. Long ago, he found Lydia, who was hidden in London; and, I daresay he will find your Mr. Staley," Elizabeth said. "Your brother now knows Mr. Staley is quite special to you."

"Yes, my dear Lizzy, he is special to me. I am convinced that Thomas and I would be perfectly suited for each other."

"I believe you are," Elizabeth replied softly. "I will speak to your brother to see what can be done."

Returning to the elegant hallway outside Lady Catherine's bedroom, Elizabeth saw Mr. Darcy still pacing, though more slowly and with less foot pounding. Upon seeing her, he said, "Mr. Jones, the apothecary, says Lady Catherine is declining rapidly. He does not expect her to last the night." He turned to a servant and said, "For what it is worth, get Mr. Collins up here to pray for her."

"Mr. Darcy, let us go to the drawing room to discuss what we can do."

Moments later in the drawing room, Elizabeth told him of his sister's heart.

"I would dearly like to communicate with Mr. Staley, but how are we to find him? This is much more difficult than your sister Lydia's situation. Then, at least, we had a clue to suggest that she was somewhere in London. Now, I am not even sure if he is in England, let alone London. Since his letter declining the position in Kent, we have not heard a word. I am tempted to leave now to contact my friends in London, but it is quite evident that Lady Catherine will die soon; as her nearest relative, I must stay for her funeral."

"Perhaps, Sir William Staley has heard something of his son since we left Pemberley. Pray, let us write him by express for information."

"It seems all we can do for now," replied Mr. Darcy. He went to the desk and penned the following note:

> To my friend, Sir William,
>
> I am ashamed to admit this of my family, but my aunt, Lady Catherine de Bourgh, has just confessed to us her despicable action in bringing false testimony against your son, Thomas. Your son is <u>blameless</u>. I should have seen through the plot of my aunt to drive a wedge between your son and our household. Her purpose was to encourage my sister's interest in another person, who is now, clearly, unworthy of her love.

My family wishes to make restitution of so grievous an affair. We would like to know the present whereabouts of Thomas, so we can speedily make amends.

The only consolation I have is that I consulted your wishes before making the final decision. However, the fault remains entirely mine. I should have been more decisive.

We should like Thomas to return to visit us. His presence in our house was a balm. He was a great help to my children and sister.

A reply by express to Rosings would be greatly appreciated. We are obliged to stay here because of my aunt's rapidly declining condition.

Your faithful neighbor,
Mr. Fitzwilliam Darcy

After finishing the note, he handed it to Elizabeth to peruse. Her face showed her agreement.

"Should we show it to Georgiana?" asked Mr. Darcy.

"Certainly. It will probably ease her sorrow to know that her brother is doing all he can to remedy the fault," replied Elizabeth.

Indeed, the letter had a soothing effect on Georgiana. After reading it, she was able to entertain hope of seeing Thomas again. Should he despise her, it would be understandable; however, she knew his charitable nature would make him likely to pity her and her family, rather than despise them.

Later that evening, Elizabeth came to Georgiana's room to talk. The heartbroken young woman shared her feelings about the note and was pleased to have Elizabeth staunchly defend Thomas. Even if Thomas should dislike Pemberley and its inhabitants, perhaps, given time and friendly communication, his affection would return.

Chapter Thirty

As expected, Lady Catherine de Bourgh died that night. What a great equalizer death is; what a leveler of mankind! Any fear or disgust the Darcys had of her changed to pity. The funeral took place in two days and she was laid to rest by a distraught Reverend Collins, who appeared to be uncertain at times as to the proper content of the eulogy.

After the funeral, Mr. Collins came to the Darcy table to offer his condolences. "Mr. Darcy, you must be in deep sorrow to have such a great relation as Lady Catherine de Bourgh pass away."

"We are bearing it as well as can be expected," Mr. Darcy replied.

Elizabeth then caught her cousin's attention and said, "Take care, Mr. Collins, of your new patron, His Grace, the Duke of Kent ."

"Whatever do you mean, cousin?"

"He is a man not to be trusted. We are suspicious that he may wish another rector at Hunsford Park."

"Do not be alarmed, my dear Elizabeth. I am sure I will find the Duke of Kent to be a great man who would want to continue the ministerial tradition of Rosing Park; besides, the power of removal lies with the bishop, rather than the patron."

Elizabeth replied, "But as you well know, a powerful man such as His Grace can often have his way with any bishop."

"Do not fret, my cousin. I believe I can win my new patron over to continue my position. Your interest in my well-being is most appreciated; however, do not alarm yourself." He bowed and moved on.

After a minute or so, Georgiana looked at her brother and said, "When is Lord Percy to arrive at Rosing Park? I am most anxious to avoid meeting him."

Her brother replied, "A notice was sent to him as soon as our aunt died. Apparently, he is in eastern Europe and may not even receive the letter for another week; as a result, it is doubtful he can be here in less than a fortnight."

Georgiana was visibly relieved with her brother's intelligence about Lord Percy.

The following day, while Mr. and Mrs. Darcy were identifying family heirlooms that Lady Catherine had directed them to take, a servant brought a written reply to Mr. Darcy's note.

> Dear Mr. Darcy,
>
> Your letter has been received. I am most grateful in your attention to my son, Thomas. I, too, am disgusted at lack of faith in my own flesh. . . .
>
> Circumstances now make the finding of Thomas even more urgent. I have just received the most sorrowful news of the death of my older son. As a consequence, Thomas becomes heir to Staley Hall. My health is failing. The doctors tell me I can expect to live three to six months, at the best.
>
> Unfortunately, Staley Hall has not received any correspondence from Thomas since he left Pemberley three months ago.
>
> As our families have had a long term friendship, with help and comfort being

provided by each, I would ask you, Mr. Darcy, if you could exert yourself in locating my son.

While it is possible he remains in England, I think it likely, since the cessation of hostilities with France, that he may be engaged in teaching across the channel.

Sincerely,
Sir William Staley

Mr. Darcy sat down as Elizabeth and Georgiana read the letter. The room was silent as they finished.

Finally, Elizabeth broke the silence, "What can we do, Mr. Darcy?"

"Our honor requires that we make vigorous attempts to locate Mr. Staley, though it may be nearly impossible."

Georgiana could see that Elizabeth's confidence in her brother was great. Elizabeth suggested contacting Mr. Darcy's friends at Cambridge or in the foreign office.

"Yes, I have thought of that. We need to move to our house in London so I can contact some of the ambassadors, especially those of France and the Netherlands."

Georgiana now regretted that her own shyness had prevented development of a wide number of contacts in London and elsewhere; then, she could be contacting them just as her brother was beginning to do by letter. Oh, how she esteemed her brother--a man of Derbyshire, London and the world!

Chapter Thirty-One

In the breakfast parlor at Rosings the next morning, Mr. Darcy told of the many letters he had written to every acquaintance who might be of assistance. Mrs. and Miss Darcy readily agreed to quit Rosings within a day and move to their house in London. Somehow, London seemed closer to finding Thomas than a return to Derbyshire would.

A week elapsed in London when Mr. Darcy was quizzed during dinner. A weary Mr. Darcy replied, "As you can surmise, my inquiries have not been fruitful. The French ambassador assures me there is no such name on any of the faculty lists of French institutions he possesses. I had the greatest hope that he would be of help. Unfortunately, while my sister thinks I know everyone in the world, I have almost no contacts in France because of the long war recently concluded."

"What about your numerous contacts at Cambridge? Since Thomas wanted to return there, perhaps someone has heard of him," quizzed Georgiana.

In a lowered tone, Mr. Darcy said despondently, "I received the following letter from my old master at Cambridge." He handed the paper to Georgiana, who read the following with Elizabeth:

My Dear Fitzwilliam,
　　It was good to hear from you after so long. I am afraid I cannot help you. Mr.

Thomas Staley was indeed an outstanding student and faculty candidate while he was here. He kept his name on an eligibility roll for a teaching fellowship after his return from the war, but failed to renew his candidacy one month ago. I have inquired of two or three of his friends to see if they have heard anything, and they have not. One rumor, which we tend to discount, is that Thomas was lost at sea.

His friends join me in wishing you success in locating him and we are unanimous that he should return to Cambridge to pursue his obvious talent.

Yours truly,
Dr. Charles Lewis

Georgiana was numb. Thomas lost at sea! She had never considered this possibility! Surely, one who had loved him so much should have felt the loss. Her hope over the past week now felt artificial and seemed to disappear like an evaporating haze. She left the table without speaking and went to her bedroom. Elizabeth followed her after fifteen minutes.

Chapter Thirty-Two

Time passed very slowly for Georgiana and her family. A fortnight after their arrival in London, they had an unexpected caller. One afternoon, the servant announced the honorable Samuel Moore as a visitor. He strode into the room and was greeted by Elizabeth and Georgiana. Knowing who Mr. Moore was, Elizabeth made it a point to stay with Georgiana, who clearly welcomed her sister's support.

"Ladies, please be seated. While I have only come for a short visit, it always seems less formal to sit down."

Since the Darcy women were surprised by his visit, and he had an obvious communique for them, they remained silent.

"I suppose you are wondering about my visit. Lord Percy has returned to Rosing Park to assume its ownership and wishes to inform and to inquire about three items. He did not think a letter would suffice. When I volunteered to come to London, he readily assented."

"First, this visit in no way represents a renewal of his courtship of Miss Darcy. Secondly, he is most desirous of knowing your condition, Miss Darcy, and whether the prior accident has had any sequella."

Georgiana replied, "Inform Lord Percy that I am no longer feeling any effects from the accident. My headaches are entirely gone."

"Good. The final point he wishes to make clear is to offer his friendship and well wishes for your future. He does not forget the hospitality of Pemberley Hall. He wants the Darcy family to continue considering Rosing Park as available at all times, should you wish to stay in Kent. No invitation will ever be needed."

Elizabeth replied, "Tell your friend that the Darcy family accepts his offer of friendship with Rosing Park. Make it absolutely clear that my sister does not wish any further matrimonial offers."

"I believe Lord Percy is sincere in these matters. My visit in no way represents an exploration of a possible engagement."

To turn the conversation from so painful a subject for her sister, Elizabeth asked, "Do you have any idea of the disposition of the Duke towards the rector of the parish, Reverend Collins?"

He replied, "Mr. Collins. . . are you acquainted with him?"

"He is my cousin."

"Then I shall be circumspect."

"No, pray, tell us the truth. We know he is a buffoon. His principle strength is that he is harmless."

"I see you know him. To be perfectly honest, Lord Percy cannot stand the man. He is always fawning over him and worshiping the ground he walks on. My friend is quite tired of his simpering. Although Lord Percy is no saint, he would prefer a rector who would focus on the parish rather than on the occupant of Rosing Park."

"What has he decided to do with him?" Elizabeth rejoined.

"This is confidential; but, since your cousin knows, I see no harm in telling his family. Lord Percy has applied to the bishop to have Mr. Collins removed or transferred."

"Do you think his application will succeed?" Elizabeth exhibited some anxiety in her voice, though her concern was more for her friend, Charlotte, Mr. Collins' wife, than for her cousin.

"The bishop is a long-term friend of Lord Percy's departed father. I have little doubt of the outcome."

"Is there any other position for him?"

"I do not know."

"How is Mr. Collins taking the situation?"

"He is so obsequious that the Duke has banned him from Rosing Park. Mrs. Darcy, I am sorry I do not have more information on your cousin." He rose and was accompanied to the door. He paused and said, "I wish, Miss Darcy, the outcome with my friend and you would have been different. I should have liked to have become better acquainted with you." With a tip of his hat, he was gone.

Chapter Thirty-Three

In the ensuing days, the Darcys were renewing old acquaintances and inviting guests who might help locate their friend.

While the Darcys wished to inform their guests of the search for Mr. Thomas Staley, it was difficult to do so without telling their guests most of the story about the offered engagement. Mr. and Mrs. Darcy were most careful to not infer in any way that Lord Percy might be the gentleman involved in a Parisian liaison; but, after the first two parties easily guessed the man involved, they became less concerned. It seemed the Duke had quite a reputation among the London gentry for breaking hearts and having little virtue in the area of controlling bodily appetites. After their initial concern over defamation of Lord Percy, it occurred to them that his character was very much like Mr. Wickham's; the only difference lay in Lord Percy's riches and power, which might continue to influence selfish or innocent women. Mr. and Mrs. Darcy then felt the Duke's infamous character should be discreetly shared with those in a position to prevent future broken hearts.

Early in their London stay, the Darcys were invited to dine with the Gardiners. Mr. and Mrs. Darcy's gratitude to the couple in Cheapside resulted in joyful attendance at the middle class address. As Elizabeth's aunt and uncle, Mr. and Mrs. Gardiner were fully informed of Georgiana's predicament at their first visit. It seemed so natural to share again in a similar problem to one worked through eleven years earlier.

At a return dinner engagement to the Darcy's London home, Mr. Gardiner announced, "Mrs. Gardiner and I have considered what we can do for Georgiana. We have made numerous inquiries about Mr. Thomas Staley and have been able to discover little."

Mr. Darcy replied, "Really, Mr. Gardiner, you must not exert yourself over our family's matter."

Mr. Gardiner replied, "On the contrary, Mr. Darcy! Your effort in behalf of our niece was beyond all measure. This time you must allow me to try something."

Mrs. Gardiner continued, "My husband has formulated a plan for possible discovery of Mr. Staley."

"Please, dear, do not excite their hope. We should probably call our efforts a possibility, if anything at all." He looked at Georgiana, now perched on the edge of her seat. "However, knowing that a rational design produces hope, I thought Miss Darcy should know of our efforts."

Georgiana eagerly inquired, "Pray tell, Mr. Gardiner, what your project involves?"

"Mrs. Gardiner and I have been planning for some time to visit France to see her nephew, who is studying art in Paris. My business will allow Mrs. Gardiner and I to leave in three days for the Continent. We plan to make inquiries along the way about Mr. Staley."

"Wonderful," Elizabeth replied. "Do you have any specifics?"

"If I do, I choose not to reveal them at this time, lest we become overconfident of the result."

Despite further pleadings from all the women seated, Mr. Gardiner would only smile in response. Mr. Gardiner said at one point, "You will recall that Mr. Darcy had his special contact, which enabled him to find Lydia years ago. Now, I hope my source in France will lead to the discovery of Mr. Staley." He then spent the remainder of the evening downplaying his trip.

Privately, at the end of the evening, Mr. Gardiner asked Mr. Darcy if there were any written communication he would like the Gardiners to present to Thomas, should he be discovered. Mr. Darcy provided the following letter:

> Dear Mr. Staley,
>
> This is a letter of sincere and strongly felt apology for our grievous error. In not trusting you, and forcing you away, we committed an unforgivable blunder.
>
> It is with shame that we relate the confession of my late aunt, Lady Catherine de Bourgh. She obtained the false testimony against you.
>
> Mrs. Darcy, the children and I are most anxious to see you again in person to reiterate our sincere repentance. My sister, Georgiana, most of all wishes to communicate with you. Your father is also very desirous of contacting you. I am sorry to cause further pain; but, the doctors have told him he has only months to live and he wishes to see you immediately at Staley Hall.
>
> We have spent the last month using every possible method of discovering your whereabouts. We pray that Mr. and Mrs. Gardiner will be successful in delivering this note to you.
>
> Yours, most sincerely,
> Fitzwilliam Darcy

The reaction of Georgiana, during her solitary hours, to the recent events was several fold. Mentally, she determined to resign herself to being single the rest of her life if Thomas were never found, or if he despised her family. This resolution gave her a steady mental consolation, which was not always matched by her heart and soul.

When she would dwell upon it, her soul was filled with shame at the attempt of Lord Percy at marriage. Georgiana was a virtuous woman, since she had been tempted and emerged the victor from the aborted elopement of Mr. Wickham many years ago. Only a virtuous woman can feel the sort of disgust against repeated and chronic sexual indiscretion in others. She had heard of the hypocritical behavior of promiscuous men who, when they finished sowing their wild oats, would endeavor to engage a woman who had not participated in similar behavior. This she felt about Lord Percy, but she tried not to dwell on it. She would set her heart on forgiveness and forgetfulness. Tincture of time would heal.

Her heart was another matter. Despite her mental resolution and the comfort of a charitable soul, her heart suffered the most unevenness of all. Most days, she tried to keep her hope at small levels to lessen despair when a lead about Thomas turned out false; other days, thankfully less often, she feared Thomas would never be found alive, or that he would despise her family if he were discovered.

Chapter Thirty-Four

The following day during breakfast, Mr. Darcy inquired, "Do you think it is time we return to Pemberley?"

Elizabeth replied, "I am anxious to return to the children; but, perhaps Georgiana would wish to stay?"

"Is there any hope, my dear brother, of further inquiries which may be made concerning Thomas?"

"Unfortunately, I have exhausted all contacts among my friends and the government. Many of them have promised to be on the watch for any clue to his whereabouts. The visit to France by Mr. and Mrs. Gardiner will perhaps prove to be productive."

"I believe you have done your best," replied Georgiana. "I think we can wait in Derbyshire as well as London, and I much prefer Pemberley Hall to our house here."

Elizabeth said, "I hope it will be agreeable to both of you that we stop over in Hertfordshire for a few hours so I can visit my parents before heading on to Derbyshire."

Her husband and sister nodded in assent and suggested they would be ready to leave in the morning.

"Good. I will send a message by express to tell them of our arrival tomorrow afternoon."

The following day, Elizabeth and Georgiana were seated in the parlor of Longbourn with Mrs. Bennet and Mary. Mary, Elizabeth's next to youngest sister, was a serious young lady given to reading great works. Her talk was filled with sensibility, which often sounded pedantic. Mr. Bennet and Mr. Darcy set off to hunt in the two nearest fields.

Mrs. Bennet started with "Oh, Lizzy, we have so much news to relate. Last night, Timothy Jackson was here and, well. . . perhaps Mary should tell you."

"Thank you, Mamma. Father gave consent to Mr. Timothy Jackson for my engagement."

"Congratulations," Elizabeth and Georgiana said simultaneously, and rose to hug Mary. Elizabeth continued, "Now tell us about Mr. Jackson. Is he the same one Mamma has been telling us about these many years?"

"The very same. He is a clerk for Uncle Phillips' business, a very sober and serious young man. . . ."

"Just the type for you," Elizabeth interjected and they all laughed.

Mary gave a rare smile and said, "Your joking is a compliment. Marriage is a serious business, and I am glad I have finally found a young man so well suited for my connubial felicity."

"When is the marriage to take place?" Elizabeth inquired.

"Mr. Jackson's apprenticeship is to be finished in six months and we shall be married at that time."

"And then I shall be desolate!" interrupted Mrs. Bennet. "To think I worried one time about any of my daughters getting married! Now, I shall lose my last; though, at times, I thought Mary would **never** get married. My heart will break with your leaving. . . ."

"Mamma, it is not certain we are going to leave Meryton. Uncle Phillips may offer my fiance a partnership."

"Good, and I shall do everything to influence my sister to convince her husband to do so." Turning the conversation, Mrs. Bennet continued, "Have you heard about the trouble Mr. and Mrs. Collins' are in?"

Elizabeth said, "We knew there was difficulty

brewing at Hunsford and Rosings."

"Well, Mr. Collins has been dismissed from the rectory at Hunsford. He has had no other offers; so, he and Charlotte have come crawling back to Lucas Lodge."

"Mamma, he was offered a curacy in Sussex."

"A curacy!" her mother continued. "What a step down to be a poorly paid representative of a rector in another parish! I do not blame Mr. Collins for not condescending to it. Further, Charlotte told me it paid one-tenth of what Hunsford did."

"Poor Mr. Collins!" Mary said. "What an imperfect soul. His pride and vanity hath finally caught up to him."

"Mary is right," Mrs. Bennet continued. "He is sorely depressed over the state of affairs and will eat very little. Charlotte says she is unable to console him. He has lost weight, and she is so distressed over him."

Elizabeth said, "I am sorry to hear such a sad report of my cousin. To think I might have been trapped in Charlotte's position. If business at Pemberley were not so pressing for us, I should like to visit Charlotte to see if there is anything to be done. Tell her, however, I shall write to Lucas Lodge as soon as I can."

With this information and further details about Mr. Timothy Jackson, the visit to Longbourn ended. Mr. and Mrs. Bennet hugged Elizabeth and repeated their desire to see their children, but they were uncertain when they might return to Pemberley.

As the carriage headed for Derbyshire, Georgiana was very quiet. She was happy for Mary, but the subject of marriage opened her feelings again in an uncontrollable way. She told herself she would have to learn to control her emotions about such a topic, or be ever after subject to vexation! She could eventually resign herself to a life as an unmarried aunt and sister, if only she could obtain a final communication about Thomas!

With the additional hope of receiving a letter from the Gardiners, the subsequent week seemed to pass dreadfully slow. At Pemberley, however, she had more diversions in her nephews and niece, and with her pleasant walks in the garden and over the bridge.

Elizabeth called Georgiana excitedly one day from the music room to hand her a letter from Mrs. Gardiner.

Paris, June 4

My dear Elizabeth,

Your uncle and I have been in France two days and we have very little to report to Georgiana.

My nephew has shown us around Paris. What a pretty city! Some of the Parisians still resent the war, but for the most part, they are friendly.

We are to head south tomorrow. Mr. Gardiner is still mum about his plans concerning the search for Thomas. Not even I can wrench the secret from him. I am afraid this excites more hope than it otherwise should.

I will endeavor to write every three days, or whenever I have anything to relate.

Yours, very sincerely,
M. Gardiner

The next letter was received in two days and read:

My dear Elizabeth,

We have discovered Mr. Thomas Staley! He is alive and well and has been staying at General D'arbley's chateau here in southern France. Mr. Gardiner now tells me that his office, in the course of other events, had occasion to meet with Colonel Fremantle of the British Army whose life was saved by Captain Staley. When your family's difficulty was discussed with the Colonel, he suggested General D'arbley be contacted, since the French General had invited the British negotiating team to visit his estate after the war.

Upon arrival last night, we were immediately ushered into the welcoming hall. Mr. Staley arrived, and we handed him the letter Mr. Darcy had previously written, in case Mr. Staley should be located. You will have to apply to Mr. Darcy for the contents of the letter.

Mr. Staley sat down and read the letter with visible relief. We conversed for thirty minutes or so. He seemed quite interested in hearing about Georgiana, and particularly about her recent involvement with the Duke.

At the end of the conversation, he stood and thanked us. He said he would be returning to Staley Hall as soon as possible and would leave the next afternoon. The General graciously offered us rooms last night. Mr. Staley then spoke to the General in French. My nephew and I are not nearly as good in French as we should like. Mr. Staley said something to the effect that Juliet should follow him to England in a few days. In the hustle and bustle that followed last night and this morning, it did not occur to me to follow-up on this reference to the person, Juliet, until shortly before our departure from the chateau.

We did not meet any such woman here. As I am writing this letter, I wish I had tried more to ascertain who this woman is. Before writing this letter, we inquired of several servants, and they did not seem to understand the reference to Juliet either.

We shall post this letter by express. In any case, Mr. Staley should be home within a day or two of your receipt of this letter. We are going to finish our tour of southern France and return to Pemberley in a few weeks.

We are most happy to have been of service to you, and to help repay Mr. Darcy's kindness towards our family with regards to Lydia.

Yours, most sincerely,
M. Gardiner

The above letter was quickly given to Georgiana after Elizabeth perused it. This news was indeed a mixed blessing to Georgiana. It was joy indeed that Thomas was found alive and was returning soon to Derbyshire; however, the possibility that he was returning with a woman was not at all anticipated by Georgiana in her months of reflection about him! Now that she clarified her thoughts, in the event that he no longer cared for her, she had always pictured him as unattached to anyone else. It would be much easier for her to stay single if he were single also! In retrospect, she upbraided herself for not having accounted for the possibility that Thomas might fall in love with another woman. Nonetheless, he had promised life-long love! However, she wondered how relevant his promise would be, since it took place before the terrible and unjust accusation. Surely, he was justified for not feeling bound by such a vow. Upon further reflection, it remained possible that Juliet was not a woman he loved, but perhaps only a friend or a servant. Georgiana's heart would certainly not put much faith in the latter possibility. The following day another letter arrived by express:

> Mr. Darcy,
> Mr. Thomas Staley is a gallant man in war and peace. He is a gentleman whose word is honor. You English are so foolish! I cannot understand you. You accuse him unjustly, and then expect with an apology for everything to go on as before. If I were Mr. Staley, I should hate and despise you for the rest of my life.
> > General D'arbley
> > Lyons, France

The above letter caused discomfiture at Pemberley Hall. Because of their status in English society, no one had given them a severe reproach for their clumsy behavior towards Mr. Staley. While the Darcys had felt these feelings as a family, the letter from the French general heightened their anxiety about Mr. Staley and his response to their family. The letter caused a refreshing eagerness to make amendments to their former tutor. Since the road to Staley Hall ran east of the river and their bridge, Mr. Darcy instructed Mr. Reynolds to have a watchman placed upon the bridge at all hours of the day and night to observe for any horseman or carriage that might indicate Thomas was returning to Staley Hall.

The following night, they were rewarded with a

report by an observance of a man matching Thomas' description passing in the late evening. In the rain, the watchman could not be certain if it was Mr. Staley in the dim light; the horse paused on the road for a minute while its rider appeared to stare at Pemberley Hall. The horse was then reined to head in the direction of Staley Hall.

Georgiana heard the latter report when she came down in the morning. She did not expect any communication from Thomas the day after his arrival. Three days after his arrival at Staley Hall was confirmed (by the Pemberley servants interaction with Staley Hall tenants) and still Thomas did not appear or write, her anxiety reached a point of impatience and restlessness. She called Elizabeth to the entrance parlor and inquired, "My dearest Lizzy, what can we do about Thomas?"

"I am not sure. Mr. Darcy and I have been discussing at length what we should do."

"What is my brother thinking he might do?"

"He is inclined to visit Staley Hall to offer amends. Thomas may be reluctant to visit this house since his last memory is an unpleasant one."

"Oh! Please ask him to go today!"

"Your approval will certainly stimulate his visit. He has been reluctant to do anything that might further aggravate the situation, but your favor in the matter will help him be confident."

"Lizzy, I would like your opinion on what my brother can say."

"Pray, continue. . . ."

"I have the distinct feeling that, for the moment at least, I must overcome my shyness and carefulness to make a critical request of my brother."

"And what would that request be?"

"I feel that I must take the unusual step of having my brother tell Thomas, if the circumstances are right, that

Thomas has permission to engage me for marriage if he so desires. . . . There now, I have spoken my heart. . . . Do you think it too shocking for me to request that?"

Elizabeth took a moment to reply, and then proceeded slowly, "Not shocking, but as you know, a most exceptional approach. Why do you think this is necessary?"

"I feel Thomas is going to slip away, as he did once before. I will never entertain marriage to anyone else, so I should like to know that I made every effort to express my affection."

"What about this Juliet that we are uncertain about?"

"That is what I meant by 'if the circumstances are right' during my brother's visit. I should like him to ascertain who this woman is and what Thomas' marital intentions are, if any, towards her."

"This may be rather indelicate."

"I trust my brother to assess the situation and communicate my wishes."

Elizabeth thought for a few moments and said, "I see your position entirely. I will heartily recommend it to Mr. Darcy. My only fear is that our grievous injustice to Thomas will greatly weaken the impact your offer, if made, will have."

"But I feel we must attempt it."

"I agree," Elizabeth said, with as much of an encouraging smile as possible.

That evening, after the supper was finished, Mr. Darcy prepared to go to Staley Hall. Georgiana asked her brother if he understood her desire and the reason for her bold move.

He agreed to try to ascertain the status of Thomas and make Georgiana's offer if it appeared propitious. "You know, sister, I would do anything for you."

"I know. You are the best brother a sister could have."

They embraced and Mr. Darcy strode out the entrance hall doors with his riding boots and coat on. It was quite late when Mr. Darcy returned. He came into the hall parlor, which was illuminated by candlelight, and sat down quietly by Elizabeth.

"Well, my dear, what happened?" Elizabeth finally inquired.

"I am uncertain what to think."

"Pray tell us what happened," Georgiana eagerly requested.

"Mr. Thomas Staley received me graciously into their front room. He had the servant put more wood on the fire and light more candles. He appeared surprised and mentioned his appreciation for my visit. I related our profuse apologies for our unjust and shocking behavior. I am glad that he gave a formal reply of forgiveness, rather than saying the matter was of no import to him. He raised his eyebrows when I told him of the Gardiner's communication about 'Juliet'. He said I could see her for myself."

Georgiana gasped, "Then there is another woman!"

Mr. Darcy smiled, "Not exactly. He called the name, and a large collie came into the room and tried to jump up on my chest. You can imagine my great relief when the dog seemed to respond to the name of 'Juliet'. It seems the dog is a gift from General D'arbley to Mr. Staley."

"These results gave me confidence to proceed with your request, Georgiana. When I related your desire and added my sincere approbation, he turned away from me and asked me to leave. I could not see his reaction because of his position and the low light. After a moment, he excused himself and left the room. I waited for thirty minutes, but he did not return."

"I feel good about our apology having been received and that Juliet turned out to be a lovely dog. I do not know whether the illness of Sir William Staley is restraining him or what the effect of our proposal was; still, at least he is cognizant of your feelings."

Georgiana stood and hugged her brother's head and neck while he remained seated. "Thank you, Fitzwilliam, for your effort tonight. The outcome is now in the hands of the Almighty."

So saying, she ascended the stairs to her room. She slept better this night than any other since Thomas left Pemberley.

Chapter Thirty-Five

The following day, Georgiana avoided pacing in front of the parlor window. She tried to practice her pianoforte and harp, but her effort was listless. Her best diversion turned out to be playing with Andrew, John and Maria in the south garden; however, she found herself involuntarily looking up at the bridge and the road beyond it—hoping for signs of Thomas. The day dragged by. She slept restlessly that night and in the morning, after breakfast, found herself pacing in front of the window she had tried to avoid the day before. Mr. and Mrs. Darcy and the entire household watched her, with concern for her well-being. She, who had been so gracious and loving to them as family members and servants, was now in deep distress and anxiety.

Finally, after two hours of watching, Georgiana said to Elizabeth, "I am going up to Becker's point. There, at least, I can see Staley Hall. Staring at the road and bridge only causes me distress."

She was thinking absent-mindedly as she approached the last portion of the ascent, where it began to flatten out. She stopped. A man was sitting on a rock looking towards Staley Hall. Was it Thomas? She was certain it was; but, she had the uncertainty of one who has wished for a sight so long that, when it comes, they disbelieve their senses. He turned, apparently at the sound of the rustle of her dress. He stood. His face showed surprise and a slight smile. She approached him tentatively and stood about six feet away.

"Thomas, it is good to see you," she said.

She felt a little awkward as he said, "Georgiana, it is good to see you."

Her previous resolve for courage began to melt away. She wanted to speak before it was gone entirely. "Do you understand what my brother told you two days ago?"

He looked to the ground and said, "Yes, but my lady, I have so little to offer you. Staley Hall is nearly in ruins."

"Thomas," she said softly, "I am not interested in the character of your wealth, but the wealth of your character."

In disbelief, he asked, "Would you condescend to marry me, the son of a poor baronet?"

"*Au contraire, mon amour*, it is you who condescends to marry me. My heart. . . my heart is all yours, if you will have me."

She saw his face turn to joy. "I never stopped loving you," he said, as he came and took her hand. They began walking towards Pemberly Hall. She took his arm and, sensing his physical strength, felt her heart well up with love. Every look between them became a smile, every step a spring, every feeling a joy!

As they began the descent, Georgiana espied Andrew down by the lake. He looked as if he spotted them and ran into Pemberley Hall. From a distance, she could see the front steps of the hall begin filling with servants and family. The boys and Maria ran up the trail to meet the young couple at the lake, happily exclaiming, "Thomas is back! Thomas is back!"

When they reached the couple, Thomas took Maria into his arms, as the two boys walked on each side of Thomas and Georgiana for the remaining distance to the front of the hall. While there was a joyous clapping of the household, Mr. and Mrs. Darcy hugged Georgiana and Thomas. Georgiana noted the wide smile and look of approval on Mrs. Reynold's face.

Chapter Thirty-Six

After an hour or so of celebration and recapitulation of their journeys to this point, Thomas asked Georgiana to return to Staley Hall with him to share the news with his ill father. She readily assented and Mr. Darcy instructed the carriage be brought about for them.

Arriving at Staley Hall a half-hour later, they were ushered into the bedroom of Sir William Staley. It was a large room with dark paneling. Two medium-sized windows admitted a good amount of daytime light. Sir William was propped up on many pillows in his four-poster bed, with the curtains drawn back. He instantly guessed what the sounds of many steps coming towards his room represented and was smiling as the door opened. Georgiana entered, followed by Thomas.

"Father, my greatest dream has come true. I wish to introduce Georgiana, the woman who has consented to make me happy the rest of my life."

Sir William replied, "Georgiana, what do you have to say about this?"

"I am thrilled that Thomas has asked me to be his wife."

Sir William coughed and said, after a moment, "Excellent! This is exactly what your mothers wanted."

"What do you mean, father?" Thomas queried.

"Neither of you know this, but I recall the day your mother and I took you, Thomas, as a two year old to visit

Lady Anne after Georgiana's birth. Lady Marilyn and Lady Anne expressed their wishes that you two might eventually marry."

"Why did you not tell us this sooner?" Thomas asked.

"Your mothers realized that if they proposed your union, you would surely oppose it. They were wise enough to take the secret to their graves. I have been sorely tempted to mention it at times, but I am glad I held my tongue. After Lady Anne passed away, your mother, Thomas, rejoiced to teach Georgiana music and French until she died three years later. What you may not know Georgiana, is that she considered you as the daughter she was never able to have."

Georgiana replied, "Oh, what solace Lady Marilyn was to my heart after my own mother died. I wanted so much to imitate her elegance and love of music."

"Now, I can die in peace," Sir William replied.

"Father, do not say so. You must live to attend our wedding."

"I do not think I am going to live much longer. I believe the doctors gave me a much too optimistic outlook." He coughed again and took a few moments to recuperate. He continued, "Please do not wait for the completion of the mourning period for me before you marry. You have my permission to get married by special license as soon as possible. . . . I go to my grave a contented and blessed man to have my son forgive me, and to see Staley Hall in the hands of my son and daughter who love it. I prophesy Staley Hall will once again achieve the glory it had generations ago. I am sorry I have handed it to you in such decrepit condition."

"Pray, Father, do not exert yourself any longer."

"Go now, my son and daughter, in the knowledge that you have given the greatest blessing a father can have-- the expectation of felicity in marriage for his only heir."

Chapter Thirty-Seven

On her wedding day, Georgiana arose early and, once again, went to sit before the portrait of her mother. While holding her beloved Phillip in her lap, she spoke softly to the picture, "I now understand what you have been trying to tell me. I am glad I was able to discover it for myself. . . . You would be proud of the man Thomas has become. I hope I can love him as much as you loved father. . . .I wish you could be here today. At times like this, I especially miss you. . . . Wearing your wedding dress will remind me of you." With a great sense of peace, she returned to her rooms to finish preparing herself for the wedding.

As he predicted, Sir William Staley passed on two weeks before. Reverend Henry Westbrook had given the eulogy at the funeral and now joyously led the wedding ceremony. The friendship between Henry and Kitty and Thomas and Georgiana was to soar after the wedding day. Thomas was grateful to Henry for his unswaying trust during the time of accusation. Henry found Thomas a reliable confidant about parish matters. Their long discussions about spiritual matters helped each to grow.

Georgiana walked into the back of the chapel with her brother at her side. Her heart began to fail her as she saw many people she knew, but many she did not. This was so much different from playing a pianoforte for a group she did not have to look at. She began to tremble, until she saw Thomas at the end of the aisle. How she loved him! His masculine strength gave her renewed courage as she approached him. She would now have refuge and security in him. To marry an honest and kind man had been the hope of her heart all along. Her desire to never leave Pemberley was also fulfilled, since she could look upon the grounds of Pemberley Manor every day of her life through the windows of Staley Hall. She could walk to Pemberley House anytime she chose to do so.

Soon, she was hearing, "Georgiana, will you take this man to be your lawful husband? To stand by him for better or worse, in sickness and in health, for richer or poorer? If so, say, 'I do'."

The wedding present of Mr. and Mrs. Darcy was to refurbish the inside and outside of Staley Hall. The workmen had finished the main rooms of the hall under the careful eyes of Elizabeth, Georgiana and Thomas. Much work remained on the guest rooms and the bedchambers. As the couple returned after their wedding, the outside of the hall and the two entry gardens were still being worked on.

Our story ends as the Darcy family is visiting Staley Hall a month later, after the workmen were done. They were seated in the front parlor with Thomas. Georgiana is singing, "Oh for a Thousand Tongues to Sing", and playing her pianoforte. Our viewpoint exits the front door of a revived house, into a beautiful garden, listening to the sounds of a melodious voice once again overflowing Staley Hall.

Epilogue

"No legacy is so rich as honesty"
Shakespeare

In the year following the marriage of Thomas and Georgiana, Mrs. Bennet suddenly took ill and died. Mr. Bennet, now alone at home after the marriage of his daughter, Mary, elected to relieve the distress of Mr. Collins by ceding Longbourn to him and dividing his time among the households of his three daughters in Derbyshire and Yorkshire.

Mr. Collins, though he never became a perfect conversationalist, was much improved after his humbling experience in losing his position as rector of Hunsford Park. He sensed the charity of Mr. Bennet and thrived in the knowledge that Longbourn could not be taken from him. He even helped the vicar of Longbourn in visiting the parish of Meryton, in contrast to his former ways of only worrying about his sermon.

Social intercourse between Pemberley House and Staley Hall became very frequent. All members moved back and forth, but Maria came most frequently for music lessons and continuation in French by her aunt. Maria felt, not without basis, that she had helped her aunt and new uncle unite in love.

Staley Hall thrived. More domestic help was hired. Part of Georgiana's dowry was used to widen and lengthen the small road which wound through the manor. Due to the economic downturn in the cotton mills of nearby Ashton, several families returned to rebuilt and expanded cottages. Soon the manor of Staley Hall was producing income again, so that Thomas was encouraged about the long-term outlook.

Sir Thomas and Lady Georgiana Staley were to reside at Staley Hall for the remainder of their lives; except, for a four year period, when they responded to a call of the French and His Majesty's government to serve as ambassadors to France for England.

The request originated from the newly appointed minister of foreign affairs, General D'arbley. After a few meetings with the gracious Lady Georgiana, he dropped all resentment of the Darcys. He was certain to introduce the Staleys to any domestic or foreign dignitary with enthusiasm.

Did Georgiana always remain shy? No. While preferring to be a private person, her social abilities blossomed in the security of the love Thomas gave. Indeed, the French court boasted the Staleys as the most delightful English ambassadors in memory. Sir Thomas was esteemed as a man of wit and honesty. Lady Georgiana was often requested to play the harp at embassy dinners. The calmness and peace, which ensued after her performances, created a perfect atmosphere for the international negotiations which followed. After four years, they returned to Derbyshire elevated in all the eyes of that district.

While history tells us that much of Derbyshire was affected by unrest, the manors of Pemberley House and Staley Hall were untouched, since their tenants reckoned their squires just and generous. What happened to the Darcy children? Andrew had to overcome . . . and eventually married. . . . John underwent great adventures as a . . . Maria grew to be a . . . and ended up . . . . These stories about the family of Elizabeth Bennet Darcy are continued in another book.

This story continues in
Virtue and Vanity
Available fall 2000 from
Revive Publishing 800-541-0558

𝕳𝖎𝖘𝖙𝖔𝖗𝖎𝖈𝖆𝖑 𝕹𝖔𝖙𝖊𝖘

Chapter One

In attempting to recreate language of nearly two hundred years ago, writers are faced with an immediate problem: Are words to be understood in their early nineteenth century context or late twentieth century usage? Since we are conveying a story, rather than playing a philological game, the authors elected the latter approach of current usage.

Words which now have different connotations (e.g., chatty, genteel, inmate) are avoided. Words that were commonly used by Jane Austen, and which still have the same meaning (e.g., wretched, mortify, amiable), are used liberally. Words not introduced until after the year 1815 are excluded (We had to discard "girlfriend" [1859] and "sleuthing". [1872]).

The authors do not claim to have perfectly imitated Jane Austen's syntax. In *Jane Austen's English*, by K.C. Phillips, the sentence structuring of the famous author is analyzed in detail.[1] While minute details of her language exist, the most helpful generalization is that her sentence structure reflects the King James Bible (without the archaic vocabulary). The authors grew up immersed in this type of 'high English" and thus have some understanding in its composition.

The reader should note, when direct action is contemplated, Jane Austen preferred using the words "shall" and "should" to our current "will" and "would".

Servants say very little in Jane Austen's novels. The greatest exception, however, is Mrs. Reynolds in *Pride and Prejudice*, who offers many lines. The tradition of Mrs. Reynolds having a major conversational role will be continued.

Jane Austen notes the relationship between Elizabeth and Georgiana as:

"The attachment of the [new] sisters was exactly what Darcy had hoped to see. They were able to love each other, even as well as they intended. Georgiana had the highest opinion in the world of Elizabeth. . ." (chapter 61, *Pride and Prejudice*).

Chapter Two

The first interaction here between Mr. and Mrs. Darcy has been presaged in Jane Austen's chapter 50 and 60.

The Josiah Wedgewood china company began in 1769 and was very well known. An early company design consisted of a green and gold pattern.

Pemberley Hall is a mythical estate, the location of which, in Derbyshire, has perplexed many Austenites. Many critics feel Jane Austen based it upon Chatsworth. It is the only estate of sufficient grandeur in Derbyshire to match Pemberley.[2] In *Pride and Prejudice*, she mentions Chatsworth on the way to Pemberley; however, this may be a deliberate red herring. The similarities are many, but the item that clinches the identity (for the authors) is that Gainsborough's famous painting of "Lady Georgiana" was present at Chatsworth in 1790[3] and Jane Austen undoubtably visited Chatsworth in 1806.[4] Interestingly, when the painting of Lady Georgiana sold in 1876, for 10,100 guineas, it was the highest price ever paid for any painting in the world up to that time.[3] Our description of Pemberley, as with Jane Austen, only vaguely resembles Chatsworth. The geography of the area does match the Peak district in England.

The appearance of our heroine matches Jane Austen's description of Georgiana, rather than the painting.

Westbrook Hall is also mythical. Staley Hall actually exists in ruins on the edge of Derbyshire in Cheshire (now Manchester). My (TFB) great grandmother, Leah Belle Staley, was a descendent of Staley Hall. We have nudged Staley Hall a little distance into Derbyshire to be north of Pemberley Hall for the story.

The spaniel breed of dog was the companion of the most aristocratic members of society. These dogs were frequently included in family portraits.[5]

The comments concerning Fanny Burney were taken from Elizabeth Jenkins.[6] It is well known that Fanny Burney influenced Jane Austen. *Camilla* was published in 1796 by subscription and Jane Austen's name is on the list of subscribers. Further, it is likely Jane Austen took the title of *Pride and Prejudice* from the last chapter of Miss Burney's *Cecilia*, where this phrase is mentioned three times. William Cowper was one of Jane Austen's favorite poets.[4] Thus, it seems very appropriate to introduce references to Jane Austen's favorite authors.

Chapter Three

We are now assembling our characters as Jane Austen would have wanted. Her oft quoted statement to a young author, "You are now collecting your people delightfully, getting them exactly into a spot as is the delight of my life; three or four families in a country village is the very thing to work on. . . ."

Chapter Four

The letter from Elizabeth's Aunt Gardiner is previewed in *Pride and Prejudice*, where Mrs. Gardiner asks for a ride "round the park [of Pemberley in a] low phaeton, with a nice little pair of ponies". A phaeton was a light, four-wheel carriage with open sides drawn by one or two horses. It sometimes applied to a carriage driven by its owner rather than a coachman.[7]

Seating guests for a large dinner party was an ordeal for any hostess. Social rank was the most important determinate in seating and a mistake here was cause for alarm. Daniel Pool's reference[7] tells us that *Burke's Peerage* could be consulted to get social ranks correct.

In the early nineteenth century, service was usually á la francaise meaning that the dishes were left on the table for the guests to serve themselves. The gentlemen present would do the carving. After dessert was served, the ladies would usually withdraw for a half hour or so before the men would rejoin them.

The so-called "season" of society in London did not usually begin until after Christmas when preparations for parliament were made. It was not, however, until after Easter, that the height of society was reached with a three-month whirlwind of parties, balls and sporting events.[6] With the adjournment of parliament in August, the season ended with the retreat of everyone to their estates until after Christmas.

St. James' Palace was the centerpoint of high society in the early nineteenth century.

Second sons of gentlemen did not inherit any part of the estate of their father--a practice which may seem strange to the modern reader. The law of primogeniture stated that the first son would inherit the entire estate and other sons or daughters would not inherit any part of the land or house. This law came from an effort to keep the large manor tracts intact rather than constantly subdividing them every generation. The intact English manor was an economic unit, vital to the survival of early nineteenth century society.[7]

Social rank was determined most by ancient family name and land holdings--both of which the Darcys possessed. Rank was then determined by title and wealth. Dukes, marquises, earls, viscounts and barons, in order, were on top together and were known as the "peerage". They helped to comprise the House of Lords. Below the peerage, came baronets and knights. A marquis, earl or viscount was addressed as "lord". A baronet or knight was addressed as "sir". A duke was addressed as "your Grace". However, these formalities were often bypassed.

Earls were abundantly present in Regency Derbyshire as noted by Roy Christian.[8]

C. S. Lewis tells us that throughout the nineteenth century, the concept and meaning of the word "gentleman" was vigorously debated.[9]

Northern England at the beginning of the nineteenth century was heavily influenced by Methodism and the Methodist societies created by the evangelist, John Wesley. John Wesley sought to reform the church of England, rather than start a new church; but, as the nineteenth century progressed, many of his followers left the Church of England to form the Methodist Church. As Methodism tried to inject more feeling into the often quiet Anglican church, they were often accused by their opponents of being melancholic.[10]

John Wesley, who lived from 1703 to 1791, has been called by many the "most influential man of the eighteenth century" in England. His 500 sermons a year (mostly to large crowds at open air meetings) and 8,000 miles per year of horseback riding, for more than thirty years, gave him an influence not matched by anyone else in the century.[11]

Montesquieu, an aristocrat visiting England in 1731, said, "There is no religion in England." He moved mostly among lords and ladies of the peerage. He further added, "If religion is spoken of, every body laughs. . . ."[12] John Wesley was soon to change that. He played a major role as one of the leaders of an evangelical revival that swept much of the Protestant world of his day. He was also concerned with such issues as education, prison conditions, and poverty. He played an important role in the development of early social reforms in an increasingly industrialized society.[13] Because of his concern with social justice, many historians credit John Wesley's revivals as being responsible for preventing the gruesome French revolution from repeating itself in England.[14,15]

For more information on the influence of Methodism and the effects that the French revolution had on reforming the English aristocracy, the reader is referred to Halevy's *A History of the English People in 1815.*[14]

John Wesley visited Staley Hall in May 1747. Otherwise, all events and characters portrayed with Staley Hall are fictitious.

What did Jane Austen think about the evangelical movement? (as all similar efforts were lumped together). It is difficult to be certain. In

1809 she wrote, "I do not like the evangelicals." However, five years later, a more mature Jane Austen wrote, "I am by no means convinced we ought not all to be Evangelicals, and I am at least persuaded that they who are from Reason and Feeling, must be happiest and safest." The term evangelical, of course, can have several meanings and scholars have struggled with understanding her position on this topic. Nonetheless, the personal piety of Jane Austen as revealed in her written prayers, letters and epitaph reveal a woman who took Christianity very seriously. Jane Austen mentioned Methodism in *Mansfield Park*. Any attempt to write in a Jane Austen style without taking religion into account is to be a hollow imitator.

The authors consider the best discussion of religion in Jane Austen's life found in George Holbert Tucker's recent biography.[4]

Georgiana is characterized by Jane Austen in *Pride and Prejudice* many times as "shy".

> "Since her [Elizabeth] being at Lambton, she had heard that Miss Darcy was exceedingly proud; but the observation of a very few minutes convinced her, that she was only exceedingly shy. She found it difficult to obtain even a word from her beyond a monosyllable. . . .
> Georgiana's reception of them was very civil; but attended with all that embarrassment which, though proceeding from shyness and the fear of wrong, would easily give to those who felt themselves inferior, the belief of being proud and reserved. . .
> "Miss Darcy looked as if she wished for courage enough to join [the discussion]; and sometimes did venture a short sentence, when there was least danger of it being heard."

We, in contrast to others, have emphasized Jane Austen's own descriptions of Georgiana in this work and "shyness" is the major feature of her character.

Chapter Five

Our characterization of Kitty matches Jane Austen's:
> "in this danger Kitty is also comprehended. She will follow wherever Lydia leads. Vain, ignorant, idle, and absolutely uncontrolled!"

Kitty's habit of coughing is mentioned twice in *Pride and Prejudice* along with her running from the house when visiting clergymen arrive.

Chapter Six

All medical concepts in this novel have been verified in referral to the 1,020 pages of *The London Medical Dictionary* by Bartholomew Parr, M.D. 1819.[16] (Courtesy of the museum of the Denver Medical Library). "Flooding" was the term used for bleeding during pregnancy; regency physicians clearly understood its dire consequences if it did not cease.

The author, TFB, delivered seventy-five babies (including twins) during his internship and is well acquainted with birthing.

Morphine was often administered during obstetrical difficulties then and continues to be used today.

Medical science could hardly be labeled a "science" in the early 19th century, since very little empiricism existed. Dr. Parr's book is merely a compilation of what other physicians previously said. However, the medical author is impressed with the acute and detailed observations of disease contained in 19th century medical writing.

The psychology of Mr. Darcy's response is unchanged for patients today when untreatable illnesses are encountered. Disease is no respecter of social rank.

The seasonal flora included in the text has been verified by consulting standard botanical texts of Great Britain (not referenced).

Chapter Seven

It is not unusual for the diagnosis of pregnancy to be delayed until the fourth or fifth month. On the other hand, some unfortunate women have symptoms of pregnancy from the very beginning.

Chapter Eight

Jane Austen was fond of telling her family what happened to her characters after her novels ended. She told them that Kitty would marry the clergyman of Pemberley.[17] We have created this ending for the reader. Jane Austen's predicted outcome for Mary is portrayed in chapter 34.

Chapter Nine

The move of the Bingleys near Pemberley is foretold in *Pride and Prejudice*:

> "Mr. Bingley and Jane remained at Netherfield only a
> twelvemonth. So near a vicinity to her mother and
> Meryton relations was not desirable even to his easy

temper, or her affectionate heart. The darling wish of his sisters was then gratified; he bought an estate in a neighboring county to Derbyshire, and Jane and Elizabeth, in addition to every other source of happiness, were within thirty miles of each other."

Chapter Ten

Employment of a tutor was a common method of teaching children among aristocratic families in the 18th and 19th centuries. The tutor (male by definition) or governess (female by definition) were often gentry who had no wealth. Their position in the hierarchy of the household placed them above the servants but less than the family. As such, the tutor or governess were often resented by the servants.[10]

George MacDonald, another 19th century author, often used tutors as characters in his novels.

Chapter Eleven

While national medals were not issued for bravery following the Waterloo victory, regiments often awarded their own medals for outstanding action.[18]

After Napoleon's historic defeat at Waterloo, the French forces retreated to surround the city of Paris. Intense peace negotiations took place over several weeks as the French wished to avoid what would have been a devastating destruction of their remaining army and capitol.

Napoleon finally capitulated and was exiled to a distant isle. A peaceful surrender ensued and the battle for Paris avoided.[19]

Supper hour was often at 5 o'clock (cf General Tierney - *Northanger Abbey*). The most common misconception about the Regency period is that readers assume a late afternoon tea and then dinner at 8 o'clock. The 4 p.m. "high tea" did not become fashionable until the 1840's.[10]

Chapter Twelve

As Sharon Laudermilk phrases it, "Spinsterhood was considered an unnatural state, and a woman on the shelf was ridiculed."[20]

The age of twenty-seven had great significance to Jane Austen. Charlotte Lucas, in Pride and Prejudice, is twenty-seven and fears being an old maid. In Persuasion, Anne is nearly twenty-seven and is in despair of marrying. In her own life, Jane Austen turned down her last suitor, for unknown reasons, at age twenty-seven.

Chapter Fourteen

Dr. Linda Washington, of the National Army Museum in London, was kind enough to confirm many of the points about the British Army during the Waterloo time period. In regards to horses, she writes:
"Most officers bought and retained their own horses, but the regiment also purchased remounts on the open market, mainly at horse fairs. Stallions, mares and geldings were used as cavalry mounts."

Chapter Fifteen

The story about the woman enslaved to her first husband and liberated by her second husband appears to be a very old story, recounted most recently in Harold J. Brokke's, *Saved by His Life: An Exposition of Paul's Epistle to the Romans* by Bethany House Publishers, Minneapolis, MN ©1964. Permission is granted.

Chapter Sixteen

The poem Thomas Staley writes about Georgiana, in the style of Cowper, was contributed by a published poet, Joe Johnston, of Denver Medical Books.

Chapter Eighteen

"Londonize" (i.e., to dress in the fashion of London) was apparently first coined by Fanny Burney in Evelina (1779).[21]

Chapter Nineteen

The description of St. James' court is taken from *The Regency Companion*.[20] According to *Debrett's Correct Form*[22], when the phrase "the Duke" is used, the title is capitalized. While in an official sense, a duke should not be addressed as "Lord", it was unofficially permitted.

The anecdote of flirting the fan was reported in the October 5, 1823 issue of *Lancet* (a London medical journal).

Chapter Twenty-One

Hyde Park was clearly the display ground of riding and carriages in nineteenth century London.

Frank Huggett notes:
"Masters who might relapse into gloomy and prolonged silence when any general topic was being discussed over port or claret, or when their wives were pestering them with some fine detail of

household business, could become loud-mouthed martinets in their own mews and stables."[23]

Dr. James Parkinson wrote the first treatise on a common neurologic affliction and thus has his name attached to it. He had an active practice in Shoreditch at this time and was well known.[24] "Concussion" was a bonafide medical diagnosis at the time.

Chapter Twenty-Four

Sexual intrigue between the family and servants, while not common, was also not rare. The accusation against Thomas would have been quite plausible. One author notes:

> "[Gentlemen] sons presented just as big a threat to servant girls, especially those who were so keen to marry above their station that they could convince themselves that the wedding banns had actually been put up in some conveniently removed parish. . . many household sons found far more cooperation than they might have expected in their first fumbling experiment with the household maids."[25]

Whether voluntarily or involuntarily involved, such servants, when discovered, would be dismissed. The Darcys are more compassionate since they wish to keep it quiet and because they are uncertain of the allegation.

Chapter Twenty-Seven

The regency period in England, considered to be from about 1800 to 1830, is so named because King George III was incapacitated and his son, known as the Prince Regent, functioned as the head of state during his father's illness. The Prince Regent ultimately was crowned as King George IV.

The regency period is considered distinct from the Victorian period which followed. Queen Victoria was crowned in 1834 and reigned until her death in 1901. The regency era was a time of transition from the looser morals of the 18th century to the stricter ones of the Victorian Era.[26]

Chapter Twenty-Eight

"Blockhead" was an old English word [1549] used by Jane Austen. Today it means precisely what it meant in 1815.

Chapter Thirty-Four

Mary's marriage to a clerk working under her Uncle Phillips was an unwritten outcome of *Pride and Prejudice* Jane Austen told her family about.[17]

The caretaker of a parish, if the rector chose not to be present, was known as a curate. Curates were often paid very poorly because they were not entitled to the mandatory tithes received by the parish for the rector or vicar.[14]

Epilogue

Jane Austen always has an unofficial epilogue at the end of her books. It is one reason why writing a sequel is such a temptation to those who read her books!

References

1. Phillips, Kenneth C. *Jane Austen's English*. Andre Deutsch Limited, London: 1970.
2. Ousby, Ian. *Blue Guide to Literary Britain and Ireland*. WW Norton, New York: 1985.
3. (A guide to) *Chatsworth: House of the Duke and Duchess of Devonshire*. This can be obtained by contacting the Chatsworth House Trust, Bakewell, Derbyshire DE45 1PP.
4. Tucker, George Holbert. *Jane Austen The Woman: some biographical insights*. St. Martins, New York: 1994.
5. Cuddy, Beverly. *Cavalier King Charles Spaniels*. TFH Publications, Neptune City, New Jersey. 1995.
6. Jenkins, Elizabeth. *Jane Austen*. Funk and Wagnalls, New York, 1969 (reissue of a 1949 edition by Minerva Press).
7. Pool, Daniel. *What Jane Austen Ate and Charles Dickens Knew: from fox hunting to whist–the facts of daily life in 19th century England*. Simon and Schuster, New York: 1993.
8. Christian, Roy. *Notable Derbyshire Families*. JH Hall, Derby: 1987.
9. Lewis, CS. *Studies in Words*. University Press,Cambridge, 1960.
10. Marshall, Dorothy. *English People in the Eighteenth Century*. Longmans, Green and Co., London: 1956.
11. Parker, PL. *John Wesley's Journal*. Hodder and Stoughton, London: 1993.
12. Durant, Will and Ariel. *The Age of Voltaire*. Simon and Schuster, New York, 1965.
13. Heitzenrater, RP. *The Elusive Mr. Wesley: John Wesley His Own Biographer*. Abingdon Press, Nashville, 1984.
14. Halevy, Elie. *A History of the English People in 1815*. Routledge and Kegan Paul Ltd., London: 1987.
15. Brown, Julia Prewitt. *A Reader's Guide to the Nineteenth-Century English Novel*. Macmillian, New York: 1985.
16. Parr, Bartholomew. *The London Medical Dictionary; including every branch of medicine, viz., anatomy, physiology, and pathology, the practice of physic and surgery, therapeutics, and materia medica; with whatever relates to medicine in natural philosophy, chemistry and natural history*. Mitchell, Ames and White, Philadelphia: 1819.

17.   Austen-Leigh, JE. *A Memoir of Jane Austen by her Nephew.* Folio
        Society, London: 1989 (reprint of 1869 book).
18.   Johnson, Stanley C. *The Medal Collector: a guide to novel,*
        military, air-force and civil medals and ribbons. Dodd, Mead
        and Co., New York: 1921.
19.   Schom, Alan. *One Hundred Days: Napoleon's Road to*
        Waterloo. Atheneum, New York: 1992.
20.   Laudermilk, Sharon. Hamlin, Teresa.*The Regency Companion.*
        Garland, London: 1989.
21.   Bloom, Edward A. *Explanatory notes to* <u>*Evelina*</u>. Oxford
        University Press reprint of the 1779 classic by Fanny Burney.
        London: 1992.
22.   Montague-Smith, Patrick, ed. *Debrett's Correct Form.* Arco,
        New York: 1977.
23.   Huggett, Frank. *Carriages at Eight.* Charles Scribners, New
        York: 1980.
24.   Jefferson, Michael. Medical History: James Parkinson 1755-
        1824. *British Medical Journal*; June 9, 1973: 601-603.
25.   Huggett, Frank. *Life Below Stairs.* Charles Scribner's Sons,
        New York: 1977.
26.   White RJ. *Life in Regency England.* Batsford,   London: 1963.

Revive Publishing welcomes comments on
Desire and Duty.
The authors, Ted and Marilyn, endeavor
to answer all correspondence.
If you would like to be on a mailing list
for Jane Austen genre-type material,
please write to:

Revive Publishing
1790 Dudley Street
Lakewood, CO 80215-3004